ADVANCE PRAISE FOR
Coupon Girl!

"*Coupon Girl* reads as true, honest, and down-to-earth as real life—only much, much funnier. Anyone who's ever dreamed of finding stardom through community theater, worked at (and sometimes even enjoyed) a seemingly thankless job, or had a car with suspected psychological problems will be able to relate to Jeanie."
—Shanna Swendson, Author of *Enchanted, Inc.*

"*Coupon Girl* is a fun, fabulous read that blends love, work, and crazy-hilarious theater productions. Becky Motew is the real deal, and her debut novel truly delivers. Delightfully quirky!"
—Johanna Edwards, Nationally Bestselling Author of *The Next Big Thing*

"*Coupon Girl* is loaded with charm, and thanks to Becky Motew's quirky voice and fast-paced style, readers are sure to find that this is one coupon book worth redeeming."
—Ally Carter, Author of *Cheating at Solitaire*

"What a wonderful, colorful cast of characters! *Coupon Girl* bubbles with humor, conflict, warmth and wit. Loved it."
—Carrie Kabak, Author of *Cover the Butter*

Coupon Girl

BECKY MOTEW

Making
it

MAKING IT®

May 2006

Published by

Dorchester Publishing Co., Inc.
200 Madison Avenue
New York, NY 10016

ISBN 0-8439-5693-3

Printed in the United States of America.

Visit us on the web at www.dorchesterpub.com.

For Mary and Gene

ACKNOWLEDGMENTS

Special thanks to my ruthless and frank friend Liz Stroud. A big thank-you for all the support I got from the b-girls and the Cave, and to my wonderful agent Kristin Nelson and talented editor Leah Hultenschmidt. To all the old Hudson Spotlighters, you are still the best, and thank you to my former coupon customers, who are nothing like the customers in these pages.

Coupon Girl

Let's Start at the Very Beginning

Monday, June 8

I was witty in my waking dream, confident and persuasive. Crowds laughed and made way. Colors were bright, grins were genuine, and hope bubbled in the air like a first glass of champagne. Then I woke up and faced my bathroom scale, which proclaimed in its somewhat British accent, "One hundred and forty pounds."

Screw the waking dream.

And the yogurt waiting for me.

And your little dog too.

You might think I would skip breakfast. You would be wrong. Two slices of cold pizza, both with extra cheese— good and good for you. The giant can of Reddi-wip was in there calling my name too. Don't think I haven't started my day with a good squirt of that stuff right down the hatch.

When I looked out the kitchen slider, I caught sight of my eighty-six-year-old grandfather, who owns the house next to mine and who had recently been told by the cardiologist not to "overdo things." To Gramp, this meant mowing and clipping and edging and trimming only once a week instead of twice, and keeping the chain saw in the "off" position while climbing the extension ladder.

He was wearing his Heidi outfit—turquoise shorts with red suspenders, dress shirt, and black socks pulled almost to the knee. I stuck my head out and called to him.

"Gramp! I thought you said you were going to relax today!"

"I am!" he called back.

I stood looking at the bags of powdery white material surrounding him and the contraption he was banging up and down. My grandfather is a Home Depot dream customer, though I keep trying to get him to shop at Mort's Hardware, one of my coupon clients.

"But what is all that stuff?" I asked.

"Lime," he said, or I think that's what he said. I turned away. It was seven thirty and my treadmill stood lonely and despondent in the corner of the dining room. I walked past it and caught my image in the gilt-framed mirror that hung above the antique sideboard. Both the mirror and the sideboard came from my mother, who had assured me that possessing these two items was a clear sign of good taste, though she didn't know about the treadmill and I wasn't planning to tell her. The whole house was like that. A Victorian silver tea service—from my mother, of course, and mostly black from lack of polishing—on top of a sagging card table. Three expensive Steuben glass squirrels, or creatures of some kind, next to a curled-up photograph of some of my girlfriends. I really should have that thing framed before it disintegrates. Though my mother tries to reform me, in matters of taste and refinement I consistently score low. But I have good skin. Everyone always says so.

"You have good skin." That's usually how they say it. Sometimes they sound shocked.

I looked squarely in the mirror, never a good idea in bright sunlight, but without my contact lenses, not as frightening. My thirty-six-year-old face looked back at me—beaky little nose, wild hair and all. My driver's license says my hair is brown, and it is, sometimes the brown of a picnic basket, other times a fairly dark butterscotch. In days of yore I would have been called an old maid. An old maid and then some. The treadmill was going to have a bad day, so I gave it a pat on my way to the shower.

An hour later, my car began to have psychological problems. Much like the scale, it too speaks, but something must have gone haywire with the computer chip because it kept saying the same thing.

"Your door is ajar."

"No, it isn't. My door is closed."

"Your door is ajar."

"No, it isn't. Shut the fuck up."

The car and I were still arguing a half hour later, and my day had not improved. I could see the new Dunkin' Donuts going in just a few yards beyond the cyclone fencing near my office, and I waited for the day when I could spend half my week's pay there before work.

Up on the third floor, things were bustling. Magda, our blond-bombshell European receptionist who was learning English swear words as fast as she could, was taking calls and turning away business with lightning speed.

"Huh? Hallow? Screwing you too, mister big nobody."

"Hey, Mag, what's up?"

"Hi, Zheenie. Wassup you?"

"I'm dangerous today, Mag. No one had better mess with me." Magda's section of the office was mainly devoted to nail care and normally reeked of various polishes and chemical products. Now and then she typed something and distributed a sales lead to one of the reps. "Very weird guy calling you today," she said.

"A weird guy for me? No way," I said. I could never remember which country Magda was from, or which country it formerly was, although I knew it had a long and proud history of partisans and bombs. I browsed quickly through my mailbox to see if any of my deadbeats had paid their bills. "Ah, there is a God. Shinola Cleaners sent a check."

I was the best in our office at collections and considered every client a deadbeat until their balance was paid in full. We sell coupons. It's called direct-mail advertising, but I don't like to use big words to my clients in Worcester. They tend to get odd throbbing veins when something is hard to understand. Veins where you don't expect to see them, trust me. I collect money better than anybody, and this had not gone unnoticed by the new owners and particularly by our new boss, Dan Albright. We didn't have a nickname for Dan yet, not a true nickname that would be used behind his back, although several had been tried, including Dan Notbright, Danny Boy, and the wimped-out Danno. But none seemed to be sticking. He was an okay guy, Dan, and I felt sorry for him. He was even a little bit handsome, in a washed-out, over-the-hill kind of way. Managing our group of salespeople was not an easy task, lousy bunch of whining showoffs that we were, and he was trying his best. So far into the new regime, Dan loved me passionately, both for my collections skills and for my on-time performance. I was never late. He was running the Monday meeting that day and had asked everyone to come in prepared to say what they were doing to get "close to the business," that having been the buzz phrase of our recent regional sales meeting.

"The contest starts today," Dan reminded us as the meeting began. "Five thousand dollars. That's right, five thousand big ones," he said. We nodded. We already knew this. It was the point of the whole meeting. "Five large, ladies and gentlemen, to the rep who gets the most new customers for this mailing." We did some more appreciative nodding and eye-widening for Dan's benefit as he continued. "Plus one thousand dollars for every one of you who signs ten new customers." I was motivated. New owners will give out prizes like that, and since LotsaCoups had just been sold again, it was a good chance to cash in. I already had five new customers in the bag.

Henrietta Lewis, our group's top performer and worst dresser, raised her hand, eager to be the first rep to report. "Dan, I'm taking the bull by the horns. I'm leaving no stone unturned, and I'm planning to give one hundred and ten percent to this contest."

"Good news, Henrietta!" burst out Abe McNamara, another of my fellow reps and one of the shortest, as he rolled his chair backward and whanged it into the wall. "On the cliché meter, you've scored a perfect ten! Tell Henrietta what she's won, Dan." This earned smirks from the regular crowd and a dirty look from Dan.

"Cut it out, Abe," Dan said, showing very weak resolve. *Cut it out, Abe?* He'd be eaten alive if he didn't do better than that. "That's fantastic, Henrietta," Dan continued, and I looked to see just how brown Henrietta's nose could get at this hour. Then I gazed across the room at the ragtag assortment of reps, twelve of them here today including me, and most staring vacantly at nothing. Connie and Garrett Shonsky, old-time coupon veterans and dandruff victims, always sat next to each other, and it was very touching, a reminder that couples who plan discounts together, stay together. Then there was Florence Keating, a timid soul who wore wigs some of the time and never apologized for it. But I had to turn back to Dan's voice. We had all just been renamed the Metrowest Team by the new owners, attributing far more energy and cohesiveness to our group than was warranted. Whatever. We handled business west of Boston, much of it in the boonies of orchard country. Abe had returned to his customary dozing position, or, as he called it, checking his eyelids for pinholes.

Henrietta continued. "I'm planning to join a health spa in my area and talk to everyone in there about Lotsa-Coups. Also, I'm including a LotsaCoups pitch in the Sunday-school lessons I teach at the church." Abe opened his eyes and we glanced at each other. We would get to this delicious fodder later. To some, Henrietta was a hard-working, innovative sales genius. To others, she was a lying, scheming, account-stealing bitch. Guess which group I was in?

Soon it was my turn. I told everyone my plan.

"I'm trying out for *The Sound of Music*."

"On Broadway?"

"Of course not. The Worcester Spotlighters."

"What's that?"

"Community theater. I'll get tons of business from it." I was in no way convinced this was true, but I figured a little confidence couldn't hurt.

I could tell people were impressed by the way they all reached for doughnuts at the same time. Incisive questions followed.

"Is Julie Andrews dead?"

"Don't they wear lederhosen?"

"No, curtains. The kids wear curtains."

"What's lederhosen?"

"Stockings, I think. Or shorts. I don't really know."

Each of the reps stood and pledged to join book clubs, Elks lodges, bridge tournaments, and PTA committees. Abe even said he was going to join some lame cocktail hour. Dan instructed us to send him a memo once a week to keep the sales force updated. Nearly everyone suppressed a groan. When it turns into memo time, the project is usually headed for the toilet.

"All right, then," Dan said. "I'll let you go." This was code for, "Get on the road right now."

"I just have to look up some files," Abe said. This was code for, "I'll go when I feel like it." Dan was entirely too genial to be successful as a sales manager. The first thing you have to do is inspire fear in the reps, and Dan was trying to be our friend. It was painful. Abe and I chatted for a few minutes and agreed to meet for our customary medicinal mai tai the next day at Cheng Du. Soon I was back in my vehicle.

"Your door is ajar."

"Shut up, or I'll kill you."

By four P.M., I had seen all God's creatures, great and small. The car was now telling me that my seat belt was not fastened when it clearly was, and I had very nearly signed up a Chinese restaurant for a menu flyer. It was disappointing not to have closed the guy. "I check with my brother and call you. Somebody fender-bender his car." Just when I thought I would give up and go home to prepare my audition song, a woman yelled at me from a doorway down the street.

"Are you the coupon girl?"

Don't I love that question.

This was a tiny beauty salon just off Pleasant Street, and the nice part was I knew that a coupon would really help her business. What wouldn't? There was only one sink and one styling chair in the place. I refrained from admiring her thick, straight bangs.

Once I convinced her she had to give something away that was actually of value, we were fine. "I can't give anything away." "I work on a tight margin." I heard it every day and was sympathetic. When you're a business owner, everyone who walks in either wants your money or something for nothing. It can get wearing. But if you're going to do a coupon, ten percent off will keep people away in droves. Most owners understand this, at least when it has to do with their neighbor's business across the street. Free second cup of coffee? God, that's ridiculous. What is Fred thinking? But such market savvy disappears quickly when the spotlight is on one's own potential ad. Buy eight lunches, get the ninth for half price. Ugh. And this is the person who will scream loudest when the coupon "doesn't work." There are many battles to be fought and won.

As for intelligence level, this woman ranked approximately with the armrest in my car, and by the time I left, so did I. She and I got very confused over print runs and discounts.

"Didn't you say that was supposed to be fifteen?"

"Yes, that would be ten and then five. Isn't that fifteen?"

"Uh, well, I don't know. Will I get to put my slogo on the coupon?"

"You mean logo? Yes, you will."

"I'm not up on all these terms."

"That's okay. Neither am I."

I was thrilled to have new customer number six. As Abe would say, euphoria at its best.

"How did you come up with the name for the salon, ColdCuts?"

"Well, like, people want their haircuts to look cool, don't they? Cool is good? And cold would be sort of cool to the max, right? You know?"

"Were you worried that it might sound like a sandwich shop?"

"That's so funny that you say that. A lot of people think that it is!"

"Hi, you've reached the voice mail of Jeanie Callahan. If you're looking to grow your business, leave a message and I'll do a coupon that will do just that. Thanks for calling." BEEP.

"Hey, Jeanie. Call me back. I can't afford to give twenty-five percent off on a doughnut." BEEP.

"Hi, it's Meg. Soon to be pregnant after what I'm wearing tonight." BEEP.

"Hi, Jeanie. This is Gertrude Mayer, from across the street? You asked me to tell you if your grandfather was up on the ladder, and he is, or he was. The fire company was just here and got him down. He's okay." BEEP.

"My name Mike. You call me."

By five thirty I'd had it out with Gramp, who said that the ladder had fallen over and he could have gotten down through the attic window but that buttinsky Gertrude Mayer had to play hero and call the fire department. He always managed to convince me. I completely forgot to ask him what he was doing up there in the first place. I could see lime spread all over the lawn, so at least that project was done.

Gertrude Mayer was one of many women who orbited around my grandfather. "I'm in a seller's market," he joked with me sometimes, and he was. He had outlived my grandmother and a second wife, and seemed to gain strength every year. My own parents, newly retired and doing some serious globe-trotting, stopped in every so often for a good hamburger and a heated argument. I was supposed to be keeping watch over Gramp. Yeah, okay. Almost everything he did made me nervous, but what could I do?

I forced myself to nuke a frozen low-cal dinner and felt virtuous. I wrote my name in the dust on top of the microwave and felt less virtuous, housekeeping not being my best event. And now things would get even worse if I had to traipse out at night to play practice. I didn't know then that it's called rehearsal, just like the big-time dudes.

I really wanted to win the sales contest. I had always been a decent performer at LotsaCoups, but it was time to step up my game. Look out, Henrietta. Plus I desperately needed new wheels. When you're parking far away from your prospects because you don't want them to see your car, you've got special problems.

I called back my best friend, Meg, whom I hadn't seen for a while, since she and her husband had been trying 'round the clock to conceive an offspring. Meg and Gary lived practically across the street from the audition site, so I begged her to take a break from all that screwing and meet me there. She said she would if she could, but wanted to try out her new Frederick's of Hollywood garter belt. We both agreed that Frederick's was a bit raunchier than Vicky's and that maybe this would help things along. I felt jealous sometimes of Meg's life and wondered whether I should sign up for the computer dating service I had received in the mail.

Meg had managed to beat the odds. Long ago we'd decided that most men fell into one of four categories: A) married, B) gay, C) dork, or D) asshole. My recent boyfriends had all been Category D, including one who was both A and D, which in some ways is a natural combination.

An hour later as I sat in the June Mitchell Room at the Worcester library, I saw one or two Category Cs, but a whole lot more women than men. One of my clients, Isabel Cartwright, was flitting about with great purpose. She looked like a younger but not thinner Elizabeth Taylor, and wore a ton of eye makeup as usual.

"Well, hi, Jeanie. Are you auditioning?"

"Hi, Isabel. Is that okay?" Maybe my coupon status would bar my admittance. Maybe she didn't want to look at me after business hours.

"But of course. Fill this out and put this on, please," she said and handed me a piece of paper and a name tag.

It was hard to see how any of this would help me win the contest, though it was fascinating to watch people studying music and reciting words to themselves. Some were doing stretchy, pointy ballet steps in front of the stage, or they could have been karate moves for all I knew. There was an atmosphere in the air, peppy but serious, like just before the honor roll is announced and everyone pretends that they don't care, but they really do. I played the part of a tree when I was in third grade. It captured my abilities perfectly.

"So this is it," a voice said from behind me. It was Meg, newly sprung from sexual servitude, and I watched people turn to take her in. She looks like a model with that frosted-hair-and-dark-roots thing that shouldn't look good, but somehow does on the right person. Meg is definitely the right person, with cheekbones that go up to the ceiling. People often expect her to be snotty, and sometimes she is. But nobody makes me laugh like Meg does. She does a scream of a George Washington imitation.

I moved down the row to make room for her. "See that woman there?" I pointed. "She's one of my clients. I have to behave myself."

"Isn't this the play where all those little kids sing the worst song ever written, 'Doe, A Deer'?" Meg asked.

"That song's a classic," I said. "Did you break out the garter belt yet?"

"Gary wanted me to get him a double-dip chocolate ripple at PC Creams first. I told him I'd be right back. I don't know what he wants to do with ice cream."

"Maybe you should have Gary wear the garter belt, ha, ha," I said, trying to distract myself from my own nervousness.

Meg gave me a look. "We're not that desperate."

I nodded and Meg added, "Not yet."

"Please don't leave until I sing. Please," I begged. "Don't you want to see me collapsed on the floor in a twitching, babbling stupor?"

"You're going to sing?" Meg asked with a smile. "Maybe I can stay for a bit."

I sank lower in my chair. "If I don't throw up." I was starting to feel intimidated by all the vibrating voices around me, running up and down scales. I quietly tried to hit a couple of notes myself.

Meg turned to me with a frown. "Is that you? Are you okay?" Then she went on. "Here are my first impressions. A lot of people are overweight." I couldn't disagree with her. But then both of us watched as a dark-haired, glowering man strode in the door and toward the table where Isabel now sat. He opened a laptop as Meg and I shifted into full handsome-man alert.

We were close enough that we could hear him mutter to Isabel, "I see we have no men." Meg and I perused our try-out sheets with great studiousness, our ears growing larger by the second.

"Just be patient, Barton," Isabel said.

"I'm not playing the role, Isabel. You know I have to be in New York on opening night, as I made perfectly clear at the board meeting."

Isabel said nothing.

"So don't get that look in your eye," the man said.

Isabel pushed her chair back. "Did I say anything?" She stood and approached a group of what looked like high school girls giggling in the doorway.

"We just want to be nuns," one of them squeaked.

Isabel gave them name tags and paperwork. The girls, in halter tops and short shorts, were showing more flesh than most prostitutes as they accepted their nun applications. I could feel Meg taking a really close look, probably for inspiration.

A very tall—and I mean six feet tall—young woman sat down next to us and spoke. "Is this the audition for *The Sound of Music?*" Meg and I whipped around to look at her and nodded as though we were experts. Was there a basketball part in the show?

Behind us we could now hear another voice. "How do you do? Hey there. How are you? Bill Tuxhorn here, qualified to handle all your insurance needs." Oh my God, how tacky. I started feeling ashamed of my own ulterior motives.

"Do they want head shots?" the tall woman asked. Meg and I shrugged our shoulders. We had no idea what the protocol was.

Fear was upon me, right between my shoulders and in my throat and solar plexus. It was black and hairy and scratching itself in the balls. The handsome man turned around and surveyed the three of us, and a chill went down my back. I wasn't surprised he was looking at Meg, but if he ever heard her sing, he would have to check into rehab.

The name on his tag was Barton Columbus. He now addressed the group. "Okay, can all the kids get up on the stage, please? And line up by height. The tallest ones here and the shortest ones down this way." This nearly caused a riot as mothers and children moved in a great clump onto the stage.

"Just the kids, please!" Barton yelled, and then smiled when Isabel poked him in the back. To my eye, he looked ready to kill somebody. Meanwhile, about a million girls squirmed and wiggled and tried to stand in a straight line. The few boys there hovered next to a doctor's scale that said, WEIGHT WATCHERS—DO NOT REMOVE.

"Oh good grief," said Meg. "That's Gary's nephew up there, Truman. See the one with the skateboard? He's a pain in the ass."

"Does that include the part of Liesl?" someone asked.

"Yes. All the kids. Everyone trying out for one of the von Trapp children." Barton folded his arms in front of his chest and gave Isabel a death stare.

"What about the part of Gretel?" one of the mothers called.

Barton slapped his head with his hand. "I know! Let's get a dictionary and look up the word 'everybody.' What could it mean?"

Great hilarity ensued. I noticed several of the boys jumping up and down on the scale, and evidently so did

Barton because he took off after them behind the curtain. He reappeared a minute later, holding three of them by the shirts as if they were puppies. He looked triumphant, satisfied, and unaware of the name tag stuck to his back that read in thick black letters: I AM GAY.

Isabel ran out onto the stage to pat him on the back and remove the epithet. She seemed unaware of the tag on her own back, which read, I AM FAT. Barton pushed the kids into the line and handed the skateboard to Isabel.

"He doesn't have to actually touch the children, does he?" one of the mothers said from across the aisle. "They'll respond to reasonable guidance."

"I have to go home," Meg said. "Call me tomorrow."

To: Dan Albright
Fr: Jeanie Callahan
Re: GETTING CLOSE TO THE BUSINESS
Made a new sale today, Dan, bringing my total to six. But about the audition—my singing was pretty bad. The lady who played piano only let me get as far as "a female deer" before she said, "Thank you very much." I don't know if this will

Somehow, Dan probably doesn't need to know I can't carry a tune. On to attempt number two.

To: Dan Albright
Fr: Jeanie Callahan
Re: GETTING CLOSE TO THE BUSINESS
On Monday night, June 8, I attended an audition for the Worcester Spotlighters in Worcester, Mass., who are performing The Sound of Music in early August. Many business owners were present. SEND.

A Very Good Place to Start

Tuesday, June 9

"Are you going to have another one?" Abe asked. We were sitting in the bar at Cheng Du, slurping on scorpion bowls.

"Are you?" I countered.

Abe pretended to look puzzled. "Well, let's see. I could go home and pull ticks off the dog, or I could sit here and sling the shit with you. Let me think about it."

"Two more." I motioned to the waiter. Abe was a bantam-rooster type of little guy, full of confidence and obsessed with sex. I could have crushed him with one foot.

"You're showing toe cleavage today, Jeanie. I like it."

"Thanks, big boy. But my feet are killing me," I said. "Unlike you, I put in a full day's work."

"So do you think you'll get in the play?"

"Psssh," was my first answer. "After hiccupping while I tried to sing? Repeatedly?"

Abe smiled. "They probably thought you were plastered."

"Thanks. I should have been."

"Yes, but plastered because you were nervous. Doesn't that show desire? Intense interest? Wouldn't they want someone like that?"

"I don't think they want the nuns staggering around hiccupping, at least not during the convent songs," I said. "On the other hand, I wasn't any worse than some of the others."

Abe smiled again. "Give me the date for this one more time," he said as he pulled out his Palm Pilot. "This is going to be great."

"August seventh and eighth. What if I don't get in?"

"I'll beat the crap out of them if you don't," Abe said, and replaced the PDA into his shirt pocket.

"God," I said. "You should have seen the women reading for the lead role."

Abe looked around. "Were they worse than you? Did they actually puke?" He found the happy-hour buffet and started undressing it with his eyes.

I ignored his questions. "You know Maria? The nicey-nice Julie Andrews part? Most of the women were over-weight, one was six feet tall, and one had a huge nose."

"Maria's the one that gets porked by the Nazi guy, right?"

"He's not a Nazi. He's the hero."

Abe laughed. "Tell me again about the young sluts."

"I didn't say they were sluts. They're high school girls showing a lot of skin. They were the best singers, actually."

Abe bowed courteously as he stood. "Do you want any-thing?"

"No, thanks," I said.

"I have confidence in confidence alone," Abe trilled in his stupid falsetto voice.

"Shut up," I said.

I could hear a doorbell ringing faintly. *Ding-dong.* I knew it was my cell phone. No matter which musical selection I chose, it continued to do *ding-dong*. It was frustrating, but I was getting a discount, so I didn't care. Other people were always confused by it, and indeed many Cheng Du patrons were looking around for the source.

"Hi, this is Jeanie."

"Jeanie, it's Mort at Mort's Hardware. You have to come over here right away."

I sighed. Mort spent the minimum possible on his coupon but was always having some emergency with it. "What's the problem, Mort?"

"Jeanie, I'm really tied up now, but I have to see you. Can you come over?"

Since I was all the way in another town and had finished my sales day, I was in no mood to go back to downtown Worcester. Furthermore, it was time to show Mort who was boss. I took a deep breath.

"Mort, are you listening?"

"Yeah."

"It's like this."

"Okay. What? I'm listening."

"I need at least fifteen minutes," I said.

"No problem, Jeanie."

Abe returned to the table with a plate heaped high. "So how many new customers have you got?" he asked.

"Six," I said, gathering my belongings. "Over the hump, baby. How about you?"

"I might have a couple," Abe said. Abe was not the hardest worker.

"You'd better get out there," I cautioned him. "Danny Boy won't like it if you don't bring in a few."

"Danny Boy can kiss my ass," Abe said. Abe had the Baldwin Springs bottled water account, and everybody knew he got huge commissions from it. He and the owner traded dirty jokes on the golf course, and the guy loved Abe.

I stood. "I can't believe I now have to drive all the way

back downtown. I'll bet you five dollars he wants some dumb little thing."

Abe saluted me with his fork. "Puke on 'em, girl."

Of course I didn't puke on Mort. Mort Gallo was one of the very first clients I ever had. When he was just starting to run the business under his parents' guidance, Mort used to call me up to see how many coupons were going to get returned and whether they'd be men or women. He thought I would know.

"Jeanie. I can't run this special all the way into November. The paint company will have my neck. It has to end before that."

"So you're saying we have to change the expiration date on the coupon, Mort."

"Well, yeah. Yeah."

"Is there anything else?"

The store phone now rang three times in succession and Mort had to take the three calls while I walked around looking at wallpaper samples and contemplating suicide. Then a customer came in and I strolled around some more. My toes, inside the snazzy slingbacks that Abe admired, had melded into one banana bunch of pain. Finally, Mort's attention was mine.

"Oh hi, Jeanie. What were we saying?"

"We were saying that you needed to change your expiration date."

"Oh yes, that will take care of it."

I swallowed down my fierce desire to yell at Mort for making me come all this way for such a little thing. But I had a five-year no-tantrum record to uphold, so I kept my cool and told him about my foray into show business instead.

Mort nodded. "The Worcester Spotlighters, huh? Is that Isabel Cartwright?"

I nodded back. "Yes, Isabel is the producer or whatever

they call it. She's in charge of everything. She's doing a coupon too, for her new photo shop business."

"You know, I think Isabel likes me."

"Oh," I said cheerfully. I doubted this very much. Isabel might have been a bit overweight, but besides being married and wearing a giant diamond, she was very pretty and stylish. Picturing her in front of the TV with Mort in his perspiration-stained shirt and asthma inhaler somehow didn't ring quite true.

Mort took out a stick of gum from his ink-stained pants pocket and added it to the enormous glob already in his mouth. "Yup. She wants me, all right."

"Hmm, well, there's a thought," I said in as vague a manner as I could project. Stranger things have happened on Main Street, of course, and if Isabel and Mort wanted to ravish each other on the paint-spinning machine, it was fine with me; I just wanted to get in the car and take my shoes off. Usually it's the dry cleaners who are lonely and won't shut up. I closed my eyes and knew I was in hell. But then God sent me my reward.

"Hey, Jeanie, I forgot. My brother-in-law is starting a carpet-cleaning business, and I told him he ought to do a coupon. Do you want his number?"

"Wow, thanks, Mort. Yes, I do."

"Your trunk is open."

"My trunk is not open."

"Your trunk is open." I really hoped my car was just messing with me again, since I was tearing up Route 290 at a high speed, trying to get home in time for *Jeopardy!*. Gramp and I usually watched it at his house. That way I got to leave when I wanted to, without getting stuck entertaining his concubines. I hadn't heard anything about *The Sound of Music*, and I was beginning to realize I probably didn't make the cut. I should have just stayed at Cheng Du with Abe.

I turned into my driveway and cursed softly at myself for forgetting to put out the garbage that morning. Gramp had remembered for me, of course. My rubber can and the recycling bin had been emptied and were ready to be rolled back up to the carport. I stopped to do that, at least saving Gramp one small task.

I grabbed my mail and was just walking into the kitchen perusing it when I saw a dead body on the floor.

I screamed.

The dead body's legs stuck out from under the kitchen sink and jumped several inches with the scream, causing the dead body's head to hit the drainpipe under the sink and transform into my grandfather with a nasty bump between his eyebrows.

"Ooooow! Jesus Christ!"

"Gramp! What are you doing?"

"Fixing a leak . . . Oh Jesus!"

"Are you okay?"

Gramp lay back down, took a deep breath, and stared at the ceiling. He looked like he was doing yoga. If only he would, I thought, as he inserted himself back into the lower sink area. "Yeah, I'm okay. Why didn't you tell me this thing was leaking?"

I sat down to calm my heart rate and took several deep breaths of my own. "Gramp, I wish there were a way for me to know you are in the house when I'm not here." This was code for, "Please stay out of my house."

"You could use a new faucet in the bathroom. I've got it on my list," was his only answer. To Gramp, wandering through my house trying the faucets was the pinnacle of a fun afternoon. But there's no doubt he came over sometimes to avoid the swarming women. Women from the church, women from the neighborhood, women he met while jogging, shopping, and even one who introduced herself while pumping gas for his car. But since Gramp had bought the house for me, I didn't really feel I had a right to tell him to stay out. It was ticklish.

Ding-dong. "Someone's at the door," Gramp said from under the sink with still another groan.

"No, it's my phone," I said.

It was both. Life's events occur in clusters, I have found. They converge. On the day you're summoned for an IRS audit, your radiator goes. On the day you discover mouse droppings in the silverware drawer, your great-aunt shows up for a visit. If the phone rings, the doorbell wants to chime in, too. I peered around the dining room curtain and saw Gertrude Mayer holding a covered baking dish on the front steps. She must have been lurking behind her own curtain, waiting for me to arrive. I decided to take the phone call first.

"This is Jeanie."

"The garter belt wasn't a good idea."

"Hold on," I said to Meg, and opened the door. "Oh hi, Mrs. Mayer, how are you?"

Mrs. Mayer—June Cleaver reborn—complete with earrings, high heels, and an apron, beamed with pride at her offering. "I thought you might like to sample my coconut crumb cake, dear."

I loathe and despise coconut. "Oh gee thanks, Mrs. Mayer. That's so nice." *I'm not inviting you in.*

"I gave one to your grandfather last week," she said. "And I have something important I'd like to talk to you about."

I wedged the phone against my sternum to take possession of the baking dish as I spoke into the phone. "So what happened with the garter belt?"

Mrs. Mayer turned and scrutinized the begonias while I listened to Meg. "I couldn't get it off. The clasp part, the thing that holds it on, got stuck and wouldn't come undone, so we had to do it with the whole thing flapping around and getting in the way. I hope we didn't lose any sperm."

"Oh geez," I said, not wanting to make sperm comments in front of my neighbor. "Well, thanks a lot, Mrs. Mayer. Did you ever get it to come off?"

Meg answered, "Eventually, but I had to tear it," as Mrs. Mayer answered for herself.

"Oh, the cover comes right off. By the way, is your grandfather home tonight? I called earlier and there was no answer."

"I think he's over there, Mrs. Mayer. He's probably got *Jeopardy!* turned up really loud. Why don't you try again?" I knew Gramp was trying to avoid her, and the least I could do after his near-death-by-drain was cover for him.

"Meg, I've got another call. Can you hold?" I asked as I watched the disheartened Mrs. Mayer walk back across the street. "What did you want to ask me?" I called, but she didn't hear me. I wanted to shout out not to give up the ship, that there were other fish in the sea, and other rousing bits of maritime solace.

Instead, I returned to the phone. "This is Jeanie."

"Hi, Jeanie, it's Isabel Cartwright. How would you like to be in the chorus of our show?"

My heart leaped. "Oh wow, I'd love to. I was afraid I was really bad." *I was afraid you thought I was shit-faced.*

"You'll be one of the nuns and a townsperson. Is that okay?"

"Oh, yes, Isabel. Who did you cast for Maria?"

Isabel hesitated. "Barton is still undecided on that. Why don't we plan on seeing you Friday night at the read-through?"

"The what?"

"When we all sit down and read through the script," Isabel explained.

"Great," I said. "Just great." I heard an odd sound as I suddenly saw myself on *Oprah*. Guest roles on *Law & Or-*

der, where I would be a young idealistic attorney. A breakthrough movie. Wasn't that what they called it? Guest-hosting on *Saturday Night Live*, where I would cheerfully mock my own career and the audience would howl. And there, at last, on the red carpet at the Oscars. The odd sound turned out to be Gramp, disconnecting and removing the entire kitchen sink. But I didn't care. I was about to start my real career, my acting career, and I couldn't wait, although I hoped it wasn't a bad omen when I looked outside and saw that the trunk of my car was open.

A Few of My Favorite Things

Friday, June 12

"Hi, you've reached the voice mail of Jeanie Callahan. Today is Friday, June twelfth, and time's a-wastin' for the coupon that will grow your business. Leave a message, and I'll call you back." BEEP.

" 'Time's a-wastin'? Gee, there's a modern, hip greeting. Hey, it's Abe. What am I going to do about getting a new customer? You gotta help me. That cocktail hour was ridiculous. Everybody trying to sell each other. Later, babe." BEEP.

"Hello, Zheenie. Is Magda. New lead for you. Jersey Macamamama, call at night only, four sping seben tree nine eight sex. Happy hunt!" BEEP.

"My name Mike. You call me."

Friday is always good. Even when you first wake up, there's a kind of zest in the air. Busier. More alive. The cars around the rotary seem to have more purpose. Let's get done; let's get out of here. The read-through was tonight, and even Meg was somewhat interested in it, although she was more interested in the lingerie sale at Filene's. We both wanted to know who would be Maria, the big nose or the giant. I hadn't told Meg yet of my secret hope that it would be me.

My new sales were stalled. I still had the six I'd already sold, plus the strong possibility of Mort's brother-in-law, which would make seven. But I hadn't been able to reach the brother-in-law, and the lead from Magda had not panned out. Jersey Macamamama turned out to be Jerry McIntosh, who wanted to do mail order, and I knew it wouldn't work. At least once or twice every mailing cycle, someone making Darth Vader thimbles in his attic calls in and wants to spend his life savings on a coupon. Poor Jerry had compiled venison and grouse recipes in a hunters' cookbook. I kept my professional face on when he handed me a rough draft of an ad. *Grisly Adams* [sic] *Stir-fries the Wilderness!* I felt very moral, since it would have been so easy to take his money and have my seventh new customer. Not that I didn't have some second thoughts.

I gritted my teeth as I stood in Benito's Fine Menswear at precisely noon. Benito was nice enough, though the scar across his face was disconcerting at times. The thing I hated was the way the rest of his help acted as though I were invisible. I went in there only as a disciplinary, leveling experience, to show my work ethic to myself. I knew he would never buy from me because he thought his business was too classy for coupons. I'd never seen a customer in his store. There was no doubt that other things were being sold at Benito's besides menswear.

"Hi. How are you guys?" I said in my chirpiest voice.

Five clerks, about four and a half more than were needed, ignored me totally. All were slicked-back gum chewers. Most of my sales territory was gum chewing.

"Nice weather, huh?" I persisted.

Two of the clerks checked their reflections in the mirror. They were perfect.

"Is Benito around?"

One of the clerks shook his head and started dialing a cell phone. "Coupons," he said. Then he hung up. "Not interested."

"Okay," I said. "Well, you guys have a good day, all right? Don't work too hard." I was reminded of a reptile tank, where everything moves slowly and none of the inhabitants get too excited.

Outside, I debated whether to check on a few more businesses across the rotary from where I stood, or drive to the office for some sales materials, or blow off the rest of the day. Abe could be had for Friday drinking, if he wasn't playing golf. My decision was made by my cell phone, which dinged and donged from inside my briefcase.

"This is Jeanie."

"Hi, um, Jeanie?"

"Yes?" There was no point in being sarcastic.

"Um, it's Roger Crandall. Ye Olde English Scones and Tacos?"

"Oh yes, Roger, hi." One of my six new ones. It was never a good sign when they called this early in the relationship.

"I'm having some problems, and I don't think I can do the pamphlet. That brochure thing."

"The coupon, Roger? The one you signed a contract to do?"

"Um, well, yes."

"Are you in the store right now? I'm just down the street."

"I'm here, but I don't think—"

"I'll be right there," I said. I was not going to let him drop out. By hook or by crook, I was not going to let him drop out.

Fifteen minutes later, I tore up Roger Crandall's contract and let him drop out. The poor guy was having "prostrate" problems and I didn't want to hear any more. I was a sucker for a good medical tale of woe and had logged many hours listening to gallbladder horror stories, not to mention kidney stones, hip replacements, cataract procedures, and every other kind of agonizing, long-winded saga. It would have been very easy to spend two hours with Roger hearing all the details, and normally I probably would have, but my time seemed more valuable now that I knew I wouldn't be peddling coupons forever. Scones and tacos would now never make their debut on Chandler Street, and though I wasn't that surprised, I still walked out feeling dispirited. I was back to only five new customers. Bummer.

"Why don't we go around the room and each say our name and a little something about ourselves? My name is Barton Columbus, I'm the director, and this is my third show with the Worcester Spotlighters. Isn't it?" Barton asked and looked around for Isabel. She nodded, wearing even more makeup than usual. Barton continued. "And this is Marianne Peters, the musical director."

"I think I can speak for myself," Marianne said, evidently not a Barton groupie. She looked to be at least forty and had a sixties-style hairdo, a big bulletproof helmet with a little sausage roll attached to it at the bottom that rested on her shoulders. "I'm Marianne Peters, and I expect everyone to have their songs learned in two weeks." This was the woman who had looked dyspeptic when I sang. She still looked ready to jump out of her own skin.

Meg and I were sitting in the second row of chorus members and taking in everything. Even though she hadn't tried out and wasn't really in the chorus, no one seemed to know or care, and we were still waiting to hear who would be Maria. My visions of the surprise announcement that Maria would be me were fading fast, especially since the tall girl was sitting at the main table where all the leads were.

I whispered to Meg, "What's Gary doing, changing the sheets?"

"How did you know that?" she answered. "I can only stay a minute."

"There's Gary's nephew," I said. "Looks like he made it into the cast. What's his name again?"

"Truman," whispered Meg. "He's not happy about it either. His parents are making him do it to show that he can stay out of trouble. If he stays clean all summer, he's going to get some new computer or something."

"Can he sing?"

"I don't think so."

"My name is Charlie Jenkins, and I'm playing Captain von Trapp," said an exceptionally tall person whose face was stony and hard. Welcome to Mount Rushmore. Gosh, why try out for something if it's such a bother to do?

And then my dream died. "My name is Laura Wheeler, and I'm playing Maria." It seemed incredible, but it was true. I looked around the room and saw a few disappointed faces in addition to my own, including the big-nosed woman on the other side of me, who sighed audibly.

"I'm out of here," she said, and got up and walked out, causing a bit of a stir.

Everyone turned toward Barton, who looked up from his laptop and stood. "Well, you know what they say," he said. "There are no small parts, only small people." A small gasp went up. Did Big Nose seriously think she would be Maria? I guess she did, and I guess the middle-aged woman across the aisle did too, because she walked out as well.

Barton seemed almost gracious. "Go. Everyone who wants to go, go. If you want to stay and help make the show the best it can be, then stay. We don't want prima donnas."

Uh-oh, I thought. I didn't want to be one of those. I just wanted to win the contest and get to Hollywood virtuously.

A few other people introduced themselves, including a little girl with pigtails who said, "I'm Jennifer, and I'm playing the part of Liesl even though I'm only eleven because I was better than anybody else." A few scowls dotted the room at that one, though no one left.

Meg whispered to me, "Is she the one who does 'Sixteen Going on Seventeen'?"

"I think so," I said.

"Truman has to sing with her. They're supposed to be in love. How is that going to work?" she persisted.

"Do I look like I know?" I whispered back.

When my turn came, I never mentioned my coupon livelihood, possibly because Bill Tuxhorn had gone so overboard with his own intro. "Hi there, I'm Billy Tuxhorn, qualified to handle all your insurance needs. I hope to get a chance to chat with all of you at some point during the production." I was sure I heard a groan.

"I'm Jeanie Callahan, and I've never been in a play before," was my dumb remark. Barton nodded his head and said, "Welcome, Jeanie," or something like that. From that moment I became his helpless slave. I've thought about it many times afterward and that's when it happened.

Meg too was showing slavelike tendencies when she stood up and introduced herself. Again, no one seemed to care, or at least no one cried out, "Stop, sit down, you can't be in the show."

"Don't you have to get going?" I asked her.

"Yes, soon," she said.

A Long, Long Way to Run

Saturday, June 13

"Jean! Jeanie! Wake up!" The applauding audience in my waking dream turned into the urgent voice of my grandfather on Saturday morning at seven A.M.

"What, Gramp?" I asked in my most waiflike voice.

"Your car needs a sticker!"

"Yes, I was going to do it later," I said. My head had acquired the contours and heft of a bowling ball sometime during the night, possibly due to the five vodka stingers I had consumed at Shipley's Pub the evening before.

It had started innocently enough back at the library during the read-through. Barton and Isabel invited anyone who cared to join them to come along for some good fellowship. About fifteen of us did. I was pretty sure I had done my Wicked Witch of the West imitation sometime during that fellowship.

"And if you're planning on getting tomatoes in, you'd better do that too, or forget it for the summer," Gramp said from the kitchen. I could hear him hoisting the new sink into position. "Home Depot still has a few," he added.

"Good," I replied, lying on my back and contemplating the ceiling. A tiny crack near the closet exactly reflected what I was sure was a tiny crack in my skull. I dialed Meg.

She answered on the eighth ring, also waiflike. "Only you are allowed to call at this hour."

"What did Gary say?"

"Never mind Gary. I'm near death."

"Oh, God, me too. Were you in trouble for going out and not making babies?"

"My loving husband, as a matter of fact, went out with his friends and didn't seem to care what I did." I knew Gary was probably right next to her in bed.

"Do you remember that you told Barton you'd give him a haircut?"

"Did I?"

"Did I do my witch imitation?" I asked.

"Yes. The waitstaff was in awe."

I sighed. "Now we both have to leave town."

"Only you, dear," Meg said. "I restricted my outlandishness to indoor behavior. You did yours in the parking lot."

I sighed again and had to whisper my next statement. "My grandfather is in the kitchen putting in a new sink. My life has deteriorated to this."

"All right," Meg said. "Call me later. I still want to go to Filene's for a thong."

Hangovers are very personal, of course, and my own unique version has some good points to it. I never get sick, I never throw up, and I never get a headache. However, before you feel intense envy, consider this: When I wake up, that is the best I will feel all day. Abe calls it the "yin-yehs." It's like when the audio doesn't match the video in a movie. Things keep happening in freeze-frame and you're still back in the last frame when the world has moved ahead to the next one. Nothing helps. Well, sleep will dispel this feeling, but the one thing I cannot do is fall asleep. My body cries out for it, and I can lie down and close my eyes, but my brain buzzes into full nervous alert. *Boyoyoyoing.* It gets progressively worse, usually culminating around two P.M., when I indulge in a feeding and soda-drinking frenzy. By nine or ten P.M. of the full hangover day, I start to feel tired, then really tired, and then I fall into a delicious sleep that lasts the whole night and brings me refreshed to the next day, when I feel like going out for drinks.

"Gramp?" I asked from the doorway, where I stood with a blanket over my head like a lost *Ten Commandments* extra.

"Yeah?" he called. I was actually speaking to his legs, which once again protruded from underneath the sink.

"Never mind," I started to say as I turned to open the fridge and saw Gertrude Mayer about to do the same thing. "Mrs. Mayer!" I gasped. I had no idea what she was doing in my house at this hour, but I did know that if she opened that door, the first thing she would see would be her coconut cake, unloved and untouched.

"Don't open the refrigerator!" I cried.

Mrs. Mayer gasped and pulled her hand back as if from a serpent. "Oh!" she said, and looked at me with wide eyes.

"There's bugs in there. Big ones." It was all I could think of to say.

Mrs. Mayer made some noise. I noticed she had painted her eyebrows.

Gramp piped up from under the sink, "How can there be bugs in a refrigerator?"

I grabbed the flyswatter and walked toward the fridge. Despite my reduced mental state, I knew action was called for, and grabbed some paper towels.

"Just stand over there," I cautioned as I opened the fridge door. I used it to block Mrs. Mayer's view while I reached in with great stealth and used the flyswatter as cake cutter, slicing off a healthy portion and leaving the cake looking used and enjoyed. I slid the hated confection into the paper towels, mashed it all with my fingers, and then removed it, hoping Mrs. Mayer might think it was what? Larvae? Yes, and from an unknown arctic insect. If you're confident, you can make people believe anything. I already knew this. If you're not confident, they will have doubts. I went to toss the whole mess in the trash under the sink, but then remembered there was no sink and no trash receptacle either, so I just stood holding it all in front of me, flyswatter protruding into my chest. Coconut frosting adorned my knuckles and fingernails, and confidence ebbed away by the bucketful.

"Well," Mrs. Mayer ventured.

I started to lapse into an insincere laugh, but Mrs. Mayer saved me.

"It looks like you have the sink where you want it, Bob, so I'd better get back to my garden."

Gramp's legs slid out into the middle of the kitchen and he stood, hanging on to the countertop for balance. He seemed a little dizzy, and that worried me. "Thanks for breakfast, Gert. Glad I jogged your way this morning."

"Did you want to talk to me, Mrs. Mayer?" I asked, praying she would say no.

"That's all right, dear. You go back to bed." If only I could, I wanted to cry out. I wanted to throw myself at her feet and hang on to her ankle for the day.

Gramp opened the fridge and continued his Saturday-morning Lecture the Incompetent Homeowner series. "Today's a good day for fertilizer, too," he said. "What time do you think you'll be back from your car inspection?"

I stood, deaf and dumb, watching him pull a knife from the drawer and slice himself a generous hunk of cake.

"Gramp, why don't you wait to eat that?" I said.

"Why?" he asked. "It's good. Want a slice?"

"Not yet, Gramp." Mrs. Mayer and I watched him eat,

she with pleasure, me in horror, trying not to imagine where that flyswatter had been.

Mrs. Mayer opened the glass slider and made her exit. "Okay, well, if you want to go to Bingo next week, let me know."

"I will, Gert," Gramp said with the jauntiest of waves. As Mrs. Mayer disappeared around the side of the house, I watched another car pull into Gramp's driveway. Out of the car stepped a woman with a frosted-blond beehive hairdo. She carried a gift-wrapped box with a big red bow on the top.

I couldn't keep the pace.

Meg and I, feeling better after some hot fried dough and large Cokes, were inspecting thongs later in the day when my cell phone dinged and donged. I hoped it wasn't Gramp, who thought I was picking up tomatoes and not wasting time at the mall. In fact, I was very much hoping it would be the Chinese guy saying he wanted to do the flyer menu after all, so I probably sounded a little breathless.

"This is Jeanie."

"I thought it was the Wicked Witch of the West."

"Who is this?"

"It's Barton." All blood now left my head, and I nearly fainted in the middle of Filene's. I whispered to Meg who it was and her mouth fell open.

"Um, Barton the director?" I croaked.

"Yeah. How are you feeling?"

"I'm . . . I'm fine. How are you?" A recovered memory popped into my head from the night before, of me doing the polka with Barton inside the ladies' room at Shipley's.

"You cracked me up last night." And another one of me playing Mary Magdalene and trying to wash Barton's feet with my hair. Oh, the shame.

"Oh, well, just give me four or five drinks and I'm off," I

said. Meg turned her back and walked away. A saleslady was still trying to help us.

"Are you doing anything tonight?" Barton asked.

"Am I doing anything tonight?" I repeated.

"Are these hard questions?" he asked again. Meg's eyes looked like a raccoon's.

"Well, aside from Prince Charles possibly coming for tea, I guess I'm not doing anything," I said. That was always my answer when someone asked if I was busy. It was never particularly funny and indeed seemed less so now. Meg frowned and began motioning *no, no.*

"Would you like to go out?"

"Um, well, sure. Yeah," I said. The saleslady kept talking to us, but Meg and I ignored her. I gave Barton directions to my house and told him I'd be ready at seven P.M. I finally hung up.

"What do you think you're doing?" Meg asked.

The saleslady jumped. "I'm just trying to show you the ones that are on sale."

"No, I don't mean you, I'm sorry," said Meg, and looked me in the eye.

"I guess I have a date," I said. "What's wrong with that?" I figured Meg was jealous as all hell.

"He calls you at three o'clock on a Saturday afternoon and you tell him you're available that very night? Only a few hours later?"

"Well, yeah. So?"

The saleslady made one more valiant effort. "Or you could go with the really nice ones here."

My own interest in the thongs had jumped greatly in the last few minutes while Meg's had declined. Meg shook her head. "That is not good, Jeanie. And you know it."

"Well, what the heck. I never get to have any fun," I said, hoping she would not remind me of my drunken antics the night before. "And I'm not going to drink, so it doesn't matter."

We concluded our business in the lingerie department (thongs for her after all, a Wonderbra for me) and left. The atmosphere between us was cold as we pulled up to her house. Gary waved to me from the sprinkler in the tiny front yard of their triple decker.

"Hey, Jeanie! Come on in," he said. "I'm making chili."

"Oh God," Meg said. "We'll all be in the hospital soon."

Chili didn't sound bad to me, even Gary's variety, and I thought maybe I could jostle Meg back into a good mood, so I got out of the car and walked in the side door with the two of them behind me. Gary had his arm around Meg and was trying to kiss her, but she pushed him away.

"Smells good, Gare," I said. Steam poured from a vast pot on the stove. "What's this?" A large, ugly portrait of a frowning old woman hung on the kitchen wall.

"It's my great-grandmother," Gary answered. "She had sixteen kids."

Meg shook her head. "Gary thinks if we hang her picture, it will happen to us."

"Wow. Sixteen."

"We'll settle for one," Gary said.

"It's ridiculous," Meg said. "I can't even cook with that there. I've burned everything. She's making me nervous."

"Just for a little while, sweetie," Gary said, and started opening cans of kidney beans.

"I can feel my uterus rejecting her," Meg said. "I'm only trying it for a week. I don't care if we never get pregnant."

"Hey, don't say that," Gary said, and turned around three times. I made eye contact with Meg.

"Don't you know turning around three times is good luck?" Meg asked me.

"Gosh, Gare. Are you going to click your ruby slippers?"

"We'll do whatever works," he said, and tied an apron around his neck.

"Hmm," I said. "How long have you guys been observing all these procedures?"

"Two months, two weeks, and two days," Meg said.

"Seems longer," I said.

"Jeanie has a date with the director of the show tonight," Meg said.

Gary picked up a wooden spoon and started stirring the chili. "That's great," he said. "My nephew is in the show. He's a handful, that kid. Look out." A burning smell filled the room, and I decided to skip Gary's chili after all. Meg still seemed irritated, though she did walk me to my car as she always did. Sometimes we have extra little secrets to talk about, but not today.

Meg folded her arms and said, "Don't sleep with Barton, Jeanie. Just don't do it."

"Well, of course I'm not going to do it," I replied.

"You always say that," she said.

"Well, I really mean it this time."

Ten hours later, as I filled Barton's glass again with rum and Coke and my own with chardonnay, I remembered those faraway words. *Saturday Night Live* was just ending and Barton was flipping through the channels. Like any guy, he had immediately claimed the remote.

"So how many people actually tried out for the show?" I asked.

"What show?" he asked. He put down the control and figured out how to dim the lamplight next to him on the couch. This made me a little nervous. "Oh, that show! The one with the Los Angeles Lakers in it! You'd have to ask Isabel. What do some of the other rooms in your house look like?" Barton had such a devilish look to him. And his shoulders were so broad. And his black hair and beard looked almost satanic. Did I already say that?

"Are these rats?" he asked.

"They're Steuben squirrels."

"Oh. They look more like rats, don't they?" He dimmed the light even further.

"You're being bad now," I said, handing over his drink and sitting down beside him, this time a bit closer than the last.

"Listen, thank you again for lending me money for dinner. I'm so embarrassed," Barton said.

"No problem," I replied.

"What an idiot, showing up on a date without my wallet." Barton shook his head as he leaned into me quite close. He was so penitent. "I'll have the money for you at rehearsal Monday night. Promise." We kissed. Even though I knew it was coming, it was still something of a surprise. Barton had such a casual way. He didn't throw his arms around me; he just leaned. Soon we were having a leaning lip conversation. Soon after that other things started happening.

"You are so sexy," he whispered. Fog and steam were filling up the room, along with indecision and rash behavior, until a very bright light shone through the window.

"That's my grandfather," I said.

Barton jumped. "Who? What?"

"My grandfather. Those were his headlights."

"Does he live here?"

"No, he lives next door. He's just getting in."

There was a bit of a pause in the fog and steam, but then they returned with even more intensity.

"Jeanie?" Barton said, and took a quavering breath. I like it when a man's breath quavers.

"Hmmm," I answered.

"Could you read something to me?"

"Yeah, sure. What?" I looked around to see what he might be trying to read.

"Something I wrote that I'd like you to read out loud. Okay?"

"Sure. Okay."

Was this going to be some kind of a disclaimer? Anything I say or do in the next twenty minutes is absolved from legal liability? A make-out prenup?

Barton pulled away slightly and I watched him extract a piece of paper from his shirt pocket. It was folded in half several times, and I had to pull away even more to open it fully after he gave it to me. I also had to reach across him in order to turn the lamp brighter. He felt warm. The paper was written in pencil with lots of smudges and cross-outs; not that easy to decipher, but I did my best.

" 'The heart of the chrysanthemum opens inside the appendix of time/Beyond the space of Mother's . . .' What?" I looked up at Barton in the bright light.

"Mother's garden."

"Oh, okay. 'Beyond the space of Mother's garden. When to find the pulping liver lying heaped on the floor as the worms grow in and in and in, always in.' "

"No, that's 'in and out and in, always in.' "

"Oh, okay. Did you write this?" I asked. Barton nodded and began moaning and kissing my neck. "Please keep reading," he said. I put my arms around his neck, holding the paper out as close to the lamp as I could.

" 'In the garden of life the poison leeches and grows . . . Is it 'grows' or 'graves'?"

Barton stroked the back of my head. "Grows. Keep going."

I read several more lines, but felt extremely distracted, as Barton kept kissing my neck repeatedly. Every time I hesitated, though, so would he. "Please don't stop," he would say. Finally, I threw the thing onto the floor and welcomed Barton into my full embrace, figuring that was enough of the poetic foreplay. The last line was something about purple blood clots, so I figured it was a good place to stop.

But Barton jumped off the couch and started to pace in the dark.

"I'm sorry, Jeanie. I really am. I'm just too weird. I'm so

sorry." Barton sat on the armchair and put his head in his hands.

"Barton," I said. "I don't think you're weird. I don't." I wasn't sure, though.

"Someday I'll tell you about my mother," he said. "It was a weird childhood I had."

"Okay," I replied.

"I'd better go," he said, and I didn't argue with him. In a minute we were both standing at the doorway kissing again.

"You'd better get out of here," I said to Barton, and gave him a playful push.

"I think I'm in love with you, Jeanie." There seemed no fitting reply, so I said nothing. I stood by the front door for several moments, turned my back, and leaned into the wall for several more. Eventually, I slid down to the floor, shaking my head all the way.

A Drop of Golden Sun

Monday, June 15

My waking dream was of my high school history teacher. She was scolding me and I deserved it.

"One hundred and forty-one pounds," the bathroom scale said in triumph, minutes later. I hung my head. Where was it all going? At least I had the massive bouquet of flowers that Barton had sent, sitting on my kitchen table. He must have paid extra for Sunday delivery, though he hadn't called.

My car was silent, thank God. I turned the radio to the sports station, inveterate Red Sox fan that I was, hoping for good news. There was. But there was always good news in June, no matter what team you rooted for. I wondered whether Barton loved the Red Sox. I couldn't stop thinking about him.

I hadn't talked to Meg since dropping her off on Saturday. I just didn't feel like defending myself, plus I knew she was busy copulating, and plus the Barton thing was totally confusing. Did he require his partner to read during sex?

How would that work in a clinch, I mean a real clinch? I tried to picture Rhett Butler, whom Barton resembled in some ways, carrying Scarlett up the stairs, she with her arms around him, squinting off to the side at a piece of paper. A girl could go cross-eyed, it seemed to me. Which of the four categories did Barton now fit into? I knew Meg was probably about to implode with curiosity. But all these thoughts left my head when I walked into the office.

Magda was gone. Fired. Kaput. We couldn't believe it. Charming, genial Dan had given Magda the push. A few people wondered whether he'd been giving Magda any other kind of push, but no one mentioned it. It was thrilling in a way. It was always thrilling when someone was fired. It could be you next time if you didn't straighten up and fly right. Everyone had their notebooks open and pens poised for the meeting.

"Some of you," Dan began, "didn't send me a memo last week. I expect a memo every week updating me on your project to get close to the business. Is that understood?" Everyone nodded, some with outright enthusiasm. Even Abe was paying attention.

Henrietta jumped in. "I sent you a memo, Dan, as you know. I can share my success with the rest of the team now, if you want." The rest of the team looked lukewarm at this proposal, and most refused to even look her way.

"Oh yes, go ahead, Henrietta," Dan said.

"I signed a client at the gym," she said. "I figured it couldn't hurt me to get a little exercise, ha, ha." She looked around to see who appreciated her zany wit. I speculated on the various retorts some of the group might want to make. She was still talking. "It was the guy next to me on the free weights. Turns out he owns Bicycle City and he bought seventy thousand homes from me." Henrietta sat back and adjusted the barrette in her greasy black hair. I knew that Henrietta spent a fortune on her clothes and accessories, but somehow still always looked disheveled. She was probably a size fourteen, but bought expensive size tens to fulfill her self-image.

"You're a coupon animal, Henrietta," Abe said. He usually called me a coupon slut.

"Thanks, Abe," Henrietta said. She was always so touched when someone praised her. But I wasn't thinking about Henrietta's social standing, not when I heard what she said next. "I'm also working on Dog Daze, which would be huge."

I turned in my seat. "Dog Daze headquarters is in Worcester, Henrietta."

"Yes," she said, "but the owner is opening a small store in my area, and that's where he's been lately. I've been grooving with him." Dog Daze was a chain of very popular hot dog restaurants throughout New England. The picture of Henrietta grooving with anybody was deeply troubling and in my view should have involved cash payments.

It was very shrewd of Henrietta to bring this up at a sales meeting. That way, the whole thing was documented and I wouldn't have a leg to stand on if I chose to complain about it. I had called the Dog Daze corporate office repeatedly in my early days with LotsaCoups and had let it slide lately. As long as you had some connection to an owner, you were sometimes allowed to cross territory lines, and Henrietta had just publicly declared her connection.

I could barely control my rage as Abe and I walked down the stairwell and out to our cars. "Well, get over there today if you can," Abe said. "Stake your rightful claim."

I took a couple of deep breaths. "So, Cheng Du tomorrow?" I asked.

"But of course. Geez, I hope I can get a new customer. Dan seems like he's had his Wheaties lately."

"Yes, he does," I said. "Why don't you actually consider calling on some businesses in your area, kiddo?"

"I don't want to be rash," Abe said.

* * *

"Good morning, Dog Daze corporate headquarters. Every dog has its daze."

"Yes, hi, my name is Jeanie Callahan and I wanted to make contact with your advertising department."

"Please hold."

("Hound Dog" elevator music)

Everyone I called that morning put me on hold. Just me and the ether, together again. I felt discouraged, sitting in my car next to the rotary. 'Round and 'round went all the traffic, and there I sat at a complete halt—still only five new customers and not a prospect glimmering anywhere. I saw something move inside Quick Study Photo Developing and wondered whether it might be Isabel Cartwright.

"Hey, Isabel," I said from the doorway. I fully expected her to ignore me or throw me out. This is how you feel on a bad sales day. Who could possibly want to talk to me?

"Hi, Jeanie," she said. "Look at this. Do you believe it?" She motioned toward several enormous cardboard boxes sitting in the middle of the floor.

"What are they?" I asked.

"Film developers. The delivery people were supposed to unwrap and install them, but they just left them. What am I supposed to do? How will I make my opening date?"

Within five minutes the two of us were tearing the cardboard boxes apart and shoving the equipment into various niches against walls where Isabel thought they should go. I was sweating in my Liz Claiborne linen shirt, but felt useful.

Isabel stood with her hands on her hips. She had a bruise under her eye that makeup couldn't quite conceal. Maybe it was from all the heavy work in the store. "I almost can't remember why I wanted to have my own business," she said. "Except I hate taking money from my husband."

"Oh, it'll be fun," I said, always eager to encourage a new owner.

"We'll see," Isabel said. "Now I get to figure out how these things work, then deal with Barton Columbus, forty-year-old boy wonder, then the Weight Watchers police."

"Really?" I asked. I didn't want to act too interested in Barton. She obviously didn't know about my date with him, or the flowers he had sent. Unfortunately, they were already wilting.

"One of the Weight Watchers scales got damaged the other night and they're having a fit. The lady told me that every single person lost three point two pounds the day after our auditions."

"That doesn't sound bad to me," I said.

"Me neither," Isabel said. In the bright sunlight, her eye looked worse.

"Then I just found out that East High School, where we're supposed to start rehearsing, is remodeling their shop department, and all their saws and drills are being stored on the stage. That should be fun, huh?"

"For heaven's sake, my best friend is the secretary there. Meg Larson."

"Really? Do you think you could talk to her about it?"

"About the saws and vises? I doubt she knows."

"Just see if she can make anything happen? Would you?"

"Well, okay," I said. Shit. I didn't need extraneous problems. "Why do you call Barton a boy wonder?"

Isabel shook her head. "Psssh. You know, everything falls back on me. If he fights with the costume director, it's my problem. If he fights with the lighting director, it's my problem. I'd like to read him the riot act." I jumped slightly at Isabel's remark, but she didn't seem to notice.

"Sounds like you have a lot on your plate, Isabel."

"Not only that, but my stepdaughter is visiting us this summer, and she's a challenge and a half. Plus I have to drive her everywhere."

"You know what they say," I said in my cheerful client voice. "If you want to get something done, ask a busy person."

Isabel shook her head. "As soon as Barton starts dating the cast members, I'll have brokenhearted bimbos on my hands too."

I gulped.

Isabel's cell phone rang just then and I decided to make a quick getaway. I was pretty sure my face was red. I still felt blobby and unsuccessful, and now, in addition to the shame I felt for being a bimbo, I had the worry that Isabel could cancel her ad if the business wasn't ready in time. Life sucks and then you don't have any coupons.

"Good afternoon, Dog Daze corporate headquarters. Every dog has its daze. How may I help you?"

"Hi, this is Jeanie Callahan calling back. I waited a long time this morning—"

"Please hold."

("Theme from *101 Dalmatians*" elevator music)

I pulled into my driveway at five fifteen and marveled at the edging Gramp had done to my grass. It looked fantastic. I could see Mrs. Mayer across the street, trying to edge her own lawn. I could also see what Mrs. Mayer could not, which was my grandfather sitting on his patio with the beehive woman. They looked to be enjoying a cocktail. Her car had been in Gramp's driveway almost nonstop since Saturday, and I was sure Mrs. Mayer realized it. Everybody has problems, I figured.

My phone was ringing inside the house, and I ran to get it. I had just enough time to eat something, watch *Jeopardy!*, and make it to rehearsal.

"Hi, I wanted to do one of those coupons. Is this the right number?"

"Well, yes, who is this, please?"

"My name is Sam Yummy. I have a septic business."

I arranged to meet Mr. Yummy at Dunkin' Donuts the following morning and hung up feeling good and right again. You just have to hold on sometimes for that one good thing to fall in. Sales is all emotional. It's how you feel and, unfortunately, how other people feel too. If you walk in somewhere and a guy is really irritated at his mother-in-law, who lent him the money for the business and is now griping that there aren't any profits, you will have no prayer of a sale. No technique you use will make any difference. Although he might buy from you just to piss off the mother-in-law. I've had a few of those.

By seven P.M. I was sitting in the June Mitchell Room at the library, waiting to be told what to do.

"Hey," Meg whispered as she sat down next to me. Lately, rehearsal seemed the best place for us to catch up. "How was your date?"

"Hey," I said back. I was relieved and happy to see my friend. "I'm still a virgin."

"Good," Meg said with a smile. "Hey listen, your business is your business. You do what you want."

"Thanks, girlfriend," I said.

"Unless I say different," Meg added. We both laughed.

"How's Mama Corleone doing on the kitchen wall?" I asked.

"Gary is crazy. He wanted to have sex on the floor right underneath that thing. Can you believe it? I refused." She then told me about the rest of her weekend, virginal behavior having been markedly absent, and I related many, but not all, of the Barton details. I decided to save the literary interlude for another time.

"You're kidding," she said, and her eyes went back to raccoon mode. "When's he going to pay you?" The answer to that question seemed unclear, since Barton had walked past me earlier without speaking and was now seated on a folding chair next to the infamous Weight Watchers scale, listening to and nodding at some woman whose hair stuck out like a fright wig. How would I thank him for the flowers?

Meanwhile, Marianne Peters called the nuns to the piano. I left Meg by herself with Billy Tuxhorn closing in. I hoped she and Gary had all the insurance they needed.

The high school girls surrounded me, and I marveled at their ease in singing harmony. I stood with the altos and felt that I sounded just like them. Then when I moved a bit closer to the sopranos, I seemed to be singing the same notes they were. I could see everybody in the room stop to enjoy the full, rich choral sounds we were making. That red carpet seemed closer than ever.

But Marianne stopped us repeatedly. "That's 'prob-lem,' not 'prollem.' Try it again," she said. Every time we would get a line or a phrase out, she would stop us. "No. Do it again." It began to seem as though she didn't want us to sound good. She wanted to spoil it. You could feel the irritation seep its way through the crowd.

I liked the high school girls. One of them had an extra sandal and they kept pushing it around back and forth on the floor. It seemed to be a game. I kept my eye on Barton and the fright wig lady. I consider myself an expert on body language, and Barton was clearly saying something pessimistic with his arms folded in front of him and frowning. The lady was matching him frown for frown, but Barton appeared to be winning the negativity contest. Then I saw Isabel appear between them, like a referee.

"Jeanie? What part are you singing?" Marianne asked, intruding on my reverie.

"Um, well," I said.

"Why don't you stand over here and do the best you can?" she asked, and I shambled over next to her. The high school girls showed solidarity with me when they passed the sandal across the floor, and indeed I passed it back and felt a little better. Meg rose from her conference with Billy Tuxhorn and waved to me as she left. I could tell she wanted to be in the show.

Finally, Marianne let us go. "Please practice your diction," she said.

I heard one of the girls say, "Please practice your hair gel," under her breath, and the rest of them laughed loudly on their way out. Marianne still had the sixties bubble-cum-sausage coiffure. She was a tiny little thing and could probably shop in the girls' department, though she looked far from girlish. "Schoolmarm" came to mind. The lenses in her glasses were thick enough to start a campfire, though it was hard to picture Marianne grubbing around on the forest floor. She had a way of scanning the group, then writing something down in the little notebook she always carried. I felt sure my name was in there with a good number of X's next to it. X's and, "Why did we cast this person?" I knew now that I would not achieve fame by singing. My acting would have to propel me to stardom.

I watched Marianne turn her attention to the children, two of whom were kicking a Hacky Sack back and forth across the scale. The little eleven-year-old who'd said she was better than anybody else was memorizing and reciting lines with her mother. They even danced together briefly, which was kind of sickening to watch. Gary's nephew Truman walked in, dragging his skateboard. It was hard to imagine him and the girl playing any kind of love interest together. Truman obviously didn't shave yet, though he did sport an embryonic mustache, which made him look comically sinister. The high school girls ignored him. All of this made me remember to ask Meg about the saws and drills on the high school stage. Just as I went to call her on my cell, the very tall gentleman who was playing the captain motioned to me from the doorway. I walked toward him, but he rudely stayed where he was, making me feel summoned rather than invited.

"Will you do me a favor?" he asked when I got there.

"My name's Jeanie," I replied, and stuck my hand out. I was very good at introducing myself.

He looked at my hand for a second as though it were a farm implement, then fell in with my polite behavior. "I'm Charlie. Hi." His grip was strong, but with his thinning hair and even thinner lips, he still looked like the bad guy on a TV movie. "I wonder if you could do something for me. I have to trust somebody," he said.

"Sure, if I can," I said.

"Will you watch me walk across the room and then tell me if anyone looks at me?" he asked.

"All right. Go ahead."

"Okay, thanks. Here I go," Charlie said, and indeed he was off, moving across the floor at a casual pace and stopping at the piano, where the kids were doing "Do-Re-Mi" aka "Doe A Deer" with gusto. He turned completely around and headed over near the stage, where Barton and Fright Wig were still having it out. I watched him complete the journey and realized with horror that while I had been watching him, I had failed to watch anyone else. Jesus, now what? He crooked his finger at me again from across the room and I crooked mine back at him. That was nervy for me, but I figured if he could walk across again, I could complete my surveillance mission that had fizzled out the first time. It worked.

"Who looked at me?" he asked. His eyebrows were furrowed. They were thin, too.

"Well, Charlie, I'm not sure anybody really looked. Not with intensity. Not that I could actually say that person was *looking*. Do you know what I mean?"

"What about that woman right there in the second row? In the striped shirt. My wife."

I found the woman and had no idea if she had looked or not.

"I don't know about her. Why didn't you ask me to concentrate on her?" I asked.

"You're right," he said. "I should have. Will you watch again?"

"Okay," I answered, and wondered what was going on. Was he looking for a sexual reaction from the wife? Would I be able to recognize it? I felt confused. The striped-shirt wife not only didn't look at him, but took that moment to open up her handbag and start rifling through it. Feeling very clever, I made my observation, then turned my back so that Charlie wouldn't be tempted to summon me again in his arrogant way. That worked, too, as he promptly appeared by my side.

"Well?" he asked.

"When she saw you, she started going through her handbag," I said.

"Thanks," he said, and walked away from me, nearly tripping over a threadbare backpack. Truman rushed from where he sat slump-shouldered on the edge of the stage to retrieve the pack, never bothering to say, "Sorry it got in your way," or anything nice. He looked miserable, and I wondered what was in the pack. Charlie glared at the kid and sat down on the folding chair next to his wife. Geesh. And I thought coupon people were weird.

Barton caught my eye just then and also summoned me to where he was. I waved in a friendly manner, but stayed where I was. Let him come to me, I figured. But he didn't.

"Plenty of nuns wear navy-blue uniforms these days," Fright Wig yelled.

"They're habits! They're called habits, Velma, and in 1939 in Austria they were black!" Barton said back to her.

I felt privileged to see my first artistic conflict.

I drove by Meg and Gary's as I left the library, but their lights were out, so I didn't stop.

To: Dan Albright
Fr: Jeanie Callahan
Re: Close to the Business
I am really enjoying the play so far. I never
knew I was an alto! Ha, ha, just kidding. I, of
course, know that doesn't really matter because
I'm supposed to be selling ads.

I suppose I should at least try to stay on topic. Sigh.

To: Dan Albright
Fr: Jeanie Callahan
Re: Close to the Business
I am making sure that I interview everyone in
the cast to see what their advertising needs are.
Several sales are pending. SEND.

A Drink with Jam and Bread

Tuesday, June 16

"Hi, you've reached the voice mail of Jeanie Callahan, the coupon girl. I can deliver the business for your business, so leave me a message and I'll call you back. Please be sure to leave a number, okay?" BEEP.

"Good morning, LotsaCoupers. This is Dan saying thanks for all the memos. It sounds like we're kicking some butt out there, and I just wanted to announce the current standings in the contest. Leading the pack is Henrietta Lewis, way to go." BEEP.

"Jeanie. It's Mort. There's a problem with the coupon. Please stop by as soon as you can." BEEP.

"My name Mike. You call me." BEEP.

"Do you have a Long Island iced tea?" I asked the Cheng Du waiter, the very respectful one who always joked with us.

"Oh, yes, yes," he answered. "Two?"

Abe piped up. "No, I'll stick with a mai tai. You gotta go with tradition, right, Rick?"

Chinese waiters and owners are always named Sheila

and Ken and Rick. Many of them were my clients, though unfortunately still not the new guy, who was thinking about the menu. Rick nodded and bowed and exited. The bar at Cheng Du has a Christmas tree up all year round, and I find that festive and efficient.

"All right," I said to Abe. "Let's go over your prospects."

"Okay," Abe said.

"What are they?"

"I don't have any."

I raised my eyebrows. "Well, let me ask you this. What account would you like to get? Picture yourself getting it."

Abe sat back and closed his eyes. "I see myself signing all of McDonald's, for the whole country."

"Really?"

"I see myself having sex with the secretary at McDonald's who has giant breasts."

I sighed.

"Or I see myself having sex with the wild-looking FedEx girl. She looks kind of like you, Jeanie."

"Abe. Stick to coupons. What account would you like to get?"

"I'd settle for anything. Mail order."

"No, not mail order," I said. "Think of a nice big food account in your area that you've always wanted to get."

Abe sighed and said, "This is too hard."

I stayed with it. "But remember that guy who told us if you could picture it happening, you can make it happen?"

"Yeah, make this happen."

Rick brought our drinks and we relished our first sips.

"Mmm, I needed that," I said.

"Okay, so are we done?" Abe asked.

I kept myself from laughing. "Abe, Abe. What's one of your towns? Baldwin, right?"

"Right."

"Isn't that where that Acapulco Mexican restaurant is?"

"Yeah. The guy hates me."

"I doubt that. When was the last time you were in there?"

"About two years ago. I rear-ended him in the parking lot."

"Okay, you're right, he hates you. What about another place?"

"Hey, there's somebody for you, Jeanie." Abe kept laser eye contact with me while still glancing behind my shoulder. I casually turned around and looked right at the guy just as he looked at me. That is always my luck. He was another bad dandruff victim, and dentally challenged as well, a fact extravagantly displayed in his broad grin. I smiled back to be polite.

"I'm going to kill you," I said to Abe. "Meanwhile, what are you going to do?"

"Meanwhile, I have no idea," Abe said. "How many new do you have now?"

"Six," I said, and tried to look casual. "I just got Yummy Septic Removal this morning." I took another sip. "I'm going to make the ten, I know it."

Abe looked down in the dumps. I added, "So are you, kiddo. Come on."

An hour later, I stood at the bottom of Gramp's stairs while he walked briskly up and down.

"Gramp, why don't you just join a gym and do the StairMaster?"

"Don't need to spend that kind of money, Jean. A fool and his money are soon parted."

I kept my eye on *Jeopardy!* in the other room. "Quoth the raven, Gramp?"

"Nevermore!" he boomed right in front of me as he pivoted quickly around to start going up again.

"Yup," I said, and decided to sprawl in the recliner if he wasn't going to. We could still talk.

"Didn't you already jog your two miles today, or whatever it is?" I called.

"Yeah," he answered, which I could barely hear, him be-ing at the top of the stairs, which turned to the left after the first ten steps. "Have you eaten?" I yelled.

"Bogen ow," he said.

"Huh?"

"Going out."

"Secret or mysterious, beginning with A?"

"Arcane," Gramp yelled, his voice filling the room. This was ridiculous. I couldn't take it. As I stood up to leave, his much softer voice called me again.

"Seccenflufflulululditlie, Jeanie."

I walked back to the stairwell. "What?"

"I'm going away for the weekend," he said with a slight pant.

"Oh. Okay." Hooray, hooray. "May I ask where?"

"I have a friend with a place in Rockport," he said, piv-oting again right in front of me.

"Cool. Is it the beehive lady?" I asked as I caught sight of the fancy gift box on the dining room table.

"What?" he asked.

"Never mind," I said, and tiptoed in to have a look. A golf shirt. Not bad, and I sincerely hoped he would wear it, though drill bits would have been higher on his list. "Write out what you want done, and I'll do it."

I walked next door and felt light and airy, picturing my-self sleeping extra late on Saturday and Sunday. I was lucky to have Gramp doing all these things for my house, and I knew it. It just drove me a little bit crazy. I noticed the accumulated junk mail on the countertop and was just going to throw it all out when I decided to pull out the dat-ing service questionnaire and read it. I flopped down on the couch and put my feet up.

How would I describe my own looks? In high school a boy I idolized had told me that I was a "solid B-plus." I knew he meant it in the nicest possible way, but it was crushing to me. I had freckles then, in addition to my good skin, and a really wholesome look. God help me, I suppose I still do. I look like a girl who will take care of your dog while you are away. A girl who can start an outboard motor on the first try. Strong like bull. Horse sick, wife pull plow.

As my eyes were beginning to close, I heard the front door open and a woman's voice call, "Yoo-hoo." Another person walking into my house without permission. Was there a sign out front I didn't know about? PLEASE WALK IN. ALL ARE WELCOME.

"Oh hi, Mrs. Mayer," I said as I raised myself about three inches off the couch. I put one foot on the floor and tried to look exhausted. It didn't take any acting.

Mrs. Mayer entered my line of vision and I very nearly lay back down again. In her arms were six or seven books and magazines. I wasn't in the mood for lending library.

"How are you, Mrs. Mayer? I know you had something you wanted to talk to me about." Did I have to offer coffee? I felt truly unable.

"Oh Jeanie, I'll come back. I can see you're tired from working. I should have called." These words of truth were balm on my troubled spirit, but they roused me as no others could. Apologize and be nice and people want to do the same thing back. This works in sales and in life.

"No, that's all right," I said, and rolled over onto my side. "What's up, Mrs. Mayer?"

Mrs. Mayer looked at me and made a decision. She perched on the edge of my plaid corduroy chair, still clutching the books to her chest.

"I'm taking a summer course at Worcester State, dear."

"Oh, that's good," I said. I wanted to be roused from my nap to know that.

"It's a psychology course."

"Oh," I said. *Okay then, babe, I'll see you later.*

"I have to write a paper on romantic attachment in postmodern America."

I propped myself on my elbow, leaning back into the couch and its warm environs. "Uh-oh, Mrs. Mayer. I hope you're not planning to interview me. I'm not married, and I don't have a boyfriend right now. No romantic attachment here."

"No, no," Mrs. Mayer said, and shook her head. "I don't want to interview you. I want to try an experiment on your grandfather."

"An experiment? Are you going to put probes in his brain or something?"

She laughed. "No, nothing like that."

"Because that might help him."

"You wouldn't believe how many books there are in the library about how to find a husband." Ah, now we were getting to it.

"No kidding."

"I thought I would try some of them out and see what happened. I just wanted to tell you first."

I scratched my head. "Try them out on Gramp, you mean?"

"Yes. Now this one here advises a woman to smile at every handsome man she meets during her day. The idea is that she will get into a smiling mode and then the object of her affections will start noticing her."

"Sounds sketchy to me," I said.

"Hmm, yes, sketchy. You're right."

"So," I said.

"But I'm still going to try it. If it's okay with you," Mrs. Mayer said.

I yawned openly. "I can't really object, Mrs. Mayer, if you want to start smiling at people."

"Now in this one," Mrs. Mayer said as she started to go down the stack of books, "they recommend just the opposite. Be kind of nasty to the subject. I don't really like that one."

"Hmmm. Yeah. I wouldn't want to try that in my line of work."

Sometime later, after she complimented me twice on the Steuben squirrels, which she thought were frogs, I managed to usher Mrs. Mayer out the front door. I didn't have the heart to tell her that Gramp was going away that weekend for a tryst with the beehive. When I returned to the couch, though, I wondered why I had any right to feel smug and superior to Mrs. Mayer. Here I was resorting to a dating questionnaire, still not filled out. I was beat. It was time to hay the hit. I threw the questionnaire out in the trash, then fished it back out and put it aside.

When the Dog Bites

Wednesday, June 17

"You'd better wear these," the pet store man told me as he handed over a thick pair of gloves.

"It's not dangerous, is it?" I asked. I had been recruited by a hairier-than-average business owner to help clip the toenails of a large and grouchy-looking black dog.

"Nah. Just grab right there. That's it. That's right. And now I will get this little— Aaaaahraaaaaaa! No, no!"

I jumped backward as the dog growled.

"Like this," the guy said, and put my gloved hand on the dog's other leg. "What did you say you were selling?"

"Coupons," I said. "Sir, I'm really sorry, but I have another appointment in two minutes. I'd really like to help you." *But first I want to swallow arsenic.*

"Okay, whatever," he said. "Do those coupons work?"

"Oh, indeed they do," I said.

"I might be able to give ten percent off," he said as the dog growled again and I moved even farther back.

"Um, we should talk about that," I replied, thrilled at the buying signal, but wary of where he was going with it.

"I work on a tight margin, you know. I can't give anything away." The guy soothed the dog somewhat and continued his work. "Why don't you stop by later? We'll talk about it. You can help me clean the hamster cages. Ha, ha, just kidding."

"Okay, I'll do that. Great. See you."

"Good afternoon, Worcester East High School, into the future through the past, leave no child behind, ask me about our meat raffle, this is Meg, how can I help you?"

"Meat raffle?"

"Yeah. Is that a problem?"

"I just don't see how you remember it all," I said.

"It's on a card. If they add anything else, I'm resigning," Meg said.

"Hey, I forgot to ask you this, but Isabel told me we're supposed to be rehearsing there at the high school starting next week. Do you know anything about it?"

I could picture efficient Meg leafing through her calendar.

"Hmm, yes, you're right. Worcester Spotlighters—Monday, Wednesday, and Friday all through June and July and then the performance in August."

"Isabel said the stage is full of saws and drills," I said.

"That's right, too, the shop department is being remodeled over the summer. Whoops."

"Is there any way to move the stuff out of there?" I asked.

"I don't think the superintendent realizes there's a conflict," Meg said.

"Is he there?"

"Is it a cold day in hell? I guess he's not here, then."

I sighed. "Well, Isabel asked me if I would ask you if something could be done."

"She did? Isabel knows me?"

"Yeah," I lied.

"I'll see what I can do," Meg said.

"So when are you fertile again?" I asked, and realized I was standing in the middle of Main Street. No one seemed to care, though I could see the pet guy watching me.

"Next week, I think. Are we going to do Shipley's again Friday night?"

"God, I don't know."

"I can't wait to see how those two tall people are going to look onstage." Then Meg's voice got louder. "Okay then, thanks for calling. Bye."

"Bye."

Since I didn't want to be caught lying to the pet guy about having an appointment, I ducked into the nearest door I could. I thought it was a florist, but obviously they had closed down. Instead, a bunch of little guys sat around at tables, most of them smoking cigarettes. One nice-looking tall fellow seemed to be addressing the group. He stopped what he was saying to look at me in the doorway. I smiled.

"Hi," I said. "Sorry to interrupt. I thought this was Betty's Buds."

"Betty's Buds got busted," one of the seated gentlemen said.

"This bud's for you," another one piped in. I seemed to have started a riot.

The guy in charge smiled back at me. "No problem. Are you a salesperson?"

"Yes, I am," I said. "Are you a new business?" The seated guys now started doing catcalls and wolf whistles.

"Whoa!"

"Look out!"

"She's going to sell him!"

"Sell me, baby!"

"I'm with LotsaCoups," I said. I held up one of our envelopes, praying it was one from Worcester, and walked over to the sandy-haired fellow to shake his hand.

"Oh, okay," he said. "We might want to talk to you."

"Music to my ears," I said. "I'm Jeanie Callahan. May I give you my card?"

The assembled group began to chat amongst themselves, and though I felt a bit guilty about disturbing their meeting, you have to welcome opportunity when it shows itself. Welcome it, whack it on the back, give it drinks, whatever it needs.

"I think someone else was in here," the fellow said. "Is there another company?"

"There could be," I said. "They come and go." I knew good and well it was Coupon Busters, our evil and incompetent competitor. But I always feigned ignorance when asked about it.

"Pardon me," the guy said. "I'm Lenny Sadowski. Very nice to meet you." Lenny Sadowski had a very enticing smile. If I hadn't been so entranced with Barton, my antennae would definitely have been up. Lenny added, "We're getting ready to open a pizza place."

"Oh, very good," I said. "Pizza is one of our best categories."

"Can you try us another day?" he said. "Actually, every one of these gentlemen might sign up with you."

Yikes, boing, bling. This guy knew how to light up my lights. Some of them do. They will dangle all kinds of promises in your face, but nothing is certain until it's signed on the dotted line. I set an appointment with them for Friday, and walked out into a brilliant June afternoon. Life was good.

By seven P.M. in the June Mitchell Room, life was sucking again. First of all, hardly anyone was there, not even Barton. I realized that, despite the flowers and all the swooning I'd done over them, Barton had never called me after our Saturday-night date, which I had paid for. And I was beginning to feel queasy about my sales prospects as far as the Spotlighters went. What would I tell Dan? I promised myself to ask at least three people per night what they did for a living.

"Hi," I said to a middle-aged woman sitting behind me knitting. She was a retired schoolteacher. That made one. Another woman walked in, and I found out she worked at Wal-Mart. That made two. At least I was achieving my immediate goal, though I still hadn't made any sales.

Meg was nowhere in sight, and I could only hope she was doing something about the high school stage. I had great faith in her abilities. Also, I wanted Isabel to love me with passion.

Barton walked in a few minutes after Marianne, and the two of them stood and talked across the piano. Marianne looked like she was fluffing the sausage portion of her hairdo all around in his honor, and I didn't blame her. His shoulders were still very broad and his thick black eyebrows frequently sent messages of great darkness. He walked over and sat beside me. I saw Marianne pretend not to watch.

"Hey," he said.

"Hey," I replied. "Thank you for the flowers."

"My pleasure."

"They're beautiful."

"How much do I owe you?" he asked. "For dinner."

"Oh, I forget."

"Well, can I take you out again to make up for it?"

I licked my lips, another unfortunate habit of mine. "Um, sure."

"Saturday, same time?"

"Okay."

I thanked God Meg hadn't been there for my sniveling capitulation. The high school girls filed in next, and I watched them cruise Barton as they slung down their backpacks and pulled out mascara and other items from inside.

"Okay, girls," Marianne said. "From the top."

"Ma'am? Excuse me, do you have a job?" I asked another older lady as we took our places. I wanted to complete my obligation for the night.

"I'm a second soprano," she said.

"No, I mean do you have a job? Outside the home?"

"I'm seventy-five. No, I don't."

"I'm sorry. I never dreamed you were so . . . that is, I never thought . . . I just never thought."

The woman kept needling me. "Did you think I was a cop?"

"No, I didn't," I said.

"Did you think I was a narc?" This got the attention of all the girls.

"No, I didn't, and I apologize." At least my three were done. I would have to learn to be more subtle.

"You probably think I don't know what a narc is."

"Yes, I do. I'll bet you are up on all the lingo."

"I'm down with it," she said, and frowned while the girls smirked.

"Helen the narc," one of the girls said.

"She's going to arrest your boyfriend," another added.

Helen beamed.

Later, as I was leaving, a beautiful sound began to fill the room, and we all turned around. It was Isabel. She was singing "Climb Ev'ry Mountain" with Marianne accompanying. I know my mouth fell open, and I would wager that the girls' mouths did too, though no gum fell out. Our nun choir sounded pretty darn good, no thanks to me, but it wasn't up at this level. This was the chills-down-your-back level. Without taking our eyes off Isabel, everyone sat back down on the folding chairs and watched.

Watched until she was finished, and then our regular lives resumed.

"I guess Isabel's playing Mother Superior," one of the girls said.

When the Bee Stings

Friday, June 19

"You have reached the voice mail of Jeanie Callahan, coupon expert extraordinaire. Please pay attention now, okay? Are you listening? You must leave a phone number if you want me to call you. Without a phone number you will not get a return call. Is this clear? Let's all enjoy Friday." BEEP.

"You're going over the edge, girl, but as always, it's fun to watch. It's Abe the wonder rep. Acapulco has a new owner, babe, one that I haven't been in a car accident with. Thought you'd like to know. Remind me to tell you about the chicken and the condom, but don't call me today. I've got a twelve-o'clock tee time." BEEP.

"Hi, LotsaCoupers, Dan here. Henrietta is still in the lead, now with twelve new cust—" BEEP.

"This Mike. Please call. Sping four dikka dikka doo." BEEP.

There were all kinds of bees and insects in the office on Friday morning, primarily because the air-conditioning was on the fritz and the windows were open. Worker guys were standing around, and I could see Dan in the conference room interviewing another candidate for the receptionist job. He was earning his pay. The woman sitting with him looked a little confused and I figured she had no chance. The last thing we needed was more confusion.

I waved to Dan as I scooped up a batch of expensive six-color-process handouts that weren't supposed to be used except with special permission. The way I saw it, why have them if we weren't going to use them? The plant was always sending us fabulous full-color sales tools that we were supposed to use sparingly. Screw that. I wanted them for my imminent meeting with Lenny Sadowski and the pizza guys. I knew Dan would never suspect me as a common thief, but as soon as the little suckers were safely in my briefcase, I headed out.

My car was trying out a new noise as I drove. It sounded a little like a hoarse person who couldn't quite get his throat cleared, rrrrrrrrrrrrr, *hakahaka,* rrrrrrrrrrrrr. I used my customary repair technique of ignoring it, and soon I was able to enjoy the Friday zest washing over me. The zest dissipated quickly when I arrived at the pizza storefront and no one was there.

"Hello?" I called. At least the door was open. "Anybody here?"

One of the smaller and balder members of the group appeared in the alcove leading to the back of the store. "Hi. How's it goin'?"

"It's going fine. I think we were supposed to have an appointment?"

"Lenny isn't going to be around today," the guy said. "Why don't you just give me all the stuff and I'll pass it on to him?"

No way. "Oh. Hmm. Gosh. Well, I'll try to call him. Maybe we can reschedule."

Lenny now appeared from the same alcove. "Oh, hi there, what was your name?"

"Jeanie. I just drove twenty miles for our appointment." Always dig the nail in as far as you can.

"Okay, I'm sorry. Things came up," Lenny said.

"That's all right," I said, chump of America. I watched the other one, the bald (and bald-faced) liar, retreat into the back room.

"Well, what have you got?" Lenny said.

"Truthfully, I've got a whole presentation to give, and I thought all the owners were going to be here."

"I'm really sorry," he said, and now he really seemed to be. "Why don't you come back on Wednesday? We always meet on Wednesdays. I thought the guys were going to be here today, but like I said, things came up." He looked nervous.

"Well, all right," I said. I wasn't going to burn any bridges. "Will all the pizza places have the same name?"

"Yes, we're thinking of Bird of Paradise," Lenny said.

"Bird of Paradise Pizza?" I asked, as if it were a brilliant idea.

"Maybe," Lenny said, with a slight flick of the eyes back toward the rear of the store. For my money, Lenny didn't fit with the rest of the group. He had an upscale look to him and wore a yuppie's oxford-cloth shirt and nice pants. The rest of them were clearly in the Joe Pesci wiseguy category.

I couldn't really think of a worse name for a pizza place. It sounded like a topping. "Give me a large pepperoni, onion, and bird of paradise, hold the bones."

We set our appointment for Wednesday and I left, smiley and professional and forlorn.

If the hairy pet store owner hadn't been waving to me from his window, I never would have walked in. But he did, and what choice did I have?

"I think you should buy a pet," he said.

"I think you should do a coupon," I replied.

I revved up my LotsaCoups motor and shifted into first

gear. Every now and then a potential customer will try embarrassingly hard to sell you his own product. This has happened to me with stockbrokers, but since I have no money it's not a real problem. When they do it to you at yogurt stands, it's not a big problem either, but you have to be firm. One primary rule is you have to keep control of the process.

Half an hour later, I walked out of Frisky Business with my seventh new sale and a check. It was now officially a good day, except for the ten-percent-off incentive the guy was insisting on and that I would have to talk him out of before the deadline. I felt confident I could do that. I felt less confident about where the guinea pig cage was going to fit in my car. One secondary rule is you do what you have to sometimes.

My car was a disgrace. I had a boyfriend once who uncharitably called it a BFI Dumpster. It was stuffed like a Thanksgiving turkey with envelopes, boxes, forms, supplies, old printers, and the occasional coffeemaker and old microwave oven that I kept trying to remember to get rid of. If someone did choose to accompany me in the front seat, it was a five-minute task to try to clear out space. Even then, the lucky rider had to sit forward and hope for the best.

I dragged a number of items out of the backseat and piled them onto the trunk. It occurred to me to just let the guinea pig into the backseat and ditch the cage. Couldn't it live there? That way I wouldn't have to move anything. It would probably get cold in the winter, though, and I was pretty sure it would go to the bathroom daily, so I abandoned this fantasy. I wedged the cage between the smallest pile of junk in the backseat and the ceiling. By gosh if the little goober didn't look cute as it gazed around at downtown Worcester. What I really wanted to do was drive off and leave the remaining stuff on the sidewalk. I saw Benito and one of his reptiles standing outside a few doors down. They were laughing, a rare occurrence for them.

"Hi, Benito," I called, and realized with a miserable pang that I had just performed all these tasks bending over in my car while wearing my shortest skirt. Benito waved, but of course his buddy didn't. "You guys want a computer monitor?" I yelled.

"No thanks," Benito replied. They laughed some more.

I began to toss papers into the backseat hither and yon. It was a little like spreading grass seed, which I'd seen my grandfather do many times. If any of this material had been in some kind of order before, it wasn't now. When the reptile tapped me on the shoulder, I nearly jumped to the top of the NO PARKING sign.

"We'll take the monitor," he said.

Divested of the clunky big box, I was able to jam the rest of the materials back into my car within a short time. My pet and I headed for Leawood Lane, he for a new home, me for a couple of aspirin to get ready for Friday-night rehearsal.

"I'll need to see ID, please," Don Shipley said to the high school girls as we all settled into our booth at his establishment. It was the really big booth, the one in the corner of the side room. It was eleven P.M. and Don didn't look that happy to see us. I was sure the kitchen wasn't happy at all.

The girls laughed. "We just want nachos," one said.

"We would never drink liquor," one of them added, and all the girls batted their eyelashes.

I sat between Barton and Isabel, and felt like queen of the May. Meg, still not affiliated with the show in any way, sat across the table and kept kicking me underneath it and raising her eyebrows. Gary was out with his friends again. Next to Meg was Laura Wheeler, our tall—I guess I should say extra-tall—Maria. Our even taller Captain von Trapp had not graced us with his presence, though his wife had. She was laughing up a storm with several cast members.

I was just starting to get people straight.

I craned my neck around Isabel. The poor waiter was trying to take orders, but I talked over him anyway. "Susie," I called to Charlie's wife, the woman with dimples who was having such a good time without her husband. "I was meaning to ask, what do you do?" I still needed one more occupation for my nightly tally and hadn't had a good hit yet. The only business I was close to was Shipley's Pub, and that was because I was sitting in it.

"I volunteer at the library," Susie said. That figured. Being married to Charlie couldn't be any barrel of laughs, especially if he was constantly walking across the room to see if you noticed him.

"Charlie's the one with the money," Isabel whispered, and then started talking to Laura. I meant to ask what he did, but then forgot.

Barton read the menu out loud, emphasizing certain points by poking me in the flab section of my midriff.

"Potato *skins*. Mozzarella *sticks*."

"Cut it out," I said, and watched Meg's mouth twitch.

It felt very intimate. At one point I felt emboldened to pull out the pocket of his shirt and flirtatiously ask him what was in it, making a direct reference to our poetry reading—that is, my poetry reading—of the weekend before.

He gave me one of his glowers. The right side of me was pushed up against the left side of him.

One of the girls leaned over to Isabel. "Who is that woman with the hair? Does she do costumes?" She referred to the fright-wig woman.

"Yes, that's Velma," Isabel replied. "I'm trying to keep her away from Barton."

"Please do," Barton said.

Rehearsal had been grueling for us nuns. Marianne

snapped at us more than once, and Barton made us walk and sing at the same time. This is called blocking. It's when they tell you where to stand and sit and anything else they might want you to do, like pull out a gun. There was no chance of that in our case, since we pretty much stood around with our hands folded. Even given that, when we started to actually move, we ran into one another like religious Keystone Kops. There was one part where everybody was supposed to file off the stage in a line. It felt to me like a bunch of commuters trying to get on a subway. To the high school girls, everything was hilarious. To the older women, everything was annoying. I was in the middle somewhere.

"What does Velma do?" I asked Isabel, but then Velma herself exploded at the other end of the table.

"What about the crucifixes, Barton? What about those?" she asked in a loud voice.

Barton paused for only a second. "That's what Pontius Pilate wanted to know, Velma," he said, leaning my way and giving me squishy feelings in strange places. "Every freakin' night—'What about the crucifixes, what about the crucifixes?' His wife got sick of it. 'Will you shut up about the crucifixes?' she said." Laura sat back and laughed, but no one else did. Barton reached across the booth and rearranged Laura's napkin.

"Laura, you're a college student, right?" I asked.

"Yeah," Laura replied. Everyone knew Laura went to Brown, and everyone was suitably impressed. "I'm working at Honeydew Donuts for the summer."

"Oh, you are?" I said, and started to grill her about the Honeydew owner when the whole crowd erupted in cheers and applause. I saw an elderly man approaching our table, and whispered to Isabel, "Who's that?"

"It's Vic!" she cried, and reached over to grab his hand. "Vic is our senior statesman."

"I'm the old geezer in the group," Vic said.

Barton saluted Vic. "Hey, Vic, you going to do our show?"

"Do you need a judge? Or a patriarch? Sure."

"We always need a judge or a patriarch," Barton said.

Once it was determined that a suitable role would be found for Vic in *The Sound of Music*, it was next discovered that today was Vic's birthday, and that brought more cheering. Vic's buddies, whom he'd left at the bar midcelebration, soon joined us as well, and patriarchal roles were promised to all of them.

"We can always use men," Isabel whispered to me.

By midnight, great camaraderie reigned. One end of the booth was devoted to unusual body talents, including Susie's ability to pop her shoulder out of joint, Velma's fast-vibrating eyeballs, and Isabel's wiggling earlobe. The moral tone at our end was a bit lower. Barton and I were forehead-to-forehead in close conversation, which I think was about pizza toppings, but I'm not sure. Meg was whispering and laughing with one of the old gentlemen, Laura was slow-dancing with a much shorter waiter who looked very content to have his head resting on her ample bosom, and several of the high school girls were doing a hard-core bump and grind with the rest of the seniors.

"This is the best night of my life!" one of them shouted.

"Make sure those guys have health insurance!" Barton yelled, after pulling his head away from me momentarily.

The birthday boy made his own rounds. The fact that he had just turned eighty did not deter Vic in the least from an energetic pursuit of folly. He reminded me of my grandfather. He started with a mild flirtation with Isabel, then Susie, then the high school girls, all the while imbibing shots of whiskey at a prodigious rate and sharing one or two with Barton.

I can't really remember at what time it was decided that Vic would walk on the bar.

"Come on! You can do it!"

"You're only as young as you feel!"

It was evidently the result of a bet made at a cast party; some said it was *Brigadoon;* some said *South Pacific.* Whatever the show, everyone agreed it was payoff time. And so that was how it happened that patriarchal Vic, much to Don Shipley's dismay, climbed up on a tall stool and stood on top of the bar, shoulders hunched to avoid the ceiling. This was about twelve thirty A.M. At about twelve thirty-one, Vic fell off the bar and was taken away in an ambulance. People decided the evening was over.

When I'm Feeling Sad

I still felt bad for poor Vic on Saturday morning, and bad for myself too, since I had another hangover, though not of the raging variety. It was heavenly to lie in bed and know that my grandfather would not come barging into the kitchen at an ungodly hour.

It was Mrs. Mayer instead.

My heart stopped when I heard the kitchen slider open and the guinea pig cage go flying.

"Oh, my God! Ahhhhhhhhhhh!" *Clank! Clunk!* Crockery sounds filled the air, none of them good.

After a cleansing scream of my own, I rose and once again draped a blanket over my head. *Ben-Hur* rides again. I peered around the doorway and saw my neighbor sprawled on the floor, surrounded by brownies. Strong instinct told me to go back to bed. Instead I walked into the kitchen, helped her get up, then assisted in the retrieval of stray snacks that had fallen from a now-broken china plate.

"I am so sorry, dear," Mrs. Mayer said. Her hair was bright orange, the color of crossing guards at intersections. "What is that thing?" she asked.

"It's a guinea pig. My new pet. I guess I shouldn't have put it next to the door."

"No, no. I'm at fault. Ouch. Well, these made it," she said, and placed the surviving brownies on the dinette table.

"Thanks, Mrs. Mayer. You're too kind," I said.

"I just wanted to tell you that my experiment is going forward."

"That's good," I replied. I didn't want to know what part the orange hair was playing. "Gramp is out of town this weekend, you know."

"Oh, yes," she said cheerfully. "He told me. I have a few plans for him when he gets back."

"Great," I said. I hoped they didn't include me. My cell phone donged, and Mrs. Mayer rather sheepishly let herself out the slider with a wave.

"This is Jeanie."

"I have a plan," Meg said.

"I have a headache," I replied.

"Well, we feel better than last week, don't we?"

"What did Gary say?"

"Gary thinks we should take a month off. We're both sick of sex."

"Oh."

"Well, I know I am."

"I see."

"If you must know, I ripped down Mama Corleone and threw her in the garbage. So I wouldn't mind getting out of the house for a while."

"Does Gary know you did it?"

"Um, no. Not yet. So anyway, I have the key to the school. Do you want to go over and move the saws and drills?"

"Are you crazy?"

"Well, a lot of other people are going to, though some are going to the hospital to visit Vic."

"Geez, Meg, you're not even in the show and you're like the social chairman."

"I am in the show. I'm the stage manager."

"When did that happen?"

"Isabel asked me last night. She says it's the most important job and a lot of things need organizing."

"I was planning to sleep."

"You can sleep when you're dead, Jeanie."

"There's a thought."

What was really dead that Saturday was Meg's hope of a large group assembling to move drills. She and I and Isabel met in front of the school and stood peering up and down Route 118 to see if anyone else would show.

"Did you scrape yourself, Isabel?" Meg asked, referring to a nasty red laceration on Isabel's chin.

"Would you believe a can opener did this?" Isabel answered.

"Another senseless can-opener killing," I said. I remembered the barely concealed mark under her eye from a few days ago. I didn't like the way Isabel kept having these bruises, but I didn't feel I knew her well enough to mention it. "How's it going with the stepdaughter?"

"Oh, you mean her royal highness? Her father just bought her a car, so at least I don't have to drive her anymore."

"Oh, so she's of age, so to speak."

"Definitely."

Then Sam Yummy, of all people, my new client, drove up.

"Hey, Sam," Isabel said with a wink. Somehow the two

knew each other, and indeed it seemed that Isabel had
called him. Sam wore his uniform shirt and hat. I think he
was surprised to see me.

"Hi, Sam."

"Hey, how are you, coupon girl? What was your name
again?"

Sam introduced himself to Meg in his customary way.
"Hi, I'm Sam. I haul shit."

"How do you do?" said Meg. Her hair was pulled back
into an itsy-bitsy ponytail, but even hungover and somewhat scruffy, Meg was a knockout.

Isabel and Sam walked down the sidewalk away from
Meg and me for a brief conference. He did most of the
talking and she did a lot of head shaking. Meg and I
shrugged.

"What are you going to tell Gary about the painting?" I
asked.

"I don't know. I'll tell him the neighbor's dog got in and
attacked it."

"Oh, that'll work, I'm sure."

"Don't ask me questions like that." I gave her a look
and she gave me one back. Isabel and Sam rejoined us
eventually.

"Okay," Meg said. "We might as well go in and assess
the situation." It was very obvious Meg didn't want to go
home. She unlocked the door and we strolled into the
cafeteria. Meg and I are both alums of EHS, but since Meg
worked there, she had all the right keys and knew her way
around the new addition. The auditorium and the stage
required another key, which she also had. That girl can really think ahead.

It looked a little daunting. As in every square inch of
space on the stage occupied by a two-ton gizmo, or by various half-ton gizmos piled on top of one another. This
would show real commitment on our part.

"I say we go home," I said.

"That's a big job," Sam said.

"I've got M&M's, you guys," Isabel said. "Peanut and plain."

No one had the heart to turn down Isabel's M&M's offer, and in the end, no one had the nerve to walk out. It was a huge job. Sam located a couple of dollies and the rest of us worked on our own. Isabel's M&M's were gone quickly, and she went back and forth to the candy machine numerous times. We were glad for the water fountain in the hallway. When Susie Jenkins showed up, we nearly wept with joy to see her. Too bad she hadn't brought her husband, the Captain. Meg retrieved a portable CD player from her office and we cranked up oldies tunes on the radio while we toiled. We hauled and hoisted and shoved and pushed every last sawhorse, power drill, and screwdriver out of there. Meg opened a few other classrooms and we stored it all away.

Somebody started talking about hell and prison and how you do time in purgatory to pay for heaven.

"I'm earning two years off my sentence with this table saw."

"That thing isn't worth two years."

"Yes, it is." Huff. "Right off the top." Puff. "A full twenty-four months."

"Oh yeah?" Sam said, his voice straining. "I'm earning ten years with this baby."

"That table saw is worth about three months max."

By the end, when the stage was clear and the music even louder, we got a little impromptu line dance going to Wilson Pickett's "In the Midnight Hour," each of us one-upping the others with boogaloo-down-Broadway dance moves. We were drenched in sweat.

"I'm gonna wait!" Sam yelled, and moved down the line backward, shimmying and twisting in a somewhat frightening manner. "Till the midnight hour!" he continued, and whipped around and pointed to Isabel, who was next.

"Shake it, girl!" Meg called to her. Isabel had plenty to shake, and she raised her long skirts to do some intricate knee-and-toe dance step, followed by Meg, who went into the athletic sort of cheerleading routine I'd seen many times.

"All those with radiating chest pains, raise their hands!" I cried as just then the music suddenly went off. In fact, all the power went off and the place was pitch dark. We had to grope our way out, giggling all the way.

"Uuuuuw," I squealed. "That better be Meg's hand and not yours, Sam," I said with a laugh.

"Hey," Sam called. "I wish it were mine. But my arm would have to grow ten feet."

"It's not my hand," Meg said from somewhere else. "I've got enough sex at home."

"Who said anything about sex?"

"The table saw did it."

We ended up outside on the sidewalk.

"Six o'clock. Geez, it only took all day," I said.

"Hey, what do you say I buy everybody pizza?" Isabel said, breathless from her exertions. Sam looked ready for a Code Blue.

"Well," Meg said, and I knew she was thinking of Gary.

"Well," Susie said, and we knew she was thinking of Charlie. She'd be earning years off her purgatorial sentence when she got home.

"I really have to get going," I said.

"Jeanie," Isabel said, "I hope you aren't dating Barton. I love the boy, but he's poison, you know."

"I wouldn't do that," I said. Meg gave me another look and in fact did her George Washington profile.

An hour later, in anticipation of my date with Barton, I finished painting my face and did a little pirouette in front of the mirror. This was the best I could look. I tidied up the kitchen a bit and even crawled around on the floor to pick up wood chips from Mr. Piggy's cage. He and I were getting used to each other. A couple of times I startled him and he squeaked and I screamed. But we were making it.

I poured myself a glass of wine and went out on my minuscule patio to sip it. After that one was gone, I poured another. When I walked inside with that empty glass, it was nearly dark and I felt like a fool. Where was Barton? Why was I sitting here waiting for him like an idiot? *Jeopardy!* was long over. Mr. Piggy was asleep. I decided to fill out the dating questionnaire for real, so I fished it out of the junk pile once again and walked across my yard toward Gramp's house. I was pretty sure I had left my good pen there, and I wanted it back. Maybe the pen would be good luck. Gramp had an elaborate home security system, unlike me, who had only a guinea pig to protect my property. I punched in the entry code for Gramp's house and let myself in. It seemed strange to be in his kitchen without him there. My eye makeup looked a little smudged, from what I could see in the reflection from Gramp's shiny toaster.

Just as I started to go through Gramp's miscellaneous drawer, I heard sirens. It must have been a slow night for crime, because three cruisers were all of a sudden in front of Gramp's house, and none of their drivers was in any hurry. This wasn't the first time I had set off the alarm, but they didn't seem to remember me.

"Can you identify yourself, ma'am?" one said. "And explain why you broke into the house?"

"I didn't break in," I said. "I live next door. Look in your records. I've done this before."

"And where is the owner, ma'am?"

"The owner is my grandfather. He's out of town."

"Can you show some identification, ma'am?"

"Well, yes, if you want to wait while I run next door and get my wallet."

"I'll go with you, ma'am," one of the officers said.

"Quit calling me ma'am," I said to myself.

"Pardon me?"

"Nothing. Let's go."

He and I walked across the dark expanse of lawn. I stayed on the stone path my grandfather had laid so carefully, but I could hear the policeman step off now and then, hopefully not into the marigolds. As we approached my kitchen door, I could see by the sink light someone moving inside. I gasped.

"What's wrong?" the cop asked, sounding more alarmed than I was and almost walking into me from behind.

"Someone's in my house," I said.

"Well, let's go see who it is," he said.

I hung well back from the officer as he stepped up to the sliding door and took hold of it. I saw the person turn around and look right at the cop and then hastily put down whatever he held in his hand. The cop had his gun out.

"Oh sorry, whoops, that's a friend of mine," I said.

"Are you sure?"

"Yes. Hi, Barton," I said as the cop and I entered the kitchen.

"Hi, Jeanie. Hello, Officer."

I grabbed my purse from the table and extracted my driver's license for the cop. He barely looked at it. He kept looking at Barton.

"Maybe you shouldn't enter someone's house unexpectedly, sir," he said.

I interrupted. "It's okay. Everybody I know does it to me."

"Well, okay, we'll lock up next door before we leave."

"Oh great," I said. "Have a good night."

"Thanks."

I turned to Barton and said, "You're a little late, I think."

"I'm so sorry. I'm just so sorry. My mother is in the hospital."

"Oh Barton, I didn't know. What's the matter with her?"

"We're not sure yet."

"You must be nervous about it, though, you poor guy."

Barton put his head down and nodded.

"Do you want a beer?" I asked, and he nodded again. Soon we were sitting in the dark outside on the minuscule patio. Before long we had consumed several beers and more wine and were into the rum and Coke. He was quite candid about the show.

"It sucks," he said.

"Have you ever had leading actors that tall?" I asked.

"I've never had trees that tall. I can't even see them to direct them," he answered. I felt too afraid to ask him why he had cast Charlie and Laura in the first place.

"Well, I know it'll be a good show," I said with confidence, though I actually knew no such thing.

"Do you mind if we don't go out for dinner?" he asked. I didn't, mainly because I was no longer hungry. Aside from trips inside to the bathroom, we sat on the patio till two A.M., mostly with Barton hanging his head and talking about his mother. Then he told me about the screenplay he was writing about his mother. Then he told me about his mother's mother. He made his life sound bleak but in a funny way. I almost can't remember how and when he left, but he did. There was a little kissing at the door again, but no more reading requests, and I felt sorry for him.

"Are you okay to drive?" I asked.

"Oh yeah," he answered, and stroked the back of my head. "Good night, Jeanie Beanie."

"Good night," I said, and watched him walk out to his

car. Just out of curiosity I went back into the kitchen and looked around for whatever he'd been holding in his hand when the cop and I saw him in the window. It was the dating questionnaire, of all things.

What I've Heard Before

Monday, June 22

I was having the dream where I can dance like the wind.

"One hundred and thirty-nine pounds," the scale said minutes later.

"Well, ha, ha to you, you pessimist! Take that!" This rejuvenated me from what had been a lackluster Sunday, spent on the couch staring straight ahead and then later in a lawn chair staring slightly to the left. Once again, Barton had paid for Sunday delivery of a handsome bouquet of something or other, and once again he had not called me.

I had better hopes for a profitable and productive Monday. It was time to bear down and win the contest, or at least qualify for the thousand bucks. I peeked across my yard and saw Gramp watering his plants; so he was back from his weekend safely. He looked peppy, although when didn't he? He was surrounded by wooden stakes, so I guessed that today was the day to tie up the tomato plants, either that or stab mice in the Havahart trap, another thing he did from time to time. No sign of the beehive, but as I looked closer, I could see there were about a dozen Post-it notes stuck to the side of his house. He couldn't see them yet. I shook my head and left him to his own day.

My car was still toying with the emphysema/laryngitis sound, but I continued to ignore it. One of our former sales managers used to say if you waited long enough, all problems went away. I wasn't entirely sure this was true for cars, though, and in truth that guy had been canned long ago.

The new receptionist was struggling her way up the learning curve as I walked into the office.

"It's a wonderful morning at LotsaCoups, may I help you? I'm very sorry. Could you say that again? I'm still very sorry. Would you mind repeating that? Hello, it's a wonderful morning at LotsaCoups."

Two checks had come in for me, and that meant it really *was* a wonderful morning at LotsaCoups because my commissions would soon follow. I felt cheerful. I had six new customers and all the way until July 31 to get the other four. If those pizza geeks came through, I could end up in the teens and maybe even beat Henrietta. Our early-summer mailing was just hitting the streets, so that meant there'd be leads coming in. Hopefully, one or two would not be barking mad.

A huge pile of boxes leaned against the wall near the door. They held stacks of extra coupons for each client. Depending on how many customers you had, your haul from this jumble could be heavy or light. Mine was pretty heavy, but that just meant I had a lot of clients, none of them very profitable. Henrietta usually had two or three heavy boxes, and I was pretty sure Abe could carry his with one hand.

Most of the reps were on time today. We assembled around the table in the conference room and watched Dan stand and put his watch down in front of him on the table. A new technique from Danno, this sent the strong message that time was of the essence. Henrietta wore a beautiful black silk shift that was at least one size too small. It showed her rolls of stomach fat perfectly. Abe looked showered, shaved, and attentive. He was wearing a suit, for Christ's sake. Several files and notebooks rested in front of him, and I tried to catch his eye so I could smirk, but he refused to look at me.

"I'd like to hear from all of you in twenty-five words or less why LotsaCoups is better than our competitor, Coupon Enders."

Abe said softly, "It's Coupon Busters, Dan."

"Yes, Coupon Busters. Why is LotsaCoups better? In twenty-five words or less. Let's start with you, Garrett."

Garrett Shonsky was a mild-mannered, balding Clark Kent type who minded his own business. His horn-rimmed black glasses slid down his nose most of the time, so usually he looked at you over the top of them. It gave him a curious scholarly demeanor. He and his wife, Connie, were old-time coupon royalty and had outlasted three or four owners. Poor Garrett was dumbstruck.

"Well, uh . . ."

"That's two," Dan said.

"LotsaCoups gives you more for your money," Garrett said, and looked satisfied with himself. His wife wore matching horn-rimmed glasses, except hers were red. She sat back in her seat and took the glasses off.

"What's the point of this, Dan?" Connie asked. This could have been a tense coupon moment if the new receptionist hadn't knocked loudly on the door of the conference room.

"Excuse me, Mr. Albright? This isn't working out for me. No one speaks English and everyone is rude."

"Can you wait just a minute, Gladys?" Dan asked, glancing down at the watch.

"Sorry," Gladys said, and was gone. We could hear the phone lines ringing all the way from the front desk.

"For your information, Connie," Dan said, "the point of

this little exercise is to see what you people are saying out there. To see why some of you aren't making your numbers. You're making yours, of course, so we'd like to hear what you have to say." Dan had to kiss Connie's ass and we all knew it. Though not at Henrietta's level, Connie's sales were always in the top five, and we suspected she gave her overflow to poor Garrett. His weren't bad either.

Dan slumped in his seat, then took off his own glasses and continued. "All right, we're going to have to stop because I have to deal with the phones. So I'll be brief. I've been promoted. I'm general manager now, and a new sales manager has been hired. Congratulations to Abe McNamara."

Jaws dropped, hell froze over, and all eyes turned to Abe, who looked very humble and even better dressed than he'd been a minute before.

"You're kidding," Connie Shonsky said. You could see the transformation of the group as everyone clapped and slapped Abe on the back. They clapped and slapped for Dan, too, but the real fervor went to Abe. No longer the butt boy of the sales force, Abe was looked up to now and even fawned over. Or at least to his face he was fawned over. What we would all have to say privately was another matter.

"Don't forget your memos, everybody, and come in here next week ready for the twenty-five-word quiz," Dan said on his way out the door. "I'll see you all at the sales meeting Wednesday."

"I'll be in touch with all of you," Abe said. "I want to ride with everybody in the next week or two, okay? Just to get a feel for things."

"Yeah, get a feel for this," I said in a low voice to Abe, but he ignored me. I couldn't believe it, but he ignored me.

I felt very hurt by Abe's snub. Henrietta looked agitated as she stood over Dan, who was sitting in the receptionist's chair and trying to make sense out of the headset.

"Good morning, um, a great morning here, can I help you? Uh yes, LotsaCoups, great morning, I mean, wonderful morning, how can I help you?"

"Dan, you're not listening to me," Henrietta broke in.

"Henrietta, it's pretty hard to listen to you—yes . . . no . . . I mean, good, wonderful morning at LotsaCoups, please hold."

The stack of boxes near the door slowly shrank as the reps hauled their extras away. I was still in a state of shock while I kicked mine into the hall, onto the elevator, then outside and *clunk*, *clunk*, *clunk*, down the steps and toward my car. Somehow I managed to get it into the trunk, knowing I might never be able to get it out. Garrett and Connie were behind me, and we huddled together like refugees.

"It must be blackmail. He must know something about Dan, or they're having sex," Connie said.

"Connie, really." Garrett looked mortified.

"I just don't get it," I said. "I just don't understand."

"Probably has something to do with Baldwin Springs," Connie mused.

"You might be right, Connie," I said. "If Dan sat down and started analyzing all the business that comes in, it might look like Abe is a top gun. On paper anyway."

"One decent account. Baldwin Springs is all he really has," Garrett said, and pushed his glasses up to his eyes.

"Did you see Henrietta?" Connie asked. "She's wicked pissed she didn't get the job."

"Imagine working for Henrietta," Garrett added.

"Henrietta makes way more money than the sales manager," I said. "Why would she want that job?"

"You know Henrietta," Connie said. "She has to be the best."

We stood for a few minutes and chatted, then decided to road the hit. That was another bit of Abespeak, and I felt a real pang for the loss of my friend. Even if we maintained our friendship, the line between working stiffs and management was a big one, and I knew it couldn't be crossed without risk.

"Maybe it won't be so bad," Garrett said.

"What's all that bullshit about a wonderful morning at LotsaCoups? Who thought that one up?" Connie asked from across her car.

"Who knows? Some yutz from the plant, I'm sure," I called back. "Bye, you guys."

"Have a wonderful day," Garrett said.

"Good morning, Dog Daze, every dog has its daze, how may I help you?"

"Could I speak to your advertising manager, please?"

"Who's calling?"

"This is Jeanie Callahan with—"

"Please hold."

("Me and you and a Dog Named Blue" elevator music)

"Can I help you?"

"This is Jeanie Callahan from LotsaCoups."

"Yes, our appointment is with you this afternoon at two, isn't it?"

"Oh no."

"It isn't for two? That's what you said."

"Oh rats."

"Well, are you going to be here or not? This would be a long shot for us anyway, you know."

I groaned. "Okay, go ahead. Bye."

"Well, bye."

I sat in my car, still in the office parking lot, and watched Henrietta load her SUV with boxes. She obviously had made the appointment with Dog Daze, and I loathed her for it. My cell phone donged.

"This is Jeanie."

"Hi, it's Abe."

"Oh, I'm so glad to hear from you," I said. All my good mental health rushed back. "You won't believe what just happened."

"I didn't mean to ignore you."

I exhaled loudly. "That's all right. I didn't think you did."

"Jeanie, you know the greeting on your cell phone doesn't even mention LotsaCoups. Don't you think it should?"

"It mentions coupons, Abe."

"And when you answer in person, you really should say 'LotsaCoups,' too."

"What if it's my grandfather? Or my gynecologist?"

"Yeah, okay, Jeanie, how often does your gynecologist call?"

"I guess I've been lucky so far, Abe. He doesn't call that often."

"And who pays your cell phone bill?"

"Well, gee, Abe, I pay part of it and the company pays part of it."

"Something you might want to think about, Jean."

"Oh, okay. I guess Cheng Du is out now, eh?"

"I don't think you ought to be doing Cheng Du, do you? Don't you want to win a thousand dollars?"

"Definitely, Abe. Why did you call?"

"Oh. Can I ride with you on Friday?"

"I guess so."

"Be sure you have at least three appointments scheduled so I can watch your presentation, all right?"

"You're going to watch *my* presentation?"

"That's right."

"All right then."

"What did you say just happened?"

"Nothing, Abe. Not a thing. You sold your soul to the devil, didn't you?"

"What?"

"Bye."

We hung up and I threw the phone on the floor of the front seat, or at least the part of it I could see.

"Hi. You've reached the voice mail of Jeanie Callahan, resident of Worcester, chorus member of The Sound of Music, and employee of LotsaCoups. Depending on the nature of your call, please leave a message." BEEP.

"Hi, it's Meg. You'd better call me." BEEP.

"This Mike. Why you no call?" BEEP.

"Jeanie, it's Henrietta. Thought I would give you a heads-up that I do have an appointment in your area with Dog Daze. Also that beauty shop you signed, ColdCuts? Her sister already does business with me in Acton, so it would probably make more sense for them both to do business with me. What do you think?" BEEP.

"This is Mort at Mort's Hardware. No one's come in with the coupon yet. Please come by as soon as you can." BEEP.

I resisted the temptation to go home and read the paper all morning, that being the usual result of bad news. There is nothing like failure or the fear of it to demotivate a tenderhearted sales rep. Instead, I delivered extras.

"Hi, Mort. How're things?"

"Oh, a lot better than since I called you. Three people came in with the coupon just this morning. One was a big wallpaper order, so that's good."

"Great. Is there anything more I can do for you?"

"Will you give Isabel Cartwright a message for me?"

"Sure."

"Tell her I know she's watching me out her window across the street."

"Gee, Mort, I don't know. Can't you tell her yourself?"

"Come on, Jeanie. Just do it."

"Hey, guys. How's biz?"

"Slow."

"How many oil changes have you had today?"

"If you have yours done, Jeanie, it'll be the first."

"Okay, well, here are the extras, if you could give them to Mark."

"He's in court, you know. That woman he patted on the ass is suing him. Geesh. Nobody can take a joke these days."

"I thought it was the one he said something to through her car window."

"Yeah, that one isn't suing, though. We're changing the name to Nashoba Tire and Harassment."

"Okay, well, have a good day."

Delivering extras is fun. Most people have already paid for the mailing, so you're not trying to get money, and the coupons are usually starting to come in, so most people are happy. It's like a big honeymoon. Because you don't have to get a check, you don't have to stick around for the gallbladder stories, though I sometimes do anyway. I skipped lunch and felt really thin and disciplined. That ended at approximately two P.M. when I walked into Low Phat House of Pizza with two hundred extras, and walked out with a large tuna sub, extra mayo. A few leads were coming in.

"Hi, Jeanie, it's Dan. Wait, is this thing working? Um, call 555-4235, it's a carpet-cleaning guy name of . . . Wait a minute . . . Shit, I can't find it now." BEEP.

"Jeanie, Dan again. The carpet-cleaning guy is Mort somebody. Or maybe that was his brother. Or father. Anyway, call him, okay? Happy hunting." BEEP.

"It's Meg. You need to call me." BEEP.

"Hello, I saw your ad. I have a revolutionary new business and I'm not ready yet to send out an advertisement. But I'd like to talk to you. I don't give out my phone number, so I'll wait till I reach you." BEEP.

"Hi, Jeanie, Dan here. This could be a big one. Water filter guy, name of Harold, 555-6697. Go get 'em!" BEEP.

"This Mike. You call."

* * *

Water-filter scams were rampant a few years ago, so I wasn't too eager to pursue the one Dan left for me. Sales managers always think every lead is a jewel. I did call, though, and set an appointment. I also got an appointment with Mort's brother-in-law, whom I hoped would be new customer number seven. If I ever went truly crazy, I felt I could blame it on this Mike person, who still hadn't given me a number I could call. I checked back on my caller ID and as usual his listing said UNAVAILABLE. Finally, Henrietta could be in the last throes of cyanide poisoning and I wasn't giving up ColdCuts.

Four hours after consuming the tuna sub, I also managed to ingest a slice of tomato-and-onion pizza with my grandfather, or rather with the sound of my grandfather going up and down the staircase while I called out the *Jeopardy!* questions to him. He never missed. Gramp didn't go to college, but he knew everything. I noticed the clump of Post-it notes on the table next to his recliner, and picked them up.

You look handsome in your Bermuda shorts.

Have you ever wondered why leaves only come out in the summertime?

They more or less all had the same stalker theme to them, and I stopped reading after the third one, which asked, *Are you wearing underwear?* I had to go home and adjust my makeup and feed Mr. Piggy before leaving for rehearsal, our first at the high school. I felt headed for the big time.

I realized as I locked my car in the high school parking lot that I had forgotten all day to call Meg back. Several of the adolescent nuns sat curbside with cigarettes, just under the NO SMOKING ON SCHOOL GROUNDS sign.

"We can't get in," one said to me as I walked around her.

"What?"

"You'll see," she said.

I did see. I stood with Meg and Isabel as we all stared at the stage, repopulated with every single drill and hammer we had removed. Everything was pushed back and wedged into its original position.

"What?" I cried.

"This can't be happening," Isabel said. Her chin looked better, though it could have been the makeup.

I continued to wail. "Is this *Groundhog Day*? Were we really here? Did all that really happen?"

Meg took a deep breath and spoke. "Maintenance thought it was a prank. A prank! I'm sure they thought they'd get their asses kicked, so they got all their people in here—on overtime pay, I might add—to put it all back. What a bunch of assholes. Sorry." Meg's apology was directed at Isabel, whose favor she was still currying. Shows are funny like that. You can work as a ditchdigger during the day, but if you are the director or the leading actor or someone important in the show, people bow and scrape to you. To Meg and me, it was as if the real Elizabeth Taylor stood in our midst, not to mention that Isabel was my client and I would defer to her anyway.

"Plus," Isabel said, "I just caught that kid with the skateboard trying to spray-paint the cafeteria wall. I'm not going to put up with that." Meg and I exchanged glances, but neither of us declared any connection with Truman.

Barton and Marianne walked up behind us, and my stomach did a little acrobatic maneuver. "I thought you people cleaned all this off the stage," Barton said.

"We did," I replied. Isabel explained the story. It took him a while to get it.

"So what now?" he said to Isabel. I saw how he dropped the problem squarely in her lap.

Bill Tuxhorn headed down the aisle to examine the stage and then back again with a proprietary swagger. "Do the Spotlighters have insurance, Isabel? I mean, if someone were to become a paraplegic during the show?" he asked.

"Bill, I honestly don't know, but I don't want to talk about it," Isabel answered. It was decided to do nothing for the moment except adjourn to Isabel's house for a strategy session. That sounded fine to me, and I agreed to follow Meg to the convenience store so we could buy chips and dip. My presence wasn't really required, but I seemed to be invited anyway. I caught Barton's eye and mouthed, *Thank you for the flowers*, and he winked at me.

Marianne pursed her lips. "People had better have their songs learned. Will somebody please call and tell me where rehearsal is going to be?" she asked, checking something off in her notebook.

"Well, isn't her diaper clean," Meg said.

Meg and I were a little intimidated as we stood on the front steps of the Cartwright manse, a Georgian colonial with an imposing view of Mount Wachusett.

"Come join us in the kitchen," Isabel said when she opened the massive front door, and we followed her down a long marble hallway. The place was huge. We did notice the bald head of a man watching television in a leather recliner. He didn't turn around.

"Just a few more friends, honey," Isabel said to the head as we passed. Meg poked me with her elbow and I nodded, maintaining radio silence. When Isabel turned her back in the kitchen, Meg pointed at the vast countertop and mouthed to me, *Real granite*. We ran our fingertips over the smooth surface and stood like a couple of orphan children in the last rays of sunlight lacing through the bay window. Some of my restaurant clients had smaller kitchens. We watched while Isabel freshened Barton's drink from the well-stocked liquor cabinet. Barton looked very comfortable and had obviously been there before. Meg held up two fingers to me and mouthed again, *Two dishwashers.*

There were also two sinks and who knew how many other wonderful things I was too dumb to recognize. I hoped I didn't have anything hanging from my nose.

"Wow, Isabel, beautiful house," Meg said.

"Yeah," I said, displaying my high vocabulary.

Just then a very tanned blond girl in her late teens padded into the kitchen in a wet bathing suit.

Isabel spoke to her. "Hi, Clarissa, these are some of my theater friends. This is—"

"Yeah, hi," the girl said. "Isabel, why aren't there any clean towels in the pool house?"

"Did you use them all?" Isabel asked.

"Whatever," the girl said, and opened one of the refrigerator doors. "Where is my Orange Crush?" she asked. "Can't I leave soda here without having it disappear?"

Isabel joined her at the refrigerator door and reached well back onto the top shelf to retrieve a six-pack of Orange Crush. The girl snatched it from her hand and stalked out.

"Stepdaughter?" I asked.

"Mmmm," said Isabel. "What would you two like?" she asked us. We let ourselves get talked into chardonnay, a much better brand than I bought at the grocery store.

"Let's see what we have for snacks," Isabel said, and again opened what looked like part of the wall but was really the mammoth refrigerator. Soon she had shrimp and cocktail sauce spread out before us, along with olive pâté and some other things I couldn't pronounce. Our chips and dip were the poor relations.

Barton could barely talk for stuffing himself. "This is my grazing hour," he said. "Thanks, Isabel."

"You're very welcome, dear. Now what are we going to do?"

An hour later, Isabel opened another bottle of wine. She didn't have to wait on Barton, because he was helping himself to food and liquor with increasing frequency.

"Okay if I open this Jameson?" he asked.

"Sure," Isabel said.

The bald head never appeared and didn't exactly speak to us. He yelled into the kitchen once, "Hey! I'm going to bed now, Isabel, so can you keep it down?"

"Okay, dear," she said. I wondered whether he was the reason for Isabel's bruises.

Eventually, we agreed on the solution to our predicament. Either we found another place for the show (impossible), or moved the stuff off the stage again. The second possibility seemed particularly repugnant to the three of us who had done it the first time, and arriving at it probably didn't require four hours of drinking, but we gave it our all. By midnight, we decided to take a dip in the pool. Isabel gave Meg and me bathing suits to wear, much to Barton's dismay.

"Hey, it's dark. You don't need a suit. Nobody's going to see anybody."

"I don't think so," Meg said at the prospect of skinny-dipping with Barton. However, Isabel's bathing suits were a bit large for us, and in the end our various parts were visible anyway. There was a lot of giggling. Barton came up from underneath like a big sea monster and tossed me up in the air a few times, and this ended up having a sobering effect, which was good, all things considered. By the time he did a massive cannonball into the pool and sent a good percentage of the water out onto the back lawn, things were winding down.

"Watch it, Barton. I don't want to disturb Ray," Isabel said. "He has to work tomorrow." That reminded the rest of us, of course, that we had to work too, which could have been Isabel's intent all along.

"Where's Clarissa?" I asked.

"At her babysitting job, I hope," Isabel said.

Barton nuzzled my ear and asked if my grandfather was at home. I said yes, he was, though technically I didn't know. I forgot to ask Barton about his sick mother.

"People had better show up for this," Meg said, referring to the next stage-clearing event.

"They will," Isabel said.

To: Dan Albright
Fr: Jeanie Callahan
Re: Getting Close to the Business
I have inquired about the status of the high
school in terms of advertising. They may want
to do some kind of informational postcard. Con-
tact is being made with the superintendent.
Everything is going swimmingly. SEND.

That Will Bring Us Back

Tuesday, June 23

Isabel was right: Almost the entire cast showed up. It was heartening. Sam Yummy even came back again, and re-lugged the same drills and saws. Meg and Isabel had tracked down the superintendent earlier in the day and arranged an emergency meeting with him, during which he had been very apologetic about the whole episode. A couple of the maintenance guys were around and they helped too. Isabel asked them if they wanted to be in the show, and they said they would think about it. The stage was clear in about an hour and rehearsal went forward. Sam and Bill Tuxhorn constructed scenery in the hallway while Marianne led the children in their songs. Barton worked in a separate classroom with the four leads, none of whom said a word to the rest of us peons. Terribly curi-ous, I stood outside their classroom and listened. There was plenty of laughing. Maria and the Captain gave their lines, interrupted now and then by Barton, telling them what to do. The other two had very loud voices and now and then told jokes. Barton laughed, and they all seemed to know one another.

"Remember in *Oklahoma!* when you missed your entrance," one of them said.

"Oh, yes, but don't forget *Carousel*, when you tripped over Vic," another one replied.

"How is Vic?"

"Oh, he's better."

"Cross here and then turn," Barton said.

Every musical has a female second lead and a male second lead, and the show cannot be successful without them. I know that now. In *The Sound of Music*, they are the Baroness and Max. The Baroness is the slightly older and more sophisticated woman who gets dumped for Maria. Max is just funny. The man playing Max was a portly and well-traveled community theater actor. Stephanie Wilson, a heavily peroxided blonde, played the Baroness. From the sound of it, Stephanie had played every lead in every play, and knew exactly what everyone should do. She also looked as though she'd had a nose job.

Back in the auditorium, Jennifer, the eleven-year-old Liesl, was startlingly good. Her voice was pure and true, and it carried to the back wall. Her mother beamed. The mothers of the children always stayed for rehearsal and coached the kids from the audience, incurring Barton's ill-concealed hatred. I wondered again how he would make Jennifer seem to be sixteen going on seventeen, but everyone said not to worry about it. I knew the young nuns, good singers all, were more offended every day that none of them had been offered the role. Maybe that was what you got for having too many piercings.

The other young actors couldn't sing nearly as well.

"I suck," Truman said. "I can't do it." His voice cracked heartbreakingly on every other note, and I could understand why he'd rather spray-paint walls.

"You're not singing from your diaphragm," young Jennifer told him, flipping her pigtails out of her face.

"Why don't you shut the fuck up?" Truman snapped at the girl. In truth, just about everyone wanted to say the same thing to her.

"Uh, uh, uh! Is that the kind of behavior we want to see at rehearsal?" Jennifer's mother trilled from the audience. No one said anything, and the atmosphere went very tense. Think United Nations during a world crisis. Think demilitarized zone where everyone is trying not to shoot.

Finally Truman altered his stance, and his voice sounded considerably better.

"See, I told you," Jennifer said. Now you can think homicide, mutilation, and mayhem. Thank God Marianne started rattling her music.

"All right, everybody, from the top," Marianne said. The young kids were called up to practice the good-bye song, the one where they go up the staircase and bid farewell to the partygoers downstairs, of which I was going to be one. I needed a ball gown in addition to my nun habit.

Speaking of habits, Meg and Isabel walked through with Velma, all three weighted down with costumes, which they dumped heavily into several seats in the last row. Jennifer's mother tore herself away from the proceedings onstage and walked back to add a bag of belts and socks to the stash. Chorus members appeared from everywhere, eager to try them on.

"Please be quiet back there," Marianne called from the piano bench.

"Pin it here," Velma whispered to the girl who got there first.

"No, the front will fall open if you do that," said Jennifer's mother. "See, I told you."

The sack around the high school girl finally got cinched and pinned and adjusted. Even a makeshift wimple was attached.

"How did you make those headpieces?" I asked Velma. "They're so real."

"Clorox jugs," she answered. "The old standby." I nodded as if I understood.

When they finished with her, the young chorus member was transformed. She looked quite the radiantly spiritual young novice, and even the lizard tattoo on her ankle was almost concealed.

"We still need rosary beads," Velma said.

"I have some at home," Mrs. Jennifer said. "Jennifer was in the show before."

"Great," Meg said. "I bet she wasn't playing the sixteen-year-old."

"No," Mrs. Jennifer said. "But she could have."

It was an exciting moment, a moment when the possibility of excellence seemed to shine within our reach. Maybe this show could be really good, after all.

I Have Confidence

"Hello?" I called into the pizza storefront. Once again, the place was empty. This time I had given up my chance to be early to the sales meeting, so my frustration level was chest high and edging upward. Where was Lenny Sadowski?

"Hello?" a voice called back. "The guys will be here soon."

"It's Jeanie," I said. "Are you sure?"

"Yes, they'll be here right away."

"I can't stay very long. I have a meeting. I thought everyone would be here now. That's what Lenny said."

"But they'll be here."

"I can't stay," I said. The little bald guy walked out from the alcove and looked apologetic.

With that, two others walked in the front door behind me. One of them carried a stack of neon-bright parking tickets. I watched as he tore them up and threw them into the trash can.

"No sweat," he said. He caught me looking at him and hitched his pants up around his considerable girth. He looked like a gangster, and I think his name was Ziggy.

I waited five minutes, but only one more owner came in.

"Hey, how ya doin', nice to see ya," he said, and shook my hand. He looked like a gangster too, but a nice one. Somebody's cell rang and I knew it wasn't mine. It sounded like "God Bless America."

"That's yours, Moey."

"No, it ain't. Mine plays 'Theme from *Jurassic Park*.'"

"My cell phone is busted. It can't be mine."

"Well, why don't you just pick it up and check it, fuck face?"

"Who you callin' fuck face, you lousy shit-for-brains?"

As chairs started scraping the floor and the atmosphere shifted into high testosterone, I walked to the window and looked out at the Merit station. If I didn't leave soon, I would have to walk in late to the sales meeting.

"Yeah, miss? Hi, are you Jeanie?" the nice gangster asked me as he tapped my shoulder.

"Yes."

"It's Lenny on the phone for you."

"Thank you," I said. I put the instrument to my ear even though it reeked of some sickening sweet scent that could probably clean my oven.

"Hi, Lenny."

"Jeanie, I'm so sorry. I'm in court and I can't leave."

"Court? You didn't know last week that you had a court date, Lenny?"

"I'm sorry, no, I didn't. Can we try again? We're really very interested in doing a coupon." Again, he knew how to light my lights. "Would you be interested in going bowling tomorrow night?" Lenny asked.

"Bowling?"

"Yes, some of the owners will be there, and maybe you could talk to them then?"

"Well, okay," I said. We agreed on where and when, and hung up.

Whatever. I walked out into a light drizzle to find my car and haul ass to the hotel for the regional sales meeting.

I walked in at the stroke of nine and slipped into a seat next to Connie Shonsky, just as Dan was doing his watch maneuver. A few people hadn't seen it before, and I knew nudges were being exchanged all over the room. Regional sales meetings were different from weekly meetings, which involved only local teams. These bigger gatherings were held after each mailing went out, and they gave me a good chance to gossip with my buddies from the North Shore and the South Shore. Sales meetings were enjoyable, if only because of the free lunch, the completely stupid and unrealistic motivational talks, and the wonderful chance to sit in a chair all day.

"Hello, everybody. I hope you all had an opportunity to get in a sales call or two this morning." Dan looked around at the assembled faces. Many of these people probably spent more than an hour driving here, but we all nodded our heads like the sycophants we were. Give 'em what they want, I always say. I could see the back of Abe's head in the chair right in front of Dan, an easy place from which to fall on his knees in front of his new idol.

Connie leaned my way. "Henrietta's got fourteen new."

"Shit."

"But Dog Daze stood her up."

I gasped. "You're kidding. What happened?"

"The people weren't there; I don't know why. Abe tried to make light of it, but Henrietta was pissed."

"Well, isn't that too bad?" I said.

"And Garrett overheard Dan say on the phone he's going to hire Magda back."

"Aha!" Connie and I covered our mouths with our hands in glee, and Garrett leaned forward from the other side of Connie to get in on the fun. Meanwhile, I had no idea what Dan was saying.

"Is there a joke, Jeanie?"

"Nope, Dan. No joke," I said, and a few of my colleagues looked back at me and smiled. We were a nasty bunch sometimes.

By the time we stumbled out to find the lunch buffet, we were almost snoring, primarily from the stultifying presentation we had just witnessed. The speaker was another marketing hotshot who had probably never made a cold call in his life. A cold call is you, my friend, all by your lonesome, walking into somebody's business "cold," off the street, and trying to sell him. Or at least make an appointment to sell him later. It takes guts. It can be bloody and painful and sometimes humiliating, but all business is based on it. No sales organization can make money unless someone is willing to do it. And we were the ones willing to do it for LotsaCoups.

"Is that macaroni salad?" someone asked.

"I think so," another replied. "It looks like macaroni." I loaded up my plate from the overradiated buffet and hurried to sit with the three Bobs. Bob Payne, Bob Morrison, and Bob Bordeaux all worked territories in Boston or Lowell, and placed bets on every athletic contest possible. I counted on lunching with them every two months to catch up on my sports info.

"Somebody owes me for the Lakers' last play-off game," I said.

One of the Bobs acknowledged the debt. "What about Yankees/Red Sox next weekend and I'll give you two points." He talked me into another bet, and I knew he would keep doing that until they didn't have to pay me anything. No wonder they were good in sales. We huddled together and compared notes on the possible Magda rehiring. This seemed to be another opportunity for wagering.

"Another one just quit yesterday, you know," Bob said.

"Was that the one who said the place was an asylum?"

"Yeah, and I call that perceptive."

"Watch out. Batman and Robin at six o'clock," Bob said.

Sure enough, Dan and Abe were right behind us, making the rounds of the lunch tables. They stopped to do manly sports talk with the Bobs. Soon we returned to the meeting room and got back to sleep, at least until Dan stood up and lowered the boom.

"Rates are going up, folks."

The whole group stirred. This was bad news for us.

"Rates were just raised in January, Dan."

"Yeah, not even six months ago."

Dan adjusted the watch in front of him slightly. "Do you know what the new owners paid for this company, folks?"

Everyone was quiet.

Dan pressed on. "They need to start making money, real money."

Everyone remained quiet.

"Here is a chart of the new prices, and there's really good news in it for all of you."

"What's that, Dan?" Abe asked. He was still new to his sucking-up role, but good at it.

"If you sell something at top price, you are going to get a much higher commission on that sale." That got everybody's attention, as Dan had known it would. He went on to rhapsodize about how wonderful this all was, how it was a win-win-win for the customer and for the company and for us. I had a hard time picturing how this would be a win for Mort's Hardware.

After two hours of Dan flapping his jaw and Abe doing the same, I was completely slumped in my seat. Connie Shonsky had given her all in arguing against the price hike, and Dan looked ready to fire her on the spot. Henrietta also fought the good fight.

"I just think we're positioning ourselves for problems,

Dan, with our competitors," she said. We may have hated Henrietta in real time, but at the sales meetings we were her loyal followers.

"Yeah! Henrietta's right!"

"You go, Henrietta."

I was doing my usual feel-sorry-for-the-bad-guy routine. This couldn't be easy for poor Dan, and my old pal Abe looked like he was suffering from multiple personality disorder. He laughed; he frowned; he didn't know what to do. I knew Abe. He didn't have a clue.

The coupon day ended in the hotel bar. Dan bought a round for everybody, but I held back and left early, knowing I had rehearsal later and not wanting to be stinking drunk. I had achieved that goal more times lately than I was proud of. Besides, Mr. Piggy needed his dinner.

"Hi. This is Jeanie Callahan. You've beaten me. Leave any message you want." BEEP.

"This is Steve Kaminski, Mort's brother-in-law. I'm ready to roll on that coupon. Can you call me back? 978-555-3678." BEEP.

"Hey, Jean, Bob Morrison. Why'dja leave so soon? Do you want to get into the Magda pool?" BEEP.

"This Mike. We give up soon and call other company."

I was ready to throw the cell phone out the window when I turned the corner onto Leawood Lane and saw a police cruiser and an ambulance in Gramp's driveway. In the street, the left rear of Gramp's car was joined with the right headlight of another car. I screeched to the curb, yanked my vehicle into park, and flew out of my seat to run over to the scene. Vehicles were slowing down to gawk, and some were rude enough to honk, a few of whom got the old bird-erino from me. Relief flooded through my veins when I saw Gramp standing next to the guys with the stretcher.

"The Industrial Revolution changed all that," Gramp said.

"That's been for the best, sir," one of the attendants said.

"I've got a book inside you might like to read," Gramp went on. I looked at the two damaged cars and noticed the other one looked a lot like Mrs. Mayer's. Oh my God, it *was* Mrs. Mayer's. I turned around and saw her a little way up her own driveway dissolved in tears. Her hair was jet-black.

"So you're refusing treatment, sir?" the attendant asked.

"Yes, I am," Gramp replied.

"What happened?" I butted in.

"Nothing much," Gramp said. "Gert had a little lapse in judgment."

"She hit you?"

"By accident, Jeanie. It was just barely a tap. I was backing out of my driveway and she was heading into her own." Yeah, okay. I walked all the way over to Mrs. Mayer and put my arm around her shoulders.

"This wasn't part of the experiment, was it, Mrs. Mayer?"

She snuffled. "No, no. Well, not exactly."

"Not exactly? What were you trying to do?"

"I just wanted to have a little accident. I didn't want to hurt anybody."

I angrily pulled my arm back and stalked off. I had every intention of ratting out Mrs. Mayer, but I couldn't get a word in back at the ambulance.

"There's been a lot of research on that," Gramp was saying.

"We had a case last week," the attendant said. He started in on a long-winded saga—I knew them so well— and I decided to go inside and wait for Gramp. Ten minutes later I was still waiting and still steaming. The two cars had been separated.

I walked to the front porch and yelled out to the street

"*Jeopardy!*'s on!" This broke up the confab and soon Gramp walked up the driveway and into the house. He immediately sat down on the bench next to the front door.

"What's wrong?" I asked, heart in throat.

"Just a little dizzy," he answered. "Don't you have play practice?"

"I don't have it tonight," I lied. "Gramp, Mrs. Mayer has got to be stopped. She did that on purpose."

"I think I might lie down on the couch."

"Here's a pillow, Gramp. Oh, my God. Why didn't you let the ambulance take you to the emergency room?"

"No need for that."

"Do you want Tylenol?"

"Okay, maybe." I brought him Tylenol and a glass of orange juice and he swallowed the tablets down.

"Gramp, Gert Mayer is not your friend."

"Yes, she is. Her eyesight just isn't that good."

I walked to the window and looked out at Gramp's car, still parked slantwise in front of the house. There was a slight dent in the fender. I walked outside, inspected it from all sides, and still didn't see anything worse. I started the car and moved it into the garage. While I was out there, I got ice cream from the freezer and fixed us both strawberry sundaes. Gramp missed a few *Jeopardy!* questions, but they were hard ones. Who was Napoleon's brother? Geesh, who cares? We watched some reruns, including *McHale's Navy*, one of our favorites. Gramp won't watch dramas. He always says, "These people have too many problems."

"Jeanie?"

"Yeah, Gramp?"

"I think maybe you should take me to the hospital."

"Oy Jesus, let's go." I jumped out of my chair and banged my knee on the brick fireplace. "Ouch! Ouch!"

"Don't panic, just a couple of chest pains, that's all. Let me put these dishes in the dishwasher."

"Gramp! Forget about the dishes!" This was the equivalent of telling a zebra not to have stripes. He loaded the dishwasher, wiped down the counter, and even swept the floor, all while I clutched my knee and grimaced in the doorway.

Two hours later, Gramp was comfortably resting in a hospital bed with the TV on while I sat in a corner biting my nails and massaging my knee. Three women friends chatted all around him. How they had tracked him down, I wasn't quite sure—some kind of dowager hotline, I guess. I was ready to shoot Mrs. Mayer if she had the nerve to show up, but she didn't. And if these babes weren't enough to keep the action going, two nurses kept walking in to share anecdotes and join the fun.

"I vomited for days after my hysterectomy," one said. "I was in surgery for four hours."

"Oh, tell me about it," another replied. "I was in the operating room so long my son fell asleep in the waiting room."

"Gramp, you're only going to be here one night," I said. "So don't you think you should get some rest?" The ER doc had admitted him for observation, and I felt strongly that the monitors attached to Gramp, beeping and clicking away, could do their jobs better without all the company.

"My neighbor has a pacemaker and it goes off all the time."

"Gramp isn't going to have a pacemaker."

"We were having lunch at Talk of the Town in Clinton the other day and it went off. The owner was very nice and wrapped up our early-bird specials to take in the ambulance."

"Gramp's not going to have a pacemaker."

"You just really have to be careful with a pacemaker."

"I didn't know Talk of the Town would give you an early-bird special for lunch."

In time, my perseverance paid off and the ladies left. In

truth, it got to be their bedtime, or they probably would have lingered all night. My own dotage seemed much closer as I air-kissed Gramp on the cheek and left for home.

I made sure the lights were off at Gramp's house. I felt confident that he would be okay. He'd always been okay. Gramp could kick my ass on any lawn mowing, leaf blowing, or homeowning project known. And the doc had said everything looked fine, probably just a little angina, the cardiac patient's curse. Still, I worried. Gramp said absolutely not to call my parents, and I supposed I would give in to his wishes on that. All from a fender-bender. That phrase reminded me that someone I had talked to recently had been in one. I couldn't remember who it was. It wasn't Meg or anybody from the show. It wasn't any of my clients. Oh wait, yes, it was, potentially; it was the Chinese guy who was considering the menu flyer. When had I last seen him? I froze in my tracks and then scampered across Gramp's yard and my own into the kitchen, where I grabbed my sales notebook. There it was on a page from a couple of weeks ago. Fender-bender. It was ten P.M., but I didn't think it was too late to call.

"Wong Dynasty, take-out or dine-in?"

"Is your name Mike by any chance?"

"Yes, this Mike."

"This is Jeanie Callahan from LotsaCoups."

"Oooooh, you finally call."

And I'll Sing Once More

Thursday, June 25

Patsy Cline was belting out "Crazy" on the jukebox as I walked into the bowling alley and looked around for Lenny. Due to a senseless mosquito incident, I had removed one contact lens in the car, so I couldn't see all that well. I eventually spotted him, leaning down to chat with the hot-tempered Ziggy.

"No! I ain't doing it!" Ziggy yelled. I hesitated, but then gripped my briefcase and headed their way.

"Just relax, Zig," Lenny was saying as he looked up and saw me. I'm happy to say his face brightened. I'm sure mine did too. He wore jeans tonight, a bit more casual than I'd seen him, but still a button-down striped oxford shirt. "Hey, there, coupon girl."

"Hi, Lenny," I said, and reached over to shake his hand.

"Do you need shoes?" he said. "Put them on our tab."

"Do you mind if I don't bowl?" I asked. "I'm only wearing one contact lens."

This agitated the guys. "Whooo, baby, take 'em all off!"

"How many do they think I wear?" I asked Lenny sotto voce.

Lenny shook his head. "This is their bowling night, not their thinking night."

"Aw, come on," several of them said. "You gotta bowl. We don't do business with nobody who don't bowl." That was all I needed to hear.

I hate bowling-alley shoes and always picture the unsavory person who wore them just before me as contagious with a disease, and with a serious sweat problem. No one I saw in the bowling alley dispelled that notion. One of the guys walked up to the counter with me and very politely helped me get my size.

"Yours look different from these," I said.

"Oh, I got my own," he said. "I don't like to wear nobody else's." Turns out all the pizza owners had their own bowling shoes. Three lanes just full of potential clients. Be still my beating heart.

I went back to the lane where Lenny sat in the scorekeeper's chair and watched him trying to keep the peace.

"I had a spare last time!"

"No, you didn't, Dino. Just sit down, okay?"

"Yes, I did!"

"Nice one, Moey," Lenny said, deftly ignoring the plaintiff Dino in front of him. Moey himself wiped his hands on a hankie that hung from his belt. His stomach, also hanging over the belt, jiggled as he strutted back to the seats after his strike.

"Thanks," Moey said, and stuck a finger in his mouth to retrieve something from between his teeth.

Soon it was my turn. "Now if you use a coupon, you will do much better than I'm about to do," I proclaimed. If I didn't turn the conversation toward business, no one else was going to.

I threw a gutter ball with authority.

"Coupons," said one of the guys. "You mean like dry cleaning and cat food?"

"Yes," I said. I was in the middle of my spiel when their attention abruptly shifted. Two scantily clad middle-aged women strolled by, and the guys started to whisper and snicker. A couple of them pulled out combs and adjusted their Brylcreemed hairstyles. Dino, in fact, left his seat to follow the ladies, and I saw him pull out a huge wad of cash. We didn't see him again.

On the next go-round, my ball jumped out of its own gutter and into the gutter next to us. I waved cheerfully to my growing audience.

Lenny was a pretty good bowler, but what I liked was the way he smiled at me every time he returned to his seat. Even through one eye he looked cute, not dangerous like Barton, but reliable and polite and with a good haircut.

On my fifth turn, or frame as they call it, my ball went straight down the middle but knocked over only four pins. "Oh no!" the guys all yelled. Several of them tried to instruct me on strategy for getting the rest of the pins to fall over, and, wonder of wonders, it actually worked. I had a spare. The guys cheered.

On my sixth frame, I threw a strike.

On my seventh, another spare.

This was a fun game. My one-eyed Cyclops technique was working.

Lenny bought me a beer and then another beer. A couple of times he stood behind me and helped me hold the ball the right way.

Coupons were never again discussed.

Later, as Lenny and I stood in the parking lot, I had the oddest feeling that he was going to kiss me. But then cars started revving up and squealing rubber on the pavement and he eventually had to quell a disturbance.

"Try us again next Wednesday in the shop!" he yelled as I drove out.

"Okay!" I yelled back. Definitely okay.

Then I Don't Feel So Bad

Friday, June 26

I did one last lipstick blot in the mirror and headed out my back door, intending to pop in at Gramp's and fix him some oatmeal before I left for the day. I walked across the two lawns and put my hand out to open his kitchen slider and was startled by his voice behind me.

"Did you set those traps?"

"Gramp, I thought we agreed you were going to rest in bed today."

"I will later. Did you set the traps?"

"Well, no. I don't want the guinea pig to get caught in one."

"So don't let the guinea pig out of the cage."

I didn't want to tell Gramp that Mr. Piggy was already out of the cage, was in fact lost somewhere in my house. It had seemed such a good idea at the time, and he had looked so cute in his liberation. I was pretty sure the droppings around the house were from the pet and not extraneous vermin. Gramp was crouched over his vegetable garden, pulling weeds, and I reluctantly concluded that he couldn't get in too much trouble. We had agreed that he wouldn't drive anywhere today, not even to Home Depot. The doc had said that everything looked fine, but once again Gramp shouldn't "overdo things." I knew that was impossible. We chatted for a moment and then I headed off for my coupon day with a reasonably clear conscience.

Abe was already in the office.

"Don't you look nice," I said.

"Thanks."

"Where did you get all the suits?"

"From my dead uncle."

"Oh."

Abe did not make further comment. I waited for him to compliment me on my rather flashy red dress, but he didn't.

"What are your appointments today, Jeanie?"

I had maneuvered my schedule so I actually did have three appointments for Abe to observe. One was the carpet cleaner, one the Chinese restaurant, and one the water-filter lead that had called in. Two were in the bag and the other was a total crapshoot.

I still felt Friday zest even with the burden of someone watching me sell. It took a while to clear out the front seat of my car.

"Jesus, what a shithole," Abe said.

"Doesn't make me a bad person."

"Where am I supposed to sit?"

"Your oil level is low."

"What?" Abe asked.

"Never mind that. Just throw the stuff in the back."

"Your oil level is low."

"Who said that?"

"It's the car. It's wrong, the oil level is not low."

"Well, why is it saying that?"

"I don't know, Abe. But hey, we're in. We're ready. We're off."

"How can you live like this, Jeanie?"

Abe wasn't participating in team goodwill. I knew he was not a morning person to start with, so I took him to the diciest place first. It fulfilled my worst fears. AAAAAA Guaranteed Results Water Filters was located inside another business, AAAAAA Pest Exterminators. All those A's get put there by people trying to be first in the phone book, but even with that, the place stood empty at ten in the morning.

I introduced myself and Abe to the tattooed young entrepreneur, who immediately tried to sell us an opportunity to join his pyramid scheme. He walked away for a second and I whispered to Abe, "Can you say 'scam'?" The kid in fact walked away from us every twenty seconds, consulting his script, I was sure. I'd seen this kind of cheese before and I knew the best thing to do was clear out in a hurry.

Although it may have been obvious to me or to any sane person, it wasn't to my esteemed professional colleague, who was eating out of the kid's hand like a dog.

"How much does it cost?" Abe asked, the classic, number one, premier buying signal anywhere in the world.

"In the end, it will cost you nothing." Another classic. "All you have to do is sign up five people every week and you will be rich." The kid walked away again, and I whispered to Abe, "What the hell are you doing?"

When the kid came back, I finally jumped in. "So, Corey, hmm, yes, thanks for the literature. Were you interested in doing a coupon?"

"Yes, I'd like to do all of Masssachusetts. Probably all of New England."

"Say a return postcard?"

"Definitely. This is the opportunity of a lifetime."

"All right, well, let me figure out the rates for what you

need," I said while Abe perused the kid's pamphlets, brand-new from the box. Abe pulled out his checkbook and the kid literally licked his lips.

I got out a calculator, my own weapon. I punched in a few numbers and showed the result to the kid.

"Here you go, Corey. This would get you into all the homes of New England, and this lesser amount would send your message to the entire state."

"What?" he said. "That's ridiculous. Who can afford that?"

"Lots of people," I said. "Pennies per home, Corey. Why don't you think it over and Abe will think it over and we'll all do some thinking over, and then you can call us if you want to go forward. Ready, Abe?" I stood at the door with my briefcase demurely in front of me.

"I think you should sign up today, Abe," the kid countered. He knew what I was doing, and I knew what he was doing. It was a fight to the death. "If you wait, someone else will get in on the ground floor."

"Come on, Abe," I said. I walked toward my new sales manager and grabbed the shoulder of his dead uncle's suit. "Let's just go in the car and talk. We'll just talk. You can come right back in."

"Don't leave now," the kid said. "I'll get you some coffee."

"Um," said Abe.

"Or beer if you want it. I have beer. Or gin."

I dragged Abe out onto the sidewalk practically by his tie, and from there it was slightly easier to talk him into the car. Finally we pulled out of the parking lot, and I breathed a sigh of relief.

"Holy fuck. You owe me for that one, buddy."

"Geez. Huh. What do you know," Abe kept saying.

"Although it might have been fun to slug down some gin at ten in the morning," I added. It took Abe a while to get his brain back. I was exhausted. We next stopped at the Chinese place where the owner, Mike, and I had our tearful reunion, and he signed up for one spiffy and expensive menu. New customer number seven. Abe bought a pupu platter while we were there and spilled teriyaki beef all over Mike's brand-new carpet. I apologized profusely and Mike graciously replaced the beef teriyaki. Abe brought it with him in my car and continued to spill.

We made a few cold calls, and I kept Abe from spending more than twenty dollars at each place. Despite my efforts, he ended the day with a case of fish food, three rental movies, a road atlas, and five quarts of motor oil.

We finished up with Mort's brother-in-law, Steve, owner of Majestic Carpet Cleaning.

"Mort's been telling me about you," he boomed.

"That's good."

"He says you've got your eye on him."

"Oh, that's too funny. He always tells me it's another woman across the street."

"You know Mort."

"Oh yes. Sign here, please, Steve." New customer number eight. Abe was just about to hire Steve to clean the carpets in his apartment when I dragged him out and pretended to be interested in a landscaping truck outside. The owner was opening his door to get in when I walked up and presented my business card.

"Oh yeah, coupons," he said. "I've been meaning to call you." The three of us ducked inside a Dunkin' Donuts (Abe bought iced coffee and a dozen éclairs) and I sold the guy. *Ka-ching!* My ninth new customer, and he paid in cash. I couldn't get anybody to say no. Sometimes it's like that. If I hadn't wanted so badly to get rid of Abe, I would have pressed onward, up and down the street like a bulldozer.

Back at the office, Dan led the cheers.

"Three in one day, that's pretty good, Jeanie. Was it because you had the big guy here with you?" Dan gave a hearty slap on the back to tiny little Abe, who looked ready to throw up. "Good job, Abe."

"Yeah, thanks for your help, Abe," I said.

"No prob," he replied. I bit my lip hard.

"How many new have you got, Jeanie?" Dan asked.

"Nine."

"Not bad. Almost a thousand bucks, girl, keep going. Go home and call some more."

"I have rehearsal tonight, Dan. Don't forget, I'm staying close to the business."

Dan nodded, then went back to his headset, still trying to field calls, and Abe reached for a pack of Tums.

A number of nuns in full habit lounged outside the high school when I drove up. Some had skirts hiked up past their knees as they sat in folding chairs passing a flask back and forth. One or two reclined, cigarettes in hand, on the grass in the courtyard, while a few older ones maintained decorum. I could hear Meg speaking as I approached.

"All of you need to look the same, so if your crucifix is bigger than hers, it just doesn't look right." Indeed, the crucifixes were of various sizes and I noticed that Helen's, the older woman we sometimes called "the narc," had a really huge one stuck into her belt.

"This crucifix was blessed by the pope," Helen said.

"I know. It's really nice," Meg said. "But it doesn't match the other ones. And it's bigger than Mother Superior's, which wouldn't be right, would it?"

"Sure, it would," Helen said.

Isabel walked out of the building in her Mother Superior outfit, and now that my vision was crucifix-sensitive, I did notice that hers was smaller than Helen's. I felt grateful it wasn't my problem.

I spoke to Meg on my way in and she rolled her eyes. Just as I rounded the corner to the auditorium, a thick arm went around my waist and lifted me in the air.

"Jeanie Beanie," Barton said in my ear. "Are we going to Shipley's tonight?"

"Aaaah, put me down," I squealed. "No foolish behavior at Shipley's; I've made a vow."

"How about foolish behavior somewhere else?" Barton whispered as he clasped me to his midsection.

"You'd better cut that out," I said with little or no severity.

Isabel walked back in just then from outside and shook her head at our antics. "You two had better not be having impure thoughts. I'll have to whale you with a ruler," she said with a laugh. I'd never seen a nun with quite such heavy eye makeup.

Barton let go of me and ran to pick up Isabel in the same manner. I'm happy to say it was a more difficult task. I couldn't hear what they said to each other, and I wondered whether Isabel liked Barton. Maybe that was why she always advised me against him. Barton returned to my personal space and we continued to walk together.

"What about Saturday?" he asked.

"What about it?"

"Shall we have a reprise?" Did he always have to speak show-tune language?

"Okay."

"See you later, alligator," he said as we entered the stage area, and I forced down a frisson of little stars that wanted to fizz up my back. I had no idea why I kept accepting Barton's advances. He never called me and had never paid me back for the first night, after saying he would. I wasn't sure whether he was a man of character, and I didn't want to consult Meg about it because I knew what she would say. If only he weren't so cute. Watching him direct always melted me. By contrast, Lenny seemed pale, not as forceful. Plus, I didn't want to date a potential customer. Did I? I didn't even know what Barton did for a living, which was pretty amazing since I had chased down most everyone else's occupation.

Stephanie, the peroxided Baroness, sat in the front row

of the auditorium and held her leg out in front of Barton, stopping his forward progress.

"Yes?" he said.

"I waited for you," she said in a low voice.

"I'm sorry," Barton said. I heard him say something about his mother and restrained myself from moving closer. I was a little afraid of Stephanie, who by day worked at a discount store, but by night reigned as a high-status cast member. She had never spoken to me.

"Are we going to Shipley's?" she asked Barton, and I saw him shrug.

"I don't know," he replied.

"Oh we have to," Stephanie said. "Today was my last day at my job." So much for the discount store.

Barton nodded vaguely and climbed to the stage. "All right, let's get this over with. Costume review!" he called out, and everyone stood onstage for inspection. Meg, Barton, and Velma stood out front and scrutinized the participants. Stephanie looked elegant in a satin-and-rhinestone creation. I felt a little nervous about how good she looked, since Barton would surely notice. The kids looked perfectly Tyrolean, except for Truman's Metallica T-shirt.

Jennifer could have been Shirley Temple. She looked about eight.

"Can't we get something a little more teenaged?" Barton asked. "Long, with a sash or something?" He looked around at the worker bees. Mrs. Jennifer bristled, while Velma winked at Isabel on the stage. "Keep working on that one," he said.

Barton turned to the nuns. "That crucifix is too big."

"This crucifix was blessed by the pope," Helen said.

"It looks like an AK-47," Barton said. "Get rid of it." With that, Helen limped off the stage and walked out the door. "Oh fuck," Barton muttered.

"I'll get her," Meg offered, and left the room.

Marianne was nice to us that night and made us repeat our phrasing only seventy-two times rather than the thousand and seventy-two we were used to. A red-eyed Helen joined us midway through, accompanied haltingly down the aisle by Meg, who had clearly saved the day. Helen now carried the papal crucifix in her hands, wielding it like a weapon. No one challenged her. Our scene went fine, and we even made little nods to each other in the spirit of our characters. It was exhilarating.

As always, the highlight of the evening was Isabel's "Climb Ev'ry Mountain," or as some were starting to call it, "Climb Ev'ry Staircase." Sam Yummy and his minions had constructed an enormous piece of scenery that was going to double as the staircase in the mansion stage right and the one in the convent stage left. Although some said there wasn't supposed to *be* a staircase in the convent, evidently we were having one anyway. How Isabel managed to ascend the thing step after step without falling, I didn't know. But by the time she stood at the top, everyone onstage and off had abandoned their tasks to sneak into the audience and listen to her. We were hypnotized. I did notice Bill Tuxhorn raise his eyebrows as she stepped up and up, no doubt figuring the insurance costs of a tragic accident.

Later on, the principal actors took the stage and ran through some of their scenes. Susie Jenkins and I sat to watch them. Her husband, Charlie, went from okay to pretty terrible. Well, actually, he went from pretty terrible to pretty goddamn terrible.

"Charlie, can you stop rubbing your head when you speak?" Barton said.

"Oh. Okay," Charlie replied, and rubbed his head. He constantly turned to find where Susie was in the audience. I wondered whether he was still walking across rooms to see if his wife noticed him. Susie herself was having a blast. She came to every outing and stayed late. I wondered if she fancied Barton too, but then I remembered how she came alive with some of the younger janitors. Things seemed complicated.

Tall Maria was a little soft-spoken, as they say, which really means you couldn't hear her at all. She was pretty, though, and sang well unless it was a high note. At least when she stood next to Charlie, neither of them seemed so gigantic. It must have been god-awful hard to feign flirtation with such a stiff as Charlie. I watched them do a scene where Maria was supposed to be shyly hanging back, blushing and stealing looks at the Captain. She might as well have been blushing and stealing looks at a vacuum cleaner. It was painful.

Stephanie was excellent. Very funny, tossing her head with just the right timing; any scene she was in seemed good. Max, played by the overweight guy, was hilarious, though Barton wouldn't let him make faces. "Don't play it funny!" he would yell. As far as I was concerned, Stephanie and Max drove the show. I watched Barton place them all here and there on the stage.

"No, cross this way. Then look back at her just before she looks up."

"Like this?"

"Almost. Now look out here for a second. Yes, that's it."

Whenever Barton got in the middle of things, the scene would get better, sometimes a lot better. I could see what a good director he was.

There was never any real doubt about going to Shipley's. It became our home away from home on Friday nights and, as the summer went by, on other nights as well. Charlie came that night, and Susie stayed away from other guys, I noticed. Stephanie had the nerve to actually push me aside so she could sit next to Barton. I fixed her wagon, though, by playing footsie under the table with him from across the way. He kept rearranging my silverware so that I couldn't find what I needed, and that being Barton's way of showing interest, I was sure it annoyed Stephanie. She still didn't speak to me. Meg huddled with Isabel and Velma, consuming mass quantities of fried food, and I wondered where Gary was.

A Female Deer

"Nah, I'm not much of a hunter," Barton said to me as we sipped drinks on the minuscule patio. "How could you kill Bambi?"

"I totally agree," I said in reply. We seemed to have all the same views, Barton and I. Life was good. "Should we get going?" We had agreed on dinner at a new restaurant at the Worcester Mall, and I felt pretty hungry. I planned to scope the place out as a private citizen before accosting them during the week for coupons. Sometimes that was a good strategy.

"It's so comfortable here," Barton said.

"Yes, thank you, it is."

"I've got an idea."

"Yeah?"

"Why don't we just eat out of the refrigerator? That way we could stay here and enjoy the sunset."

"We could do that, I guess. I have some leftover chicken."

"I make a really mean chicken stir-fry. Do you have any vegetables?"

"Um, maybe, if they're not slimed."

"Is your grandfather over there? We could ask him."

"Yeah, I think the Beehive is over there with him." I explained this terminology to Barton, and that led to a phone call, and that led to Gramp and Beehive walking over and joining us. Barton and Beehive chopped and diced in the kitchen while Gramp and I discussed the progress of the tomato plants outside.

"They take time, you have to be patient," Gramp said.

"I know."

"I thought you said he was taking you to the new restaurant."

"We were, but it seemed more fun to just stay here."

"Oh."

"We'll go next time."

"Mmm."

"Barton's very nice, Gramp. See those flowers? He brought them to me tonight."

"Oh yes, oh yes."

An uncomfortable silence fell over us as I sipped chardonnay and Gramp chugged prune juice. We both jumped up at a woman's scream.

"Where was that?" I asked.

"Inside," he answered, and we both ran for the door. Beehive nearly stabbed me with a knife on her way out.

"A horrible giant rat is in there!" she yelled.

"Oh, good," I said.

"Bob, I can't stay here. I'm sorry," Beehive said to my grandfather. "Good? She said good?"

"I think you found my guinea pig."

Barton and I ended up eating alone at the kitchen table. The meal was quite tasty, and when we ran out of wine, Barton went out to his car and produced another bottle. It takes a certain kind of man to carry wine in his car. Later he told me more stories about his mother, and we discussed the show. Then he found my dating questionnaire.

"You were reading it when the cop came in, remember?" I asked.

"So I was. Let's fill it out," he said. "The first fifty applicants don't have to pay."

"Come on, cut it out."

"I'm putting tens on all of these."

"Barton. Stop."

"But you are very beautiful. I don't want you to mail it, though." The atmosphere started to heat up. We eventually settled in on the couch in front of the television, and I admit I was in the mood.

"What roles have you played?" I asked.

"You mean on the stage?"

"Someone said you played Curly in *Oklahoma!*"

"Jeanie, can I tell you something?" He dimmed the light.

"Okay." I settled onto the couch with just the tip of my shoulder touching his forearm.

"Every actor in America has played Curly in *Oklahoma!*"

I giggled. "So what else?"

Barton sighed. "All the usuals. Kings. Heroes. You name it, I've played it. It's meaningless. I have an audition in August, though, that might not be meaningless."

"Really. What is it?"

"It's bad luck to say."

"Well, I'm glad, though." Barton dug his elbow into my arm, and that made me sit up and face him. I poked him and he poked me and pretty soon we were wrestling. Apparently it's only a short move from a half nelson to a kiss. His was bristly, which surprised me since you would think a beard would be smooth.

"Jeanie?"

"Yes?"

"Can I ask you to do something?"

"Barton, you don't want me to read again, do you?"

"Does that bother you?"

"Well, no, but . . ."

Barton jumped up off the couch and said, "Don't make editorial judgments, okay? Do you mind if I play something on the CD player?"

"No, I don't mind." I sat back and wondered if this was what went on in Hollywood. Did movie stars have oddities like this? When you saw pictures of Brad Pitt on the magazine stands, were they leaving this out? I could hear Barton rustling around with bags and sacks and my all-purpose music player. Soon a loud, staticky sound filled the room, followed by a low voice, disturbing though polite, something like Vincent Price.

"The chrysanthemum shimmied down to the aura of a petunia," the voice said. I recognized it as Barton's voice just as he joined me on the couch. We continued kissing, though I couldn't help hearing the voice drone on about flowers and human fluids.

"Capturing the pollen with the bloody spleen of my love," the voice said. Barton grabbed me tightly on that part.

I sat up. "Barton?"

"You think I'm weird, don't you?"

"No. Well . . ."

I guess I shouldn't have said that, but what could I have said? Yes? Barton stood, grabbed the CD out of the player, his keys from the top of Mr. Piggy's cage, and left. He sent flowers again the next day. I was running out of vases.

How Do You Solve a Problem?

Monday, June 29

"In twenty-five words or less, how will our customers benefit from a rate hike?" Dan asked. Danno appeared far more at ease at our small team meeting than at the big hotel one. He even picked up his watch from the table and adjusted the time, a move of confidence.

Connie Shonsky wasn't buying. "Wait a minute, Dan; you said last week it would be twenty-five words or less on why LotsaCoups was better than our competition."

"Everyone should be able to think on their feet, Connie," Dan replied, though he put the watch down.

"But that's not what you told us," she persisted. The rest of the group stared into the middle foreground, and I for one tried to listen for Magda out at the receptionist's desk. Too bad I hadn't gotten into the pool, because there she'd been, big as life, when we walked in. She'd already told at least one caller to "fark" himself.

"Why don't we do both?" Abe piped up. "Why the rate hike is good and why we're better than the competition."

Spanky in the *Our Gang* movies couldn't have looked more innocent or energetic than Abe as he smiled back and forth from Dan to Connie, from good to evil. I couldn't speak for everyone's feelings toward Abe, of course, but a hard knee to the groin would not have met with objection from me. Connie was scheduled to ride with Abe that day, and she looked particularly grim.

"I can go first," Henrietta said. Her fat feet were wedged into the tiniest, pointiest pair of shoes I had ever seen. Glinda the Good Witch sells coupons.

It was all in all an average Monday, though with the Fourth of July holiday coming up, there was a bit of zest in the air, at least for me. My good performance on Friday had been announced and commented upon and drooled over.

"Nice going," Garrett Shonsky said.

"Yes," added Connie. "You're ahead of me."

"Were any of those your relatives?" Henrietta asked. She was still in first place.

We got through the twenty-five-word drill in about twenty-five minutes. You'd think salespeople could whip out something dumb like that with no problem. But everyone got all tongue-tied and embarrassed, proving my theory once again that sales is solitary, meant for just you and the customer, not observers. One of our nicest reps, Florence Keating, actually hyperventilated whenever we had to do one of these foolish recitations. Florence was a former schoolteacher, and in the end Dan gave her a Snickers bar for her answer. "LotsaCoups is the best in the business, and you should never be afraid to buy the best." Henrietta grumbled that another company had used this same pitch on TV for something, but Florence got the prize anyway.

Magda handed me two leads when I walked out of the conference room. I was happy to see that one was an optical shop, a category I hadn't had much luck with, and the other was a chiropractor, also a good possibility. Dan motioned me back into the conference room.

"Can I talk to you?"

"Sure." I would say no to this?

"I have a new rep coming on board today. I want you to train her."

I sighed. This was always the way they got training for free from the experienced reps. "Well, okay. What about the trainer from the plant?"

"He's busy. I'm going to pay you for it."

"Oh."

"A percentage of any sales she makes."

"Oh?" This seemed dubious. The last person I trained made no sales, called me night and day on my cell phone, then borrowed my sales notebook and never returned it.

"She'll be here any minute. You know, Jeanie, if we need another sales manager, that could be you someday. I'm not sure how Abe is going to work out, so try to do a good job with this gal."

"Of course I'll try to do a good job, Dan."

"Yes, I know."

We both walked back out to the front desk and listened to Magda tell people it was a "vunderful" day. This seemed to go against the grain for Magda, and I noticed she told a few people to "get to point, mister," probably just to make herself feel better. Our wait wasn't long, and I managed not to faint when I saw the new sales rep walk through the door. It was Stephanie, the Baroness.

"Hi, you've reached the voice mail of Jeanie Callahan of Lotsa-Coups. Never be afraid to buy the best. The best sub sandwich, the best piano tuner, or the best direct-mail coupon. Leave a message and I'll call you back promptly. Or whenever I feel like it." BEEP.

"Hi, um, I'm almost ready to talk to you about my revolutionary idea. I like the way you talk. Believe me, no one has ever had this idea for a business. I'll be in touch soon." BEEP.

"Hey, it's Meg. Where have you been lately? Were you with Barton Saturday night? Gary's mad at me now, and I don't care. He found the stupid picture and put it back on the wall again, even though it has ketchup on it. I'm surrounded by wimples." BEEP.

"Jeanie, this is Marianne Peters. I've sprained my ankle and wonder if you would mind coming to my house for rehearsal tonight. 444 Dodge Street. Thanks." BEEP.

"Hi, Jeanie, Henrietta here. I'm still working on *Dog Daze.* Just wanted you to know. I'm not relinquishing control of that. Also, ColdCuts, the beauty salon, should be mine. You haven't replied to my message on that yet." BEEP.

"Jeanie! My God! How are you? I love your dress!"

Danno beamed at what looked like instant rapport between Stephanie and me, but what was really closer to instant distrust. Of course, I smiled and fawned, that being called for. I did not call her a hypocritical piece of shit, nor did I refuse to work with her, not when my future depended on her performance. Dan flitted around like a maître d' at a restaurant, giving Stephanie forms to fill out, etc. Stephanie was put in the conference room to watch a corporate video, and that gave me a little time to make phone calls, or at least that was what I thought.

"Do I really have to watch this?" she asked from over my shoulder. I jumped.

"Hang on," I said into the phone. "Not as far as I'm concerned," I said to her. Many of the reps were still loitering from the sales meeting and surveilling Stephanie from behind file cabinets. She had the look of someone who would be very successful and have more accounts than you did, with just that perfect aura of phoniness that management loved. I still thought she'd had a nose job.

Stephanie was my new best friend. From the office elevator to the parking lot, she complimented me on my dress, my hair, my makeup, and my shoes. I tried to help her get in the passenger seat of my car. I could already tell this was going to be a long day.

"Oh, what a cute arrangement in your front seat," Stephanie gushed.

"Sorry. Let me just toss this stuff."

"No, really, it looks so . . . so active. Like you must sell a lot."

"Oh it's active, all right."

"What is that? It's not wet, is it?"

"It was beef teriyaki on Friday. Abe spilled it."

"Oh, Abe the sales manager? He's such a cutie."

"Oh yeah, isn't he just?"

Soon we were on the highway. Stephanie balanced on a stack of napkins, and I tried to ignore my car's upper respiratory ailment. Stephanie rhapsodized about different businesses along the way.

"Oh, Burger King! Do you have them?"

"Well, no, actually I don't."

"Oh, Serendipity Boutique. You must have them!"

"No, I wish I did."

"Oh! Send 'n' Paste Package Service! I love them!"

"Mmmm, yes, I've never had them either."

"I'm sure I can get them."

"Yes, but I have to tell you—and I mean it in a nice way, where some people wouldn't—this is not your territory."

"Well, where is my territory?"

"Dan will give you one after you're trained."

"I need to have Worcester and the area close to where I live."

"Actually, that's my territory, Stephanie."

"It makes sense for me to have Worcester."

"It makes sense for me too."

"Well, I should still have it. Maybe you'll leave and I'll get it."

"Shall we try a cold call? Do you want to do it yourself?"

"Yes, definitely. I'm sure I can do this. It can't be any different from acting."

We parked outside a small wallpaper shop and gathered our sales materials for the call. I knew the owner, a very pleasant woman with almost no money. We walked in, and Stephanie immediately hid behind me. I turned halfway around and waited for her to say something, but she turned her back and pretended to stare out at the car.

"Hi, Jeanie, how are you?" the owner said.

"Fine, Nancy. How have things been here?"

The owner launched into laborious detail about her ovarian cyst. Stephanie eventually retreated from the window and traded gynecological horror stories with Nancy while I switched places and stared out the window. We were there at least half an hour and never once talked about coupons.

When we finally made our exit, I said, "Let's go in here." It was a craft shop, probably a chain with headquarters far away, but it was worth a shot. Once again, Stephanie disappeared behind me when it was time to talk. The decision maker wasn't there anyway, so we walked out and crossed the street to a shoe repair shop. Same thing. Stephanie seemed to have stage fright.

I dropped off a color brochure at the home office of a small grocery store chain, where Stephanie and I sat in the cramped waiting room to see the advertising manager. Many salesmen of unknown products sat around us. They were all ogling Stephanie's short skirt, and finally one spoke to her.

"Are you frozen or nonfrozen?"

"I don't think that's any of your business," Stephanie said.

"We're nonfrozen," I said, and then chatted with the guy about low-carb ice cream, he being of the "frozen" persuasion. We saw the manager for thirty seconds and then left.

"These places are too small," Stephanie said. "Shouldn't we be trying for some big fish?"

"Okay, big fish, here we come," I said. We drove to the mall and hit one big store after another. All chains, which I knew they would be. I just wanted to give her the practice. Stephanie never said a word to anyone, and I offered the experience up for my immortal soul. Eventually, we ended up at the chiropractor's, the one who had called in. I couldn't resist going for new customer number ten, and maybe showing off a little for the rookie. Dr. Leviathan took the time to see us and loaded us down with brochures and pamphlets about his services. Things were going along very well, and I was just starting to close when Stephanie found her voice.

"I've never gone to a chiropractor," Stephanie said. "I always thought they were quacks."

I don't really remember what I said after that, but we were out on the sidewalk inside of five minutes. The drive back to the office was quiet.

Dan greeted us like a father. "So how did you girls do?"

"Great," Stephanie said. "I really got my feet on the ground. I got appointments with five different businesses, and I think they're all going to buy." Stephanie was using the time-honored technique of lying to the boss. I knew it well, but wasn't a proponent of it, not generally. All I could do was purse my lips. I'm a good lip-purser when I have to be, and it was either that or a primal scream in the middle of our suburban building. I walked out without saying good-bye.

Mr. Piggy was good therapy for me that afternoon. I held him in my arms and stroked his soft, furry head. I thought of Stephanie's soft, peroxided head and pictured it crushed. At first I thought I would match my breathing to Mr. Piggy's, but then realized he was respiring at a far more accelerated rate and I would probably be passed out on the

floor if I attempted it for long. Also giving a soothing influence were the two glasses of chardonnay I downed in
quick succession. At least Stephanie wouldn't be at Marianne's tonight, only the kids and the nuns. How could I
stand seeing Stephanie during the day and then again at
night?

I was bound to get one more new customer, and that at
least meant a thousand bucks. The thought of it calmed
me again. Then I looked out the window and saw Mrs.
Mayer mowing her lawn in a clown suit. What? I took another look and not only were my eyes correct, but there
was my grandfather weeding her garden, the garden of the
woman who smashed his car and could have killed him.
When he stood up, I doubted my eyes once again. He, the
man who wouldn't attend a Halloween party because he
didn't like costumes, was also dressed like a clown. This
undid some of the guinea pig/chardonnay tranquillity. I
was still very angry at Mrs. Mayer, and I was not going to
resume friendly relations with her, no matter what Gramp
was tricked into doing. God, what would be next—
mohawk haircuts while they limed their lawns? I decided
to take a nap.

I found Marianne's house easily because of all the other
cars parked nearby. The von Trapp kids were running up
and down the driveway, which helped too. One or two
wore Nazi armbands, and I wondered whether Velma
ought to be handing those out from the doorstep.

"I'm so sorry I'm late. I fell asleep," I said to no one as I
walked in the front door. The place seemed pretty quiet,
though I could hear the faint sound of a piano from somewhere in the back. The living room looked like a hospital
ward. An old, shriveled version of Marianne, was propped
in the bed, swallowing pills with a shaky hand.

"Marianne's in the back," the person said.

"Oh. Hi there. You must be . . ."

"I'm Marianne's mother. If she'd made a success of her life, she wouldn't have to live with me now."

"Oh, you don't mean that," I said. Not to be heartless, but this had the sound of a long-winded saga to it and frankly, I got enough of that at work. It seemed like Marianne might have a tougher life than I'd imagined. I walked down the dark hallway and found the piano room. Marianne was working with Jennifer, and naturally Jennifer's mother was wedged in between the two of them. I wondered how Marianne could stand it. Barton usually walked away when any of the mothers got too close. Marianne looked up when I stepped in, and I repeated my apology. I noticed that the little sausage around her hair helmet was a bit bedraggled. Even more noticeable was the cast encasing her foot.

"That's okay," she said. "I haven't gotten to the nuns yet."

Her mother's frail voice found its way down the hall and into our space. "Marianne! I need my *TV Guide*." Marianne stood with difficulty and started to make her way out from behind the piano.

"I'll do it," I said. "Don't get up."

"Thank you, Jeanie," Marianne said. "I appreciate that."

I returned to the living room and found the *TV Guide*— easily within the old woman's reach. "Here you go."

"Did Marianne make you do that?" she asked.

"I offered to do it. With her on crutches and everything."

"Well, if she'd be more careful, she wouldn't be wearing the cast."

"Oh. Well, still it must be tough."

"She tripped over my oxygen tank. I could have been dead in two minutes. Can you imagine anything so dumb?"

I took a deep breath. "Can I get you anything else, ma'am?" Like a serious attitude adjustment.

"No. Tell Marianne those Muslins are looking in the window again."

"Pardon me?"

"Just tell her. And I'll need my lotion at eight o'clock."

I turned my back on the old crone, walked down the hall, and relayed the message to her daughter, who took a deep breath. Seemed as though Mrs. Peters required a lot of deep breathing.

"She thinks the Indian family across the street looks in the window," Marianne said.

"Muslins?" I queried.

"She gets things wrong." Marianne pursed her lips even more than usual.

"Just let me know what she needs. I'll get it," I offered.

"That's okay," Marianne said. "It looks like I'm going to be a bit longer with the kids. Why don't you make yourself at home in the kitchen—there's lemonade there—or outside."

"Thanks," I said, and wandered away. I never got to the kitchen, because as I passed a darkened room, a computer screen flickered and made me remember the hated memo that was due from me to Dan by the end of the day. I was greatly tempted to duck in and take care of it. I also wanted to see if Dr. Leviathan had answered my desperate e-mail. Surely Marianne wouldn't mind. I sat down on the chair in front of the screen and adjusted the plastic seat cushion. The Internet access wasn't password protected, but that didn't surprise me too much. I was sure Mean Mom out in the front room couldn't possibly work a computer.

Before I got through to my own e-mail server, an instant message flashed on the screen. Now I felt guilty. I didn't dare answer it.

HEY, MARIANNE. YOU STILL GOING TO CONDUCT NUDE OPENING NIGHT?

I tried to ignore the message, but the sender, sandman, wouldn't stop.

YOU'D BE RIDING THE LIGHTNING, BABE. THAT WOULD SHOW EVERYBODY.

I'D REALLY LIKE TO SEE THAT.

I hoped sandman wasn't one of the nuns, who were

mostly in the kitchen and presumably not spiking the lemonade. The joker kept it up.

I CAN'T TALK LONG. AREN'T YOU GOING TO SAY ANYTHING? I restrained myself from writing back.

ISABEL IS A HORE.

My mouth fell open.

ISABEL IS THE BIGGEST HORE IN TOWN. HA, HA. GET IT?

Now I replied. ISABEL IS NOT A WHORE. I figured I might as well correct the spelling while I was at it.

TRUST ME, SHE IS.

At this point, I signed off and hightailed it to the kitchen. Screw the memo. One of the high school girls was there with a laptop computer.

"What do you think you're doing?" I demanded.

"I'm playing solitaire."

"Where did you get that?"

"It was just sitting here. What's the matter with you?"

"Nothing." I looked outside into the small backyard and saw several other nuns in regular street wear, including Helen, holding her crucifix in her lap. Perspiration beaded on my forehead as I wondered who had called Isabel a whore. And whoever it was had suggested that Marianne conduct nude on opening night. What a ridiculous notion. Marianne surely knew that. Didn't she? My brain short-circuited and stopped working.

Shortly afterward, we were all summoned to the small piano room. Our songs were clearly sung, precisely pronounced, and chorally correct. Marianne nodded all the way through.

"You're getting there," she said. Just as we all basked in this high praise, my cell went off and caused Marianne to glare. I prayed it would be the chiropractor, but I didn't dare look.

One of the girls spoke to Helen on our way out through the living room.

"Are you going to carry that huge crucifix in the show, Helen?"

Helen stopped and stood over the hospital bed to hold the cross above Mrs. Peters.

"I'm always going to carry it. It's blessed by the pope."

"Get it away from me," Mrs. Peters said. "I'm Methodist."

"It can help you, dear."

"Get it away from me, or I'll call the police."

This sent us all out the door. We said our various good-byes, and I yanked my cell out to see who had called. It was Meg. She must have called from the regular acting rehearsal at the high school.

"Hey."

"How are you? Are you at Marianne's?"

"Yes, just released. How's it going there?"

"Fine. It's great without the kids."

"What's with the baby making?"

"I'm still sick of sex. Turns out Gary isn't, though, and he's pissed at me. I told him he could wait till after the show."

"Is Isabel there?"

"Yes, and with a big bruise on her leg, which she thinks I didn't see because she's wearing a long dress."

"This is all getting a little odd, isn't it?"

"Do you think we should say anything?"

"Who would we say it to? Let me ask you this: To your knowledge, how many people could have been on computers an hour ago?"

"What people? People in the world?"

"People in the show. At your rehearsal."

"An hour ago? Any of them. Barton had to be late, so we all just got here."

"Rats."

"Gotta run. Call me tomorrow."

To: Dan Albright
Fr: Jeanie Callahan
Re: Getting Close to the Business
I haven't made a single sale. I'm angry about
Abe being promoted and Stephanie being my
new partner. I'm angry at my neighbors and at
my grandfather. The only person I like is my
guinea pig, who I know is not technically a person. That's how close I am to the business.

A bit negative, perhaps? Besides, who needs the truth.
Time for the Pollyanna version.

To: Dan Albright
Fr: Jeanie Callahan
Re: Getting Close to the Business
I've met with five business owners who are in
the show and I think they are all going to buy.
We talk about nothing but coupons. SEND.

Many a Thing You Know You'd Like to Tell Her

Tuesday, June 30

I was getting used to Stephanie, whose behavior started to follow a certain pattern. First she was all smiles, gushing and drooling. Then she would use me shamelessly, then ignore me. All in all, I preferred the ignoring part. I made sure that I wouldn't have her with me the next day, when I fervently hoped to sign the pizza guys.

Just for fun, I took her into Benito's Fine Menswear.

"Hi, everybody," I said to the assembled reptiles. No one moved. "This is my colleague Stephanie Wilson." Being in the using-shamelessly segment, Stephanie was in her regular place, hidden behind me. "Stephanie is just starting with LotsaCoups, and I wanted to make sure she had a chance to meet you guys."

Complete silence followed. The head reptile nodded his head. "How much does it cost?"

"What?"

"The coupons. How much do they cost?"

"Oh, well, it depends." I was flummoxed.

"Why don't you come back later in the week? We might take a look."

"Oh. Okay. Well, bye. Have a good day."

"Bring your friend."

Stephanie was thrilled beyond her wildest dreams. We sat in the car, and I could barely put my key in the ignition.

"My first sale!" she exclaimed.

"Well, we haven't made a sale yet," I cautioned. I didn't have the heart to tell her it would be my sale, not hers. Although from the sound of it, maybe I should give it to her, if the guy liked her so much and all. Frankly, I didn't relish the prospect of servicing Benito's.

"So do you think you'll be okay on your own tomorrow?" I asked.

"Oh, definitely. Especially now that I've made a sale."

"Remember, you're working in Northboro, not here in Worcester."

"I know, I know. I can't wait."

"Well, okay. Go for it, girl."

"Battle of Waterloo, Gramp?"

"Eighteen fifteen. Did you bloralnsitandue?"

Every time Gramp headed back up the stairs, his remarks became indecipherable. Comfortably ensconced in his recliner, I didn't bother yelling out the next question. I happened to know it myself, and so did he, and so did everyone else within a hundred miles: years between the last two Red Sox World Series wins—eighty-six. That, in my opinion, was very cruel and unfair of *Jeopardy!* to include. I could've sworn I even heard a few boos from the studio audience. Red Sox Nation was everywhere.

"I said, did you blow out the candle?" Gramp asked clearly before pivoting around again.

"Yes. It's out." Someone, no doubt a woman, had given

Gramp a clever but tacky Cape Cod tourist gift that included a candle, and I had lit it upon my arrival. It shone inside a tiny lighthouse. Gramp was always very conscious about fire hazards and to my knowledge never used candles unless we had a power failure. The candle giver probably didn't know that, and that told me it was probably someone new.

The doorbell rang with excellent timing, just as I heard Gramp hit the bottom step. He answered the door and spoke to someone.

"Robert Callahan?" the voice said.

"That's me."

"Sign here, please." My curiosity was piqued, but I didn't want to show interest. Gramp walked into the family room and plopped down on the couch next to me. He held something in his hand.

"I hope you're feeling all right," I said.

"Never better," he replied.

"So, Gramp. I noticed the clown outfit yesterday."

"Oh yeah?"

"Probably everybody who drove by noticed it. Did you get a few waves?"

"Sure did." Gramp flexed his shoulders and smiled.

I remained silent.

"I was helping out Gert."

"By dressing like Bozo?"

"Yes, as a matter of fact. She's chairman of the children's-wing auxiliary at the hospital, and we were just on our way there. I said I might do Santa Claus at Christmas too. What the heck."

I sniffed. "Any mail for me?"

"Not today."

Because we had the same last name, postal carriers frequently considered one house the same as the other. "Here's some for you," I said.

"Oh, thanks."

"What is that in your hand?" I asked, my curiosity winning out.

"Oh, just something I had to sign for. From some law firm."

Alarmed, I cried, "Some law firm? What's it about?"

"Oh, Gert told me about it. She's suing me for something."

I jumped forward in my seat. "*Suing* you? For *what*?"

"It's just a silly thing with that car accident. It's no problem."

I spent the next forty-five minutes arguing with my grandfather about why a lawsuit was not a silly thing and why Gertrude Mayer should be expelled from our social lives. I even told him about her so-called "experiments" to find a husband.

"That's okay," he said.

"Gramp! This woman is dangerous! You have to get a lawyer now."

"No, I don't. The insurance will pay."

"But it wasn't your fault!" I cried. We went back and forth about the incident until he finally agreed to at least look into things and find out what the heck Mrs. Mayer was doing. I said good night, then walked out his front door and around the block to cool off. I let myself into my own house and looked around for that dating questionnaire again. Where had Barton put it? Why didn't he ever call me?

My Heart Will Be Blessed

Wednesday, July 1

Already in a good mood because I didn't have Stephanie attached to my backside, I felt my heart swell with true love when I entered the pizza storefront at precisely nine A.M. and all the owners were present. Not only present, but seated, paying attention, and each with a little pile of cash in front of him. Some even had notebooks and pens. Ziggy, looking calm and collected, saluted me with an index finger to the eyebrow. He even remembered my name.

"Hey, Jeanie. We're ready to rumble."

"Nice going on that nine-two split the other night," another one yelled.

"Thanks, guys."

Lenny stood up and shook my hand. "All present and accounted for, ma'am."

I felt like Snow White addressing the forest creatures, or Dorothy at a munchkin meeting. "Gosh, thanks." I proceeded to give one of the best presentations of my life to one of the best audiences I had ever seen.

"If a new customer comes in with the coupon, and they like your pizza, do you think that person will become a regular customer?"

"Yeah! They sure will!"

"Even you, Moey. And you're an ugly bastard."

"Har-har."

"And how often does a regular customer come in?"

"Once a week at least!"

"And how much do they spend?"

"Ten bucks or more!"

"So over the course of a year how much are you getting from that customer?"

"Five grand, baby!" yelled Ziggy, who stood and waved his fist in the air. A few of the guys started chanting, "Woo! Woo! Woo! Woo!"

I stopped. "Well, no, not five thousand dollars," I said.

Lenny jumped in. "Five hundred, guys."

"It's five thousand, ain't it?" Ziggy yelled, trying to count on his fingers.

"No, you fuckhead," one of the other ones yelled. "Five grand on pizza?"

"Oh yeah. Okay," Ziggy said, chastened. "Be nice, though, wouldn't it?"

"That's right," I said. "More than five hundred dollars. And all from a modest investment in a coupon."

"Yeah! Wow!"

I was careful to manage their expectations. "Now, gentlemen, that is, of course, a very rosy scenario. It may not always work that way." The truth was that their pizza might be terrible. Or their parking might be terrible. Or really anything might deter customers from coming in. I have seen businesses tank because of grouchy counter help. Coupons can't work miracles.

"I'm sold," Ziggy said. "Sign me up."

"You got it." I started filling out one contract after another, all for different towns yet each one a separate sale for me, while they got up and walked around and chatted. Voices got raised a couple of times, but no fights broke out. Lenny sat next to me and guided the process.

"So are you staying with Bird of Paradise for a name?" I asked.

"No. We've decided on something else," Lenny replied.

I looked him in the eye, a most enjoyable experience on my part.

"These guys are all my clients," he said.

"Oh."

"They all learned to cook in the same place."

"I see."

Lenny paused, and then said, "Walpole State Prison."

"Oh for heaven's sake."

"We want to call it Jailbird Pizza."

I admit my mouth did fall somewhat open, but I smiled big. "I love it, Lenny. It's great." It was either great or terrible; I knew that.

"I'm their probation officer. We did have one more guy with the group—remember Dino?"

"Oh yeah," I said.

"Uh, he won't be able to participate."

"That's fine. I need all the addresses."

One by one the guys came up to my table, gave me their particulars, and paid me in cash. It was heaven. I just had to hope and pray that none of them murdered their mothers before the mailing went out.

With these—count 'em, fifteen!—fifteen new customers, I could almost taste victory in the sales contest. My mind was numb.

"Okay, everybody," I yelled when I was finished. "Our art department will come up with something and I'll bring a proof back for you. A picture of how the ad will look when it is printed. Okay?"

"Yeah! We'll be waiting!"

* * *

I floated through the rest of the sales day, the only bad part being that Dr. Leviathan refused to meet with me again. I did get an appointment with the optometrist, though. If I got that one, it would make a very flashy twenty-five new sales. Ha! I could hardly concentrate on driving. The car's admonitions concerning oil levels and open doors fell on deaf but joyful ears. With the five-grand prize, I could dump this heap and get something decent. Henrietta couldn't possibly beat me now.

I was much less perturbed by the Mrs. Mayer situation when I returned home, so I decided to stroll across the street and ask her a few questions. I knocked on the front door bold as brass, but then noticed her car wasn't in the driveway. Nor did I see it in the garage when I peered in the window. She drove up to her mailbox just as I was heading back across the street.

"Jeanie! How are you?" Once again Mrs. Mayer's hair was a different color, this time a bright red. Somewhere, a stressed-out hairstylist must have been having a shot of whiskey.

"Mrs. Mayer, I'm a little concerned about this lawsuit of yours against my grandfather."

"I'm sorry. Don't worry about that."

"The accident was your fault, Mrs. Mayer, and you know it."

"Oh yes, I know."

"Then why are you suing?"

"I promise I'll talk to you about it next week, dear. Things might get a little more complicated before they straighten out. Just keep your chin up."

My lips were moving but I couldn't quite form words. If chins were the issue, hers needed a good punching, in my opinion. Incredibly, she shifted gears and took off. I stood in her yard like a door-to-door salesman who'd just been smacked in the face.

* * *

Two hours later I sat in the high school auditorium, thoughts far from sales or lawsuits. I watched the choreographer, Tommy Cuthbert, work with Jennifer and the other little von Trapps. The new joke was "shut your von Trapp." The kids thought this was hilarious, and they giggled at everything Tommy said. He could do the splits, he could stretch his face, he could stop in the middle of everything and do a somersault across the stage. A couple of the kids tried somersaulting themselves, and one of them went right into the orchestra pit. He was fine. It would take a lot more than a tumble off the stage to slow down these kids, who, if they'd known, could have had free Ritalin paid for by all of us in the cast.

"Could somebody hold these?" Tommy asked the audience, holding up a stack of poster boards.

"I will," I said.

"Thank you," he said, and then whispered, "And would you mind killing that kid?" He referred to the youngest girl, who looked the least like any of the others, got into the most trouble, and who was hardly ever accompanied by a parent. Tommy handed me the stack, each with a few song lyrics scrawled across it so the kids could do their dance and still see the words in front of them. Cue cards.

Marianne, sausage roll firmer since I'd seen her last, provided piano music, and the number was starting to look really cute. That is, in places it started to look cute, when the youngest girl stopped making faces.

"Honey, that isn't good for your eyes, you know," Tommy said.

"Shut your von Trapp," the kid said in a burst of giggles. Tommy's beautiful complexion turned bright red. At least Jennifer, a brat in her own right, knew when it was time to get to work.

"Come on, everybody," Jennifer said. "Tommy can only be here at certain times. So let's try to buckle down, okay?"

"Shut *your* von Trapp." It was kind of fun to see Jennifer

told off like that, but even so I found myself wishing the children would vaporize.

Holding up cue cards gets boring in a hurry. Just as I was regretting my earlier urge to please, in swept Stephanie, still dressed from a day on the road. She put down her briefcase and other belongings on a seat in the front row. She said nothing to me, of course.

"How'd it go?" I asked as quietly as I could.

"People are stupid," she said. "Where's Barton?" She made one of her noteworthy exits and I put on my professional face as best I could, resisting the tiniest of smirks.

Truman, after being absent for several nights, had finally turned up. Meg told me Truman got caught stealing *Hustler* magazines and various candy items from the convenience store, and justice was being meted out. His father looked like a stern Pilgrim forefather sitting stolidly in the back row. I couldn't believe he was Gary's brother. I was glad he wasn't a business owner in my territory. Jennifer and Truman didn't need cue cards for their number, and that was the best thing you could say about it. I watched Tommy try to get the look of love, or something faintly reminiscent of love, between the two of them, but their youth worked powerfully against this goal. It seemed ludicrous. "I Am Eleven Going on Twelve" would have been a difficult enough challenge, given that Jennifer and Truman hated each other. "I Am an Insufferable Twit, but You're a Real Asshole" would have been more like it.

"Shit," Tommy said, and looked around to me. "I left my other music in one of those classrooms out there. You wouldn't get it for me, would you?"

"Sure," I said. "I'll get it." Anything to vacate the premises. I walked out of the auditorium and into the classroom across the hall, but didn't see any music. I tried two other classrooms but still nothing. I even opened a far door down the hall to a maintenance closet, thinking it might be in there. But what I found wasn't musical.

At first I wasn't sure what I was seeing. Then I realized it was a man and a woman in an embrace—Isabel Cartwright and Sam Yummy in a steamy, ass-grabbing clinch, right between two floor buffers.

"Excuse me," I said, and closed the door as fast as I could. I thought I heard it open behind me as I speed-walked back to the auditorium, but I wasn't sure. As soon as I popped my face back into the rehearsal, Tommy called to me.

"I'm so sorry, Jeanie. Stupid me, the music was right here all the time."

"That's okay." I probably looked like it wasn't okay. Oh, how I wished I hadn't seen that. Stephanie clicked back down the aisle in her high heels, Barton right behind her. Barton hadn't called me all week, and there were no plans for another "reprise" Saturday night. I stood nearby to give him ample opportunity to ask me, but he didn't. Why did he seem so manly and handsome here in the high school auditorium and so wimpy and freaky in my living room?

Barton and Tommy got nearly the whole cast onstage to try a run-through of the ballroom number. There weren't nearly enough men.

"Where's Vic?" Barton yelled. "I thought Vic was going to be in this number."

"He's still in a wheelchair," Isabel said. I wondered whether anyone else noticed her smeared lipstick. "I don't think he can dance."

Even though Bill Tuxhorn had signed up to be a stagehand and not an actor, he was recruited to stand in, as was Sam, who looked different to me now. One of the kids' fathers happened to be in the audience reading a book, and he was hustled up there too, along with the janitor on duty. The only man they didn't ask was Truman's dad. He looked too scary.

"All right," said Barton. "If you haven't got a partner, pretend you do." Most of the nuns, including me, waltzed around in circles, arms up in the air around phantom dance partners. Then the shut-your—von Trapp kids did their good-bye song, and the stage was filled with half-real and half-imaginary bodies. The whole thing was like Dante's *Inferno* and the different levels of hell set to music.

Tommy sat down abruptly on the stage floor. "Let's start with one group at a time," he said. "First the chorus." We nuns stepped forward, eager to play our alternate roles as ball attenders. I imagined myself as a rich, sophisticated, and, of course, quite young widow, neighbor to Captain von Trapp. I, too, was a baroness. I lived down the tree-shaded street from the Captain, but had never been interested in him. Oh, I invited him for coffee occasionally and gave treats to the children, the little scamps, but my career as a concert pianist precluded any real love interest, especially not with a stick like him.

But the women were supposed to be only half of the chorus. For every nun up there, a male dance partner was needed, a daunting situation four and a half weeks before the show. Meg stood in the wings checking things off in a notebook, not unlike Marianne frequently did. There were more notebooks at our rehearsals than men.

For purposes of blocking only, Barton and Tommy and Charlie stood in with the other subs. Tommy called out the instructions and we waltzed. Barton took me as a partner, and his arms felt warm around my waist. He winked at me and I winked back. Then he switched and took another partner. As I danced, I wondered what other secrets existed besides the one I'd found in the janitor's closet. Not that the janitor himself knew or cared—he was having too much fun.

It took most of an hour to get all the nuns to learn the dance. The waltzing was pretty simple, but some, like Helen, couldn't seem to get it. Tommy kept dumbing it down, but finally he suggested that Helen stand on the sidelines.

"Like a wallflower?" Helen said.

"No, not like a wallflower," Tommy replied.

"Because I was never a wallflower."

"More like an interested onlooker."

"I don't want to onlook either."

"Okay, then, why don't we have you and you and you stand over here and pretend to have a conversation with Helen."

"While everybody else dances?" the selected nuns whined. It was very obvious Tommy had gotten rid of the older women and left the young girls on the stage. Tommy looked at Barton in frustration. Barton looked at Isabel, and Isabel looked at Meg.

"Let's draw numbers," Meg said.

This took far longer than it should have, and in the end Helen won the right to stay in the dancing group, so we were more or less back where we started, some dancing and some stumbling.

We got through it, though Tommy's face stayed bright red and Barton looked aneurysm-ready. Every time I passed Barton in the circle, he gave me a thundering, glowering look that made me laugh. But he kept winking. As the group broke up, I lingered a bit, giving him more opportunity to switch from winking to talking, but Stephanie kept his attention the whole time. Silent during the day, wouldn't shut up at night. Soon the big group turned into a little group and we walked outside the high school in a clump. No nuns, no high schoolers. The night was hot and sticky, and someone suggested we go to Shipley's for a quick one. No one said no, not even Meg.

"Might as well. Gary's watching some game anyway, I'm sure," she said. Tommy reminded everybody that he was appearing in *Cabaret* in the next town over the following weekend, and we all said we would try to go.

Our seating pattern at Shipley's was cozy. Stephanie managed to plop herself right between Barton and me, which meant I had to sit half on and half off the vinyl seat. I finally moved across the table and got to watch her monopolize Barton's attention for the whole night. At least Barton looked bored.

Somebody asked somebody else their astrological sign, and that led to close analysis.

"You Virgos are such perfectionists."

"You Libras are always balancing both sides."

Everyone started praising everyone else, and it quickly became a narcissism fest. It was more fun than I could remember having. I didn't feed Mr. Piggy and turn out my light until two A.M., but I still didn't have a date.

I Must Have Done Something Good

Thursday, July 2

"Hi, you've reached the voice mail of Jeanie Callahan, couponmeister—or should I say coupon mistress? Hmmm. Anyway, leave a message and I'll call you back." BEEP.

"Hey, Jeanie. It's Abe. I got some problems and I wonder if you would meet me at Cheng Du. Like today? Like four o'clock? I'll be there." BEEP.

"Jeanie, it's Connie Shonsky. If Abe doesn't resign, I'm going to." BEEP.

"It's your favorite Bob, girl. Uh, about the ten dollars you owe? Want to go double or nothing on the weekend game?" BEEP.

"Hi, it's Meg. Can your boss access these messages? I don't think mine can. I can barely hold my head up after last night. Why did we do it again? And on a weeknight. Isn't Tommy Cuthbert darling? Oh, yeah, can you help me pick up some music stands from Marianne's house tomorrow? Let me know." BEEP.

"Good morning, LotsaCoupers. Jeanie Callahan has overtaken Henrietta for the lead in the contest, and all of you are *going to have to really push to catch up with her. Is this thing on?" BEEP.*

"Hello. I really do like hearing you say 'coupon mistress.' You are going to love my new business idea. But I still can't leave my phone number because I don't like people calling me. I realize now that this is a voice mail and that I will never reach you live. I have not solved this enigma." BEEP.

"Hi, it's Mort. I have a problem with the coupon." BEEP.

By four o'clock I had consumed one vanilla bear claw, two maple-frosted doughnuts, a plain cruller, a large iced coffee, and two small coffees. I had done the *Globe* crossword puzzle and perused all the current Red Sox minutiae. I made one appointment with the optical guy who had called in, and felt confident I could sell him. The next day was a holiday, and I told myself that nobody else was working today either. This made me feel entitled to drive from one Dunkin' Donuts to another for most of the afternoon. Some of their bathrooms were better than others. Finally, it was time for cocktails.

Abe's car was already in the Cheng Du parking lot, and Abe himself looked as though he might have been there for a while.

"Hey, girl, wassup?"

"So drinking is okay now in our sales day? What's up with you?"

Abe sighed heavily. "I can't take it."

"Can't take what?"

"Being sales manager. It sucks. I'm not good at it."

Now I sighed. "What happened with Connie?"

"How do you know about that?"

"Abe. What happened?"

We stopped talking to order drinks and then we both attacked the happy-hour appetizers. After my hard day of pastry eating, I was still able to handle a plate of egg rolls and duck sauce. I felt slightly sick, but stuck by my decision.

"Connie is a fuckin' bitch, you know. She's worse than Henrietta."

"I like Connie."

"Yeah, well, try managing her sometime. I was with her on a call, and all I did was suggest she make use of the LotsaCoups sales materials. She went ballistic on me."

"I don't know, Abe. It must have been something."

"I had to take a cab back to the office."

"Wow."

"Cost me thirty bucks."

"You haven't been out with Stephanie yet. She's a jewel."

"Oh yeah. You can still get Dog Daze, you know. The guy is not cooperating with Henrietta."

"I don't think I'd have the nerve at this point."

"I thought I would like the job," Abe said.

"How did you get it anyway? The job."

Abe smiled and looked at me, clearly deciding whether to tell. "You know my Baldwin Springs account?"

"The golf-player guy? Yeah."

"He called Dan and told him if I didn't get promoted, he'd take his four hundred grand a year elsewhere. I put him up to it."

"Geez. He must really like you."

"He's my brother."

I nearly spit out my Peking ravioli. *"What?"*

"I never told anybody because . . . well, why should I?"

"So why are you telling me now?"

"Because I don't know why. I want you to have the job. As long as you promise not to pester me."

I shook my head. "I doubt you can just hand me the job, Abe."

"I'm going to talk to Dan about it. I'm not taking any more cabs."

Clean and Bright

Friday, July 3

I woke refreshed and spoke cheerily to Mr. Piggy. While not entitled to true Friday zest, since it was already a holiday, I felt pretty good anyway. Connie Shonsky called me midmorning and we chatted for more than an hour. Not only did Abe suggest sales tactics for Connie, who'd been in the business for twenty years, but he had also insulted her house, her car, and her husband. Connie's sense of humor was somewhere between very small and completely absent, so I felt pretty sure Abe had been joshing her. I didn't break Abe's confidentiality. It seemed doubtful to me that he could walk in, quit, and then name his successor, but I admit the possibility was tantalizing. No more cold calls was the siren song. Sales managers hired and fired the people who had to do that. Sales managers usually got involved with clients only when there were problems and then usually gave away the farm. I could do that. As soon as I hung up from Connie, the phone rang again.

"This is Jeanie."

"Hi, Jeanie, this is Muriel."

"Hi. Do I know you?"

"Not yet. I have your name from the dating service. Didn't you get mine?"

"Uh, no. I didn't send in my info yet. I was going to."

"Well, why don't we meet for lunch if you'd like?"

"Are you going to help me in some way? Do you work for the service?"

"I'll help you if I can. Do you know the Cheng Du restaurant?"

"I certainly do."

"Do you want to meet for a quick bite?"

I figured it might take my mind off Barton to consult with someone about how to find the perfect mate, so I agreed.

The meeting lasted as long as it took me to drink a Diet Coke. Muriel, though amazingly masculine, was not my perfect mate, though she thought she might be. I explained to her that there must have been some terrible mistake, and she was very obliging about it. We laughed and then she asked me to come to her house for dinner on Saturday night and go to see fireworks. I declined.

Glowing in the knowledge that I didn't have to work for the rest of the long weekend, I was almost happy to see Mrs. Peters when I arrived at Marianne's house later in the day. Meg and Isabel were sweating as they lugged music stands into Isabel's van. Marianne was off at the ankle doctor's.

"Leave it to Marianne not to be here when people need her," her mother said.

"That's okay, Mrs. Peters, we can handle it. She couldn't really help us anyway, being on crutches," I answered.

"Do you know how she got that sprained ankle?"

"Yes, I think you told me, Mrs. Peters."

"She'd better be back here in time to take me for my mammyogram."

"Oh, I'm sure she will be," I replied.

"She's always late, you know." Every time we dragged materials through the hospital/living room, my thoughts turned to matricide. *Oops, I've inadvertently disconnected your IV drip, Mrs. Peters. Gosh, and now I've turned off the oxygen switch. Oh, and I've accidentally put a pillow on your face and sat on it.*

I received my second holiday invitation of the day from Isabel. "Hey, do you two want to come for a little barbecue tomorrow and then go over and see fireworks at the high school? Bring your husband. Bring a date."

"Sure," I said, wondering whether Barton would be there. "Are you asking the whole cast?"

"Adults only," she said, and stopped in the hallway out of range of Mrs. Peters, who was still alive, as far as I knew. "I know you saw me the other night, Jeanie. I'm really ashamed of myself."

"Hey, Isabel, you have your life to lead. It doesn't bother me."

"It's complicated."

"I don't doubt it."

Meg looked very confused, and Isabel turned to her. "I'm having a little thing with Sam Yummy."

Meg didn't bat an eyelash. "Sam Yummy is cute. I don't blame you." That seemed to take care of that.

I took a chance and asked, "Is your husband not nice to you, Isabel?"

"No, he's very nice," she answered.

My cell phone donged. Please let it be Dr. Leviathan, I prayed.

"This is Jeanie."

"Hi, Jeanie. This is Carol."

"Hi, Carol. Carol from ColdCuts?"

"No, Carol from Only You dating service. I'm thrilled to talk to you."

"Oh dear."

"You sound perfect."

"Carol, I have to tell you something." I proceeded to explain what I thought had happened. Trouble was, I had no idea. Carol didn't want to give up.

"But will you call me back if you change your mind?"

"Carol, if I change my mind, you'll be the first one I call."

"Thank you."

Meg and Isabel unabashedly helped themselves to lemonade in the fridge, which Isabel said Marianne had probably left for us. Meg, being a far nicer person than I, offered some to Mrs. Peters, who accepted it silently. As I walked past the computer room, I looked in and remembered the strange instant message I had seen. I couldn't help myself. I entered the room, touched the keyboard, and saw another long series of instant messages still on the screen, again from sandman.

"Hey you guys, come in here and look at this," I called to my buddies as quietly as I could. They joined me.

"You must be kidding," Meg said. "What does that say? Conducting what?"

SANDMAN: I CAN'T WAIT TO SEE YOU CONDUCTING NUDE.

MARPET: THAT'S NOT GOING TO HAPPEN.

SANDMAN: I HOPE IT DOES. WHAT ARE YOU WEARING RIGHT NOW?

MARPET: A HOSPITAL JOHNNY. WE HAVE TONS OF THEM HERE.

SANDMAN: I FIND THAT VERY SEXY.

MARPET: WHY WON'T YOU TELL ME WHO YOU ARE?

SANDMAN: I WILL.

MARPET: HOW DO YOU SEND E-MAILS TO ME DURING REHEARSAL TIMES? HOW DO YOU DO THAT?

SANDMAN: MAGIC.

MARPET: WHEN WILL YOU TELL ME WHO YOU ARE?

SANDMAN: YOU NEVER KNOW.

We soon helped ourselves to more lemonade and some Brie that was also in the fridge. Then we found the Ritz crackers and peanut butter.

"What are we doing?" Isabel asked.

"We're sneaking snacks," I said. My phone rang again. This time it was Rhonda, who wanted to take me to Maine for the weekend. Then Sally called and offered a time-share on Nantucket, also for the weekend. I appreciated the affluence of the candidates, if not their gender. The phone did not stop ringing. I patiently got rid of all of them.

"I'm going to make more lemonade," Meg said.

"What do you think would happen if we made tuna salad? I'm starving," Isabel added.

My phone rang yet again.

"This is Jeanie and I'm not gay."

"This is Lenny Sadowski, and I'm not either."

"Oh Lenny, hi. Sorry about that. It's kind of a long story."

"Sounds pretty interesting."

"What's up?"

"I'm sorry to tell you that Geronimo, one of our guys, got in a little fracas last night, and he's out of the group. You'll refund him, won't you?"

"Oh. Oh, okay. Well, sure. They're not all going to get in trouble, are they?"

"Jeanie, my girl, that is the question I live with every day."

I chatted with Lenny for a few minutes and he asked what my plans were for the holiday. My handsome-man antennae went up and I toyed with the idea of inviting him to Isabel's with me. But I really didn't know, even after the bowling extravaganza, if he was interested in me or just being nice. I don't like to date clients; it always ends badly and usually with the loss of a good print run. I was pretty sure Barton had mailed in that dating questionnaire. It must have meant that he didn't want men calling me. I supposed that was flattering, even if the result was annoying as all hell.

"Oh, look. Olive loaf," Isabel said.

"And rye bread," Meg added.

"Wait a minute, you guys. Did Marianne say it was okay to make lunch?"

"Marianne won't mind," Meg said. I was about to ask Meg how she knew that, but then my phone rang again. I switched it off. "Tell us your story, Isabel."

Half an hour later we sat at Marianne's tiny dinette table in her tiny kitchen eating sandwiches and chips and enjoying fresh lemonade with just a spritz of vodka, which we found way back in a kitchen cabinet. Assorted clam dips and soft cheeses were on the table as well. Isabel, who had found a lonesome beer in the back of the fridge, was draining that too as she talked.

"I tried to make it in New York. It's vicious there. Everybody smiles to your face and then slashes you behind your back."

"It's like that in coupons, too," I said. Meg gave me a dirty look. "Sorry, just kidding," I added.

"I got one chance to sing in this little showcase musical. Put on in the back of a warehouse, but still, a good opportunity. I was sick one day, one lousy day, and another girl took my spot. The director liked her better because she, I don't know, she looked better."

"That sucks," Meg said. "Could you pass the mustard, please?"

"Then that same director called me for another thing he was doing and it got canceled. I was trying to pay my bills working at Kinko's. You'd think I would have been thinner."

"So how long did you keep going?" I asked just before chomping into my own ham-and-cheese.

"Two years. I maxed out three credit cards and lied to

everybody in my family. That's when I met Ray. He came to New York for a builders' convention, and I waited on him at another place where I worked."

Meg took a drink of her lemonade and asked, "So he must have looked pretty good to you by then."

Isabel nodded. "He thought I was beautiful and glamorous. Problem was, he was married with a kid. You've met Clarissa."

"Oh yeah," Meg said. "We know about the married-with-kid phenomenon."

"Eventually he got divorced and persuaded me to come back here. He made me promise to leave all that behind. That's why he's so against all this community theater stuff."

"We've worried about you and Ray," I said.

"Oh, Ray's okay. He's just not into show business, you might say."

I poured myself another drink and another spritz. "So how angry does he get, Isabel?"

"Not angry. He gives me everything I want. A beautiful house, money for the new business, everything. Honestly, Clarissa is tough sometimes, but Ray's a good guy."

I looked Isabel in the eye, and she looked away. "I don't know. Sam Yummy sees me as a star. Ray more or less sees me as a cook."

Meg and I both nodded. What was there to say to that? Ray was a clear Category C (dork), and Isabel had settled. Many do. I knew Meg was thinking that at least Ray had money. As we contemplated our own lives silently, the sound of garbage cans filled our ears. I thought of Gramp hauling garbage week after week at my house and then realized someone was doing that outside in the backyard. It was Marianne.

"You're good friends with Marianne, right, Isabel?" I asked.

"No," Isabel said. "I barely know her." We all looked at

one another, mouths full, and waited for the entrance of our hostess. I wrapped up the Brie as fast as I could.

Presently, Marianne stood in the doorway on her crutches. Meg wiped a fleck of mustard off her lip.

"What . . . what are you doing?" Marianne asked.

"Oh, Marianne, we're so sorry," I said. "We started with your lemonade and got carried away." I picked up the vodka bottle and replaced it in the cabinet. "We shouldn't have done it."

Marianne stood silently for quite a few seconds and then flinched. "That's okay. That's all right. Everybody takes advantage of me." She collapsed in tears, and we all flew out of our seats. What followed was a collection of heartfelt apologies, heartfelt life stories, and more long-winded sagas than even I was used to. Marianne told us about her awful life with Mrs. Peters and how she had hoped for better. Isabel continued her narrative about Ray and his grouchiness, though she didn't mention Sam Yummy again. She went into great detail about Clarissa and her various outrages, mostly financial. The girl had gotten her father to return the car he'd bought for her and buy her a new one that Clarissa liked better. Isabel shook her head and so did we. Meg lamented her infertile state, and I confessed my relationship with Barton, though not all of it. Everyone acted a little foolish, and, after polishing off the vodka, a little drunk too.

Rehearsal seemed perfunctory that night. Barton sat in the back row and watched, seemingly not even in charge. The actors fumbled their way without him, and finally Stephanie flounced out to the front of the stage.

"Well?" she yelled.

Barton remained silent.

"Are you going to say anything?"

"What do you want me to say?"

"Do you think you could direct us?"

Barton tilted his head. "Oh, are there people up there I can direct? Where are they?"

I tiptoed out of the auditorium and found the music rehearsal in the high school choral room. Meg sat on the piano bench with Marianne and turned pages for her. We were all Marianne's best friends tonight, and Isabel had brought a bag of groceries to slip into Marianne's car.

I whispered to Isabel, "What's with Barton?"

"He does this now and then. It shapes everybody up."

So this was a strategy. I wished I could use it on my clients. "How long will he do it?"

"Just till the end of rehearsal; then he'll soften up."

That was exactly what happened. By the time we left for Shipley's, Barton was joking and laughing, while Stephanie still looked miffed. Marianne said she had to go home, even though we begged her to join us. I wondered if she was headed for her computer.

Bless My Homeland Forever

Saturday, July 4

I woke up to the familiar sound of the lawn mower right outside my bedroom window. The neighbors never complained about Gramp's early-morning grass cutting, probably because most of them wanted to date him. I hadn't seen Beehive for a while and wondered who he'd moved on to now. I decided to be nice and make breakfast for both of us. Gramp was vigorously cheerful after his mow, and brought in my mail, which I'd forgotten about last night. Again, there were several thick letters for him, and all looked to be from legal firms. Hoyt, Miller, Page, and Dombrowski. Cunningham, O'Halloran, Malloy, and Shorenstein. I couldn't read them all.

"What's going on, Gramp?"

"Oh, I don't know. Something with Gert and her friends."

"Please don't tell me that Mrs. Mayer and her friends are *all* suing you. Please don't tell me that."

"Jeanie, do you have any more of that marmalade from your mother? The one they sent from England?"

"Gramp."

"You said not to tell you. It's just something funny Gert's doing."

"Okay," I said, and swallowed my last bite of scrambled eggs. I found the marmalade and shared it with Gramp on our third round of toast. "I guess to you this is funny. To me it's worrisome in the extreme. But okay." I licked my lips and blotted them as part of my resolution not to say anything more.

But it didn't work. "I just hope you're prepared to lose your house and everything you have, that's all."

"Do you want to go with me to Home Depot?"

"No, thanks."

I spent the early afternoon preparing the Dallas Monster, a nine-layer Mexican dip guaranteed to satisfy. Mr. Piggy seemed to enjoy a few of the hamburger bits that sprayed out from the frying pan. At least, he enjoyed them before impolitely puking them back up. I really needed to read up on guinea pig care.

I knew I had layouts to do for all the new clients I had signed up, but the day was so nice, who could blame me for ignoring them? Why anyone would leave New England in July is beyond me. It felt good to know that the next few weeks would be idyllic, at least in terms of weather, and maybe in terms of romance as well. I threw out some of the first batches of flowers Barton had sent me, since they seemed to be wilting rapidly. A couple of the very large arrangements had hulking gladiola that looked especially brown.

The Dallas Monster is labor-intensive and kitchen-destroying. I turned my cell phone off to give the task my full attention, though not before fielding several more high-income female dating candidates. I saw Gramp out the window, setting up his own barbecue control center. I felt briefly curious about his guest list, but turned that thought off. Let him hobnob wherever he might. He was wearing a seersucker suit he must have retrieved from the attic, and looked gallant in an old-fashioned way. Mark Twain meets Colonel Sanders. I thought of all the jailbirds and hoped they were having a peaceable and nonfelonious holiday.

That made me think of all the cash I had collected, and anxiety fluttered in my stomach. The office wouldn't accept cash, primarily because it was too risky. No paper trail. So they passed that risk off onto the reps' shoulders. Many was the pizza place or Chinese restaurant that doled out twenty after twenty to you in a stack, and then you had to stand in line at the convenience store to get a money order while everyone thought you were a drug dealer. But while you carried the cash, the responsibility was totally yours. If my hands hadn't been so greasy, I would have rushed out to my car to lay eyes on it. But I was sure I knew just where it was.

"Freak show!" yelled a young boy as he jackknifed into the pool in front of some other middle school boys. Meg and I have discussed many times the higher confidence level of men in general. A woman looks in the mirror and finds fault, usually lots of it. There are zits to be squeezed, eyebrows to be plucked, and improvements to be made. A man looks into the mirror and sees nothing much amiss. "I'm okay."

There was plenty of evidence of this disparity around the Cartwright swimming pool. Susie Jenkins, who was very attractive and slender, sat covered up in a beach blanket, while Charlie, her husband, perched on the edge of the deep end with his gut hanging out and gray chest hairs bristling. Meg, who looked utterly fantastic in a bikini, wore a cover-up and her hair hidden in a baseball cap, while Gary, dragged along against his will, sunned himself practically naked on a chaise longue. It looked to me like they were still fighting.

"Queers and faggots!" yelled another boy as he made his own clunky and no doubt painful splash from the diving board. My sinking stomach told me they were referring to Tommy Cuthbert, resplendent in his young blondness, but in one of those unfortunate tiny Speedo suits. Isabel wore a long muumuu, and Laura Wheeler was in shorts and a blouse. Marianne sat in the shade wearing an enormous hat with a sunflower on the side. Barton reclined in a wicker chair, smoking a cigar in knee-length Hawaiian shorts and a nonmatching Hawaiian shirt. The only other man not showing his chest was Sam Yummy, who wore a golf shirt and a hat with a tiny fan on the front of it. Clarissa lay on her stomach with the top of her bathing suit untied, no doubt enticing all the men, while she paid no attention whatsoever to the group of youngsters for whom she was supposed to be babysitting.

"Faggots and queers!" another one of them yelled as he dove. I saw Isabel lean over and speak quietly to Clarissa, who turned her head to the other side and did nothing.

The oldest of the boys, probably eleven, went running off the diving board with the cry "Fudge packer!" and that got Barton up out of his chair.

"Hey, buddy, nice dive," he said to the boy when his head appeared.

"Thanks," the boy said, and climbed up the ladder and out onto the deck, dripping water.

"Why don't you cool it with the insults," Barton said. Barton was a big guy, and I watched the kid consider this fact. One of his other friends ran off the diving board and yelled "Don't drop the soap!"

Isabel, who had disappeared into the house, came back out with Ray behind her. Ray evidently didn't care to join us, but he did solve the immediate problem.

"Get up, Clarissa! Get these brats out of here, do you hear me? Take them to their own house!" he yelled to his daughter, and she sullenly raised herself up, tied her bathing suit behind her neck, and hustled the kids out, but not before three or four or five trips into the house while the boys howled and laughed at their own private jokes. Finally we were left to ourselves, and everyone looked relieved.

The Dallas Monster was a big hit. It always is. Barton didn't really pay attention to me until Stephanie got there with her boyfriend. The boyfriend almost immediately found Tommy Cuthbert and the two of them giggled and splashed each other, leaving Stephanie free to kick into her never-shut-up mode, though not to me, of course. She wore a black sundress with deep décolletage.

"You look like Eva Perón today, Stephanie," Isabel said.

"Oh, I *must* play that role before I'm too old," she said in reply. Personally, I thought that time might have already come.

Isabel's house sat first and primary above the upscale development close to the high school, and so we walked to the fireworks laden with beach towels, knitted afghans, and even a tarp that Sam Yummy had in his truck. Stephanie had left after the barbecue, irritated with the boyfriend and bitten by mosquitoes. Liquor, of course, was not allowed on the high school grounds, so that meant we had to pour ours into plastic soda containers. Barton and I shared a big one. Barton left his cigars behind, and he and I sat together on a blanket like king and queen. A band played.

"Is that your grandfather?" he asked, leaning over and pressing on my lower quarters to reach the 7UP bottle.

"Yes, that's Gramp. How many women does he have with him?"

"I would say four. No, five." Barton examined them from

under hooded eyes. "Imagine if they played Spin the Bottle to see which one would get him."

I waved to Gramp, and Mrs. Mayer waved back, the sly litigant. I hated her.

"Or maybe they could cut cards for him," Barton continued. "It would be fun to set things in motion, wouldn't it?"

"No," I said. "There's already enough motion. And by the way, Barton, you mailed that questionnaire, didn't you?"

"Huh?" he said.

"I know you did," I insisted. He raised his eyebrows and crossed his eyes.

"You're so suspicious, Jeanie Beanie," he said as he pushed my elbow out from under me, causing me to fall backward onto the blanket.

"What's your grandfather's sign?" Tommy asked, and that started us into another discussion of personalities and traits.

"Barton's a Taurus, you know," Isabel piped up. "That's why he's oversexed." She leaned back against a large red-and-white cooler. If Cleopatra had ever put on a few pounds and chosen to attend the Worcester civic fireworks, she would have looked just like Isabel. Sam lay at her feet.

"Oversexed? Oh yeah?" Barton cried, and jumped up away from me. He lowered himself onto Isabel and, arms propped either side of her on the plastic tarp underneath, looked as though he were actually having sex with Isabel on the EHS football field. We all gasped. Sam had to move.

"Cut it out, Barton," Isabel said, but didn't move an inch. Barton was the one who ended up rolling away from her, more into my vicinity, but not before pinching Isabel on the arm. "Ouch!" she cried, and frowned at him. "That's going to make a mark," she said, and Meg and I exchanged a meaningful glance. Maybe Isabel's bruises were just playful jabs from Barton. I certainly didn't want to be getting any of those.

The fireworks started after a while, and we joined the chorus of "oohs" and "aahs." I could hear my grandfather's harem cackling away in the middle distance, but mostly I could hear Barton saying my name.

"Jeanie Beanie. Aaaaah." "Jeanie Beanie. Ooooh." Then he pinched me. I slapped him, and pretty soon we were wrestling on the blanket and off the blanket and annoying everybody else. Susie Jenkins and Tommy whispered astrological secrets while Charlie Jenkins looked at his watch every time there was enough light in the sky to see by.

Looking back, a good time was had by all, and especially by me. Barton followed me home and I guess I got what I wanted.

How Do You Catch a Wave Upon the Sand?

Monday, July 6

I drove to work in a cloud. Not a real cloud, like a cirrus or a cumulus, and not like one from a bad radiator, which I knew well, but a foggy, unreal one, like in a dream. It was a love cloud—the sickening, swirling, nosediving variety, which I really hated. I was sure Barton must have spent Sunday recovering from our night together, because he hadn't called me all the next day. I set my cell phone close by on the front seat so I could answer it right away. See, I told you, I wanted to say. See? You don't need reading materials or a tape recorder to have a good time.

"Hi, you've reached Jeanie Callahan. Leave a message and I will call you back instantly." BEEP.

"NO NEW MESSAGES." BEEP.

*   *   *

Whatever Dan was saying about deadlines went right over my head. Abe looked particularly miserable, and Connie made a big point of moving all her materials away from him to sit somewhere else. So did Garrett.

"Jeanie is ahead in the contest, but that doesn't mean someone else couldn't win," Dan said. I smiled. Abe passed me a note.

You look like you just got laid.

No comment, Psychic Boy, I wrote back.

Why can't it happen to me?

Try getting close to the business.

I continued to bless the team with my love smile. The cloud was so thick, I could barely see them all.

Florence Keating asked a question. "If a client ups his order, does that count as a new sale?"

Henrietta took it upon herself to answer. "No, Florence, what do you think? A new customer has to be new."

"Okay, I just wondered," Florence said.

"Yes, that's right," Dan said. "Henrietta is right." Dan wasn't exactly ready to kill Henrietta with an ax, but I could tell the honeymoon was over.

Stephanie spoke next. "I am so ready to get into this contest. When am I getting my territory, Dan?"

"Soon, Stephanie." I too was very eager for this to happen.

Bob Bordeaux, renegade from the North Shore office, was sitting in with us today. "Hey, who wants to bet on the Yankees game?" he asked, while Dan raced out of the room to see why Magda was whooping and screaming.

· *"NO NEW MESSAGES." BEEP.*

Magda had just discovered she could use her Filene's coupon on L'Oréal nail products. This didn't seem to bother Danno, but why should it? He'd hired and fired three receptionists in two weeks and was a new expert on screaming. He looked somewhat mollified when he walked back in. Meanwhile, Bob had gotten a few bets down.

"All right, listen up, everybody, I have an important announcement," Dan said. All ears pointed and perked.

My cell rang, a clear infraction of the no-phone rule. It was an even further infraction to take the call, but I did.

"Hello," I tried to whisper in my sexiest voice.

"Is this Jeanie? It doesn't sound like Jeanie."

I hung up. It was Mort, who would clearly be with me to my dying day.

"I'm sorry, Dan," I said. "I'm waiting for an extremely important call." Everyone glared at me.

"Okay, here it is," Dan said. "Abe has decided to withdraw from the sales manager position." Dan took a small pause to let the news sweep silently around the room. "It just didn't work out with his home schedule and family commitments." I saw Connie lower her gaze to the table in front of her. Like everybody else, she knew Abe rented an apartment and lived with a beagle.

"So the position is vacant. I will be holding interviews when I get back from the corporate meeting in Florida. If any of you are interested in the job, just let me know and you'll get an interview." I looked at Abe and he gave me a thumbs-up sign, which in my view could mean only that it was an inside slick track for me.

"In the meantime, I'll be away for the rest of the week and I've asked Bob to watch over things. As some of you know, Bob and his wife are relocating to the West Coast at the end of the summer." A few "aws" and disappointed clucks went around the table.

"Bob's going to start his own LotsaCoups franchise out there, and we wish him the best." More sounds approving, this time. "So. Bob has a lot of experience, and if you need help on the road or if you have questions, he will be covering." We all smiled at Bob, who smiled back from behind his thick glasses and gave a quick wave. I had my doubts about Bob's dedication to direct mail, but if Dan didn't mind a bookie operation on the premises, why should I? "Okay then, I'll let you go," Dan said. "Happy hunting, everybody, and keep us informed of any new sales."

"NO NEW MESSAGES." BEEP.

Were it not for Mort's call, I would have wondered whether my cell phone was working. Barton was probably at his job, though, which he still hadn't divulged to me. Maybe he'd want to meet for coffee. Maybe he'd want me to move in with him. He could read to me all day if he wanted.

"Who are you expecting a call from?" Stephanie asked as we drove.

"Um, my grandfather. He's seeing his doctor today."

"Oh, I hope everything's all right."

"I'm sure it will be. Now remember, when we get to this optical place, try to be professional but complimentary to the owner."

"I think I know how to act in a sales situation."

Twenty minutes later, I couldn't get Stephanie to stop trying on eyeglass frames. She didn't like any of them. Optical shops are always filled with mirrors, so she was in heaven. I personally was a bit alarmed by the bags under my eyes. I chatted with the optometrist.

"Sir, I don't know who told you that you would get a five percent return. Do you really expect five hundred people to come in as the result of one ad?"

"Oh," he said. "I see what you mean. That does seem excessive."

"I don't think five percent is excessive," Stephanie called from the middle of the room. I feigned a knowing, isn't-she-cute laugh.

Stephanie walked over to us. "You could use some different frames in here."

"Why don't you try these?" the optometrist said, and
left me standing at the counter. I wanted to drag
Stephanie out the door by her color-treated Eva Perón
French twist to beat her senseless. Instead, I smiled and
waited. By the time Dr. Anestis returned, there were three
customers for him to deal with. I tried on a few frames myself and again thought wistfully of beating her senseless.

Finally, he was mine. I signed him, got a check, a decent
offer for his coupon, and got Stephanie out the door before
she could open her fat mouth further.

"NO NEW MESSAGES." BEEP.

By midafternoon I was concerned. By the end of the day I
was panicked. I dumped Stephanie off as quickly as I could
and didn't even walk upstairs to turn in my new sale. I was
still at twenty-four new, since the one jailbird had escaped.
I saw Henrietta's vehicle and felt sure she was up there on
the third floor talking Bob into a state of paralysis.

Why shouldn't I call Barton? Why shouldn't I have the
right to call the man I love? Meg and I both knew all the
answers to this question, but I wasn't buying just now. I
thought I would be the exception.

A woman answered, a familiar voice to my ear. "Hello,
this is Barton's phone."

"Is he there?"

"Just a minute."

I hung up. I sat and hyperventilated. The love cloud
turned black.

Lady-Oh

I didn't feel much zest. In fact, I had skipped work two days in a row, spending most of the time parked at the Grafton Street rotary so my grandfather wouldn't know. My tomatoes were unwatered, my guinea pig fed but not loved, and I still hadn't started the layouts for my coupons. I didn't have the heart for it. My heart was with Barton, wherever he was, driving around in his car, drinking coffee with him, directing the show. That reminded me of Wednesday's rehearsal, the first Shipley's outing I didn't attend.

As I'd sat in the audience and listened to Laura Wheeler try to hit the high notes of Maria's song, I made an important discovery.

She was the one who had answered Barton's phone.

Turns out Barton worked at Honeydew with Laura. He was a baker of doughnuts. His second job was for a funeral parlor, which, of course, explained the lavish bouquets. I was glad he had at least removed the decorative plastic messages that must have scrolled across them: *We'll miss you! You're in our prayers! This Thing Cost a Fortune!* I hoped a hearse hadn't driven up to my house to make the delivery. In the end, everybody seemed to know except me, and the only thing fresh was my mortification. You might think I'd be put off by his humble status in the workforce, but I knew that many show business aspirants put in time at low-wage jobs while they waited for their big break. Barton's show business break was perhaps overdue, since his breaks in other areas seemed plentiful.

But on this morning I didn't park at the rotary. I'm ashamed to say I drove to the one place I could find peace, the parking lot by Hannaford's Market, right next to Honeydew. Yes, that's right, I was a stalker, and my results weren't that great. I tried to camouflage myself as best I could, but it was problematic. If you park facing away from your target, you give them a good look at your license plate. If you park facing them, well, duh, they can see you. I tried slantwise positions but got too many irritated looks from shoppers and motorists. A surprising number of people are in bad moods when they go to the grocery. I knew how pathetic I was, sitting there. Pond scum couldn't have been lower. But at least pond scum was innocent, I realized. It was doing its job in the ecosystem. I wasn't accomplishing anything. From a total of five hours in my various slots, I'd caught sight of Barton only once. He walked out the back and smoked a cigar. He still looked handsome.

"Hi, this is the voice mail of Jeanie Callahan. You must have called me for a reason, so let me know what it is." BEEP.

"Good morning, LotsaCoupers, this is Bob Bordeaux, your man in the driver's seat for the week. Last night's results— Tigers over the Devil Rays in a rout, Rockies over the Dodgers by three—if you had the points, you're smokin' joints, boys and girls. Remember—bets in by four P.M. Oh, yeah. Henrietta Lewis has added another two sales. Nice going, H. Have a good day, everybody." BEEP.

"Jeanie, this is Mort at Mort's Hardware? Why haven't you come in to see me? I need a new color for the fall coupon." BEEP.

"It's Meg, dear. I'm not going to say anything. I wouldn't. But you're going to have to get over this. You're going to have to put on a smiley face for the sake of the show. Call me back." BEEP.

"Jeanie, it's Lenny Sadowski. I'm really sorry to report this, but another two have fallen out of the group. Check the local edition of the paper." BEEP.

"J girl! How goes the battle? Your pal Bob here, talkin' trash and spendin' cash. Wondering where your memo is, doll. I got everybody's but yours. Maybe I missed it. Listen, don't forget the All-Star game, there's going to be some big action on that. Ciao." BEEP.

I felt like a robot or a statue. My face was succumbing to gravity years before its time. I looked in the rearview mirror of my car and saw a shell of myself. It could have been a good opportunity to pine away and lose weight if I hadn't kept a full bag of corn chips by my side at all times. At least I wasn't eating dip.

As I kept my vigil in the mirror I saw Laura Wheeler run into Honeydew. Barton's car was there too. Why would he like someone that tall? And that smart? Wouldn't he prefer someone shorter, with a wholesome look and plenty of cellulite? I rummaged around in the newspaper until I found a small article about two men who'd been caught trying to steal three cars. This also seemed problematic. I wondered which of the pizza guys they were and which songs their cell phones played. Mine seemed to never go off anymore.

I went back to staring intently into the rearview mirror, and was startled when the car door opened and Barton sat down in the passenger seat. Or he tried to. I wasn't sure what he was sitting on.

"I wish you wouldn't do this."

I looked at my steering wheel.

"I'm sorry I haven't called you."

"Oh," I said. "I hadn't noticed." Then I shook my head. "Yes, I know. It's stupid."

"No, I'm the one who's stupid. You're a very nice girl, Jeanie. You're too nice for me."

"I wasn't too nice the other night."

"Believe it or not, that was too nice for me too. I did it for your sake, Jeanie."

"Thanks. I did it for my country."

He laughed. "Look, can we, I don't know, just put this aside and see what happens?"

"Sure," I said. "Sure. That would be no problem."

"And I'm sorry too about that questionnaire fiasco. I honestly thought it would be funny. I just like to set things in motion sometimes."

"Oh, yes. So you said." Then I asked the following question and wanted to slap myself. "Are we dating?"

Barton looked straight ahead. "Dating is hard for me."

"Oh."

We talked for a few more minutes, and then he went back to his muffins and I drove dry-eyed into the center of Worcester. I parked near Isabel's new store, scheduled to open in one week.

"Hi," Isabel said. "Are you okay? We missed you the other night."

"I'm deliriously happy," I said.

"You don't look it."

"I'm meeting Stephanie here, if that's all right. I'm going to let her sell Benito's."

"Oh, my gosh, lucky her."

"Yeah."

"Jeanie. Look at me. I don't mean to pry. Is this about Barton?"

I felt my shoulders slump as I swallowed hard and riffled through a stack of order envelopes. Hopefully, they would soon be filled with customers' film canisters.

"Honey, I'm really sorry. He's not a good romance candidate."

"Yes, Category D."

"What?"

I explained the categories of men to Isabel, and she smiled as she shook her head. "I've been so nice to Barton over the years. Fed him every night when his mother was dying, consoled him when he didn't get the Lyric Stage part, I don't even remember all of it. Ray's scotch supply has taken a personal dent from Barton."

"His mother's dead?"

"Oh yes, he's used that excuse on me too. He forgets I went to her funeral. I could have told you all this, Jeanie. I wanted to tell you."

"Is he the one who gives you bruises, Isabel?"

"No," she said.

Sam Yummy walked out from the stockroom, and the asshole category discussion ceased. Then Stephanie walked in, bright as a butterfly. She wore a thigh-high red leather skirt and yellow tank top. I knew this look and had used it myself, though not proudly. In the end, you only get problems from a "britches" account.

"Hey, Isabel," I said as lightheartedly as I could, "Mort tells me you're watching him from your window."

"Does he?" Isabel asked. "That's cute." She waved out the window in the direction of Mort's Hardware, then winked at Sam and he winked at her. Stephanie applied another pound of lipstick and we sauntered out the door and across the street to Benito's. A couple of cars nearly collided in Stephanie's wake.

Benito greeted us like the Godfather. The scar across his forehead gave him a certain credibility, though not necessarily as an arbiter of men's fashion. I thought the same thing I always did: How soon can I get out of here? Though we did not kneel and kiss his ring, Stephanie was appropriately reverent. This is always a mistake. You need to take your own space. Not surprisingly, Stephanie managed to turn an easy sale into a hard one.

"This art is no good. You need something fresher, edgier, younger."

"This is the art my vendor gave us. Do you have something else?" Benito asked. The other reptiles slouched near us, their attention tuned strictly to Stephanie's legs. When she moved in her chair even slightly, their beady eyes flicked back and forth like lizards watching a tennis match.

"Oh, I'm sure we can find something," Stephanie said, and looked at me for approval.

"I don't see anything wrong with this art," I said in a last-ditch effort.

"No, it's not good enough for Benito," Stephanie said. "Make us work for this, Benito. Don't sign anything until you're satisfied."

I looked Benito in the eye. "On the other hand, Benito, you can take advantage of our prepay discount if you sign up right now."

He signed.

"Who will be our salesgirl?" he asked.

"Stephanie," I said.

"Well, that's really nice of you, Benito," Stephanie said. "But what about the color of your logo? Let me look around for something that matches it better, okay?"

"Sure," Benito said, bestowing his blessing with the kindly benevolence of a don who hacks people into bits before lunch. Stephanie signed her name on the contract with a flourish. I remembered my very first sale. It had been mail order, because I didn't know any better and didn't have somebody competent standing at my side to steer me away from it. Not that Stephanie was in any way grateful. She didn't even speak to me outside.

Mort did, though. "Hey, Jeanie!" he yelled from his doorway. "I need to see you."

"I'll be back soon," I called.

"Isabel waved at me today! See, I told you."

"Good, Mort."

Stephanie and I made it back to my car at precisely the same moment as the meter maid.

"You lead a charmed life, coupon girl," the woman said.

"Not really," I replied.

"Attention Spotlighters," Barton announced that night. "We need more men. We must have more men. Please ask someone you know to come in and help us out in the ballroom scene."

"And onstage crew, too, men or women," Sam added.

"Hey, Barton! My cousin would like to be one of the nuns," Helen yelled.

"Tell her to sign up at St. Mary's," Barton yelled back. "The last thing I need is more nuns," he muttered. The two of them had reached an impasse on the crucifix issue. She was going to be allowed to carry it, but only if it was covered up. I didn't see how this would work, but Helen seemed content.

"My other cousins from New York will be here the week of the show," Helen said, crucifix balanced on her shoulder like a rifle. "They're coming up for our family reunion."

"Forget it. We need them now."

Stephanie was still glowing from her sale.

"Barton, don't you think that Honeydew would want to do a coupon?" she asked slyly.

"I don't know," he said. "Don't put your hands on your hips like that. And don't stand so far upstage."

It was all I could do not to scream at Stephanie that Honeydew was in my territory and so was Benito's, and I was only giving her Benito's because I couldn't stand the thought of going in there, and to quit talking to Barton so that I could make him notice me and desire me and feel generally awful like I did. But I didn't. Instead, I moved in a dignified fashion around the stage. We were getting it, we nuns.

A number of nuns were getting more than that, it seemed, and I wondered uneasily whether Don Shipley knew some of his bartenders were serving underage patrons. Marianne came with us and had a Shirley Temple. No surprise there. And no surprise that Susie Jenkins was all over one of the young janitors from the high school in the corner of the booth. I contemplated the number of adulterous or potentially adulterous relationships now ongoing in our production and shook my head.

Stephanie didn't show. Barton sat with Laura and they made all kinds of jokes about short people. I didn't think they were that funny. I sat with Velma and listened to her talk about her fifteen cats. That wasn't too funny either.

When My Heart Is Lonely

Saturday, July 11

I tooted my horn in front of Meg's house. We were supposed to pick up Isabel and then go see Tommy Cuthbert in *Cabaret*. I was determined to snap out of my Barton slump. After a few minutes I got out of my car and walked to the front porch. I thought of Meg and Gary having sex on the chandelier, so I hesitated. Then I remembered they didn't have a chandelier and walked confidently. Then I thought of their dining room table and hesitated again. I hoped the neighbors weren't watching my stutter step approach to the house.

"Halloooo! Ding-dong! The Wicked Witch is dead!" I poked my head in the door and pulled it out again. It smelled like they were still burning all their food, whether from the old lady's evil eye or Gary's culinary skill, I couldn't tell.

Just as I opened my mouth to call out again, Gary rushed past me, tucking in his shirt.

"Is this a bad time?" I asked as he touched the four corners of the doorway and then turned around three times. Then he licked his finger and touched the heel of his shoe.

"Gare?"

"Go on in," he said, and walked backward down the steps. He looked like a third-base coach sending signals to the runner. "She's almost ready."

"Be careful," I called, and walked into a quiet house, the only sound coming from the shower in the bathroom. I used my time wisely and did Meg's dishes for her. When I am in someone else's house, I don't mind doing housework at all. It's fun and enjoyable. I even dried the dishes and put them away and wiped down the counter. I had the broom out to sweep when Meg rushed out of the bathroom in her yellow sundress and wet hair.

"Oh, that's so nice of you," she said.

"Isn't it?" I commented.

"Why can't you do it at your own house, you geek?"

"I don't like it at my house. It seems overpowering and depressing."

"Are we going to need money? Gary left with all my money."

"Where's he going?"

Meg found her shoes under the couch. "Red Sox game with his work friends, and one of them is a little harlot."

"Geez, Meg, you could have gone."

"No, I want to see Tommy in his show."

"I've got plastic, don't worry." We walked out onto the porch.

"I just had sex upside down like a bat."

"I figured."

"I'm done. That's it. I don't want kids."

Meg explained why she didn't want children as I drove to Isabel's. Most of her reasons had to do with sex in general. I told her to suck it up. She told me to rephrase that.

Isabel wasn't ready either. Meg and I walked in through

the open garage door. Huge barrels of empty Orange Crush containers took up space, and I could tell Meg was calculating how much we could get for them. We could hear yelling as we opened the door to a small room off the kitchen.

"Hello? Isabel?" The yelling stopped. Meg and I stood in the marble-and-granite marvel of a kitchen and looked around at the mess. It looked to me like a new dish had been tried from a cookbook and failed. I tried a spoonful of whatever was in the frying pan and I thought it was pretty good.

"Jeanie, cut it out!" Meg hissed. "That is gross."

"No, it isn't," I said. I washed a few dishes and wiped down the range top of the stove.

Isabel walked in looking very Catherine Zeta-Jones (when she was pregnant) and smelled of a high-priced perfume.

She nodded to us and walked to the liquor cabinet, where she pulled out a bottle of tequila and poured three shots.

"Ladies, to your health," she said. Meg doesn't usually drink nonwine beverages, but we both picked up our glasses and downed them. Tequila is so underrated.

"Okay, let's go," Isabel said.

"Where's Clarissa?" I asked. Isabel's mouth went into a straight line.

"She's not at a Girl Scout meeting, I'll tell you that."

That got us going. Isabel got into the backseat and we started saying where Clarissa probably wasn't.

"She's not at Campfire Girls, I bet," Meg said.

"Not ringing a bell at the Salvation Army."

"Not at Up with People rehearsal."

I could tell the night was going to go cuckoo when Isabel stopped laughing long enough to say, "Do we really want to go to this play?"

"What do you suggest?" I asked. "And how did you do that to your elbow?"

"Let's think about this," Isabel said, and ignored my question.

We ended up at Struggles, a dark place not far from Shipley's. Drinking was heavy. We decided to stay pure and remain with tequila, so we ordered shooters. Isabel and Meg kept toasting the evils of men, but eventually we got around to thanking them for all they do.

"Let's drink to men taking out the garbage."

"Yes, I love when they do that. Here's to mopping up sewer line leakage."

We drank to that. "And mowing the lawn."

"Changing tires."

"Chimney emergencies," I said.

Meg hiccupped.

We were having a lot of fun until Gary and his friends walked in. The little harlot was quite obvious, but no competition for Meg.

"What?" Meg said. "Is that Gary?"

Isabel polished off her shooter while I stared at Gary, and so did Meg, who seemed to be frozen in space. He saw me finally. I give him credit for walking over to us.

"Hi, honey," he said to Meg. What a galoot.

"It must be raining outside, I guess," Meg said from the inside of our booth, next to Isabel. "Otherwise, why would the Red Sox game be canceled?"

"We only had bleacher seats. Stuff happened," Gary said. "One of my friends had a bad night with his girlfriend and we decided to console him here."

"Do you expect me to believe that?" Meg said.

"I thought you were going to a play," Gary said.

In time, Gary's group joined our group. At first Meg refused to sit next to Gary, but eventually he climbed over the booth and claimed his rightful place. The harlot left soon after that.

Meg announced to the entire bar that she and Gary

wouldn't be having children. "We don't need children to have a good marriage."

"You don't need them to have a bad marriage either," Isabel muttered to me.

"I want to travel in Europe," Meg said.

"Oh, honey, so do I," Gary said. The room cheered.

We toasted Italy and France and Liechtenstein, which Gary said he'd always been interested in.

"I will give you the best sex of your life in Liechtenstein," Meg told Gary, and the group whistled.

"Licking what?" the waitress asked cheerily.

Life's problems seemed to be solved. No kids for the Larsons and a standing ovation for Tommy, as we found out later from Velma, who actually went to *Cabaret*. She hooked up with the Baldwin Players costume director and finagled two sets of lederhosen, which, I finally learned, are shorts and not stockings.

Have Confidence

"One hundred and forty-two pounds." I accepted the verdict sullenly but without surprise. My waking dream had been of losing a tooth. I knew peripherally, around the edges of my brain, that three large boxes of Milk Duds weren't that good for weight loss. Add to that a big bowl of mashed potatoes, homemade by me on Sunday, plus everything else I'd consumed and now forgotten, and the edges of my brain were curled in upon themselves, singed. I'd had a bit of a Barton-weeping relapse on Sunday, but the mashed potatoes had made the difference, to say nothing of the tequila hangover.

And speaking of brains, they do work in funny ways sometimes. There I was driving unhappily along one minute, and slamming on my brakes the next because of something that occurred to me.

Where was the cash? The nearly five thousand dollars in deposits I had taken from the jailbirds. I had meant to look for it the other day and it slipped my mind. Ha! What mind? I started to sweat. I leafed through my sales presentation book to the place where I kept a plastic insert just for cash, but it was empty. It had been too small, I now remembered. So that meant I put it somewhere else. All this time I had felt so confident that the money was in the notebook. It wasn't. I'd barely worked last week, had sat home like a chump, and hadn't opened it. If I'd dared, I would have turned around and driven back home to look for it, but I had to go to the meeting.

"My thanks to Bob for covering last week," Dan said.

"Yeah," Abe added with a bright smile. "My thanks too." Abe had won five hundred bucks in some big jackpot of Bob's, and his good spirits were back. I was happy to see it, though I hoped he wasn't serious about a new life of professional gambling. Bob had returned to his North Shore sales team, where I was sure he was welcomed with open arms.

Thoughts of the money had me nearly insane by the end of the meeting. Dan lectured everybody about the importance of a good offer, and Stephanie lectured everybody about the importance of wearing the correct dress size. I knew this was aimed at Henrietta and marveled at Stephanie's nerve. I also marveled at her finicky inability to accept the ink colors that our plant offered.

"This maroon is unacceptable for Benito."

"Well, Stephanie, how do you think we keep prices down? You get one maroon, that's it. Plain-vanilla maroon."

Stephanie sniffed and huffed off to keep looking.

I did remember to ask Dan for an interview.

"Good, Jeanie. Do you want to do it right now?" he asked. I didn't want to tell him that I had to rush home and look for five thousand dollars of lost company money, so I said okay.

We sat in the conference room and Dan closed the door. I could see my colleagues outside the glass wall, openly gawking. Some of them looked like turkeys, gobblers bobbing up and down, others more like aquatic life-forms, doing nothing and saying nothing. I sat up as straight as I could.

"How do you think you could motivate the group to higher sales, Jeanie?"

"By inspiring fear."

"Fear? Are you serious?"

"Yes. Fear and punishment. Humiliation. Also blackmail. They always work."

Dan stared at me.

"I'm kidding, Dan." I had to say that. In truth, they were successful techniques all, and ones used in our company every day, but I didn't dare say it.

The interview went well. I came up with numerous varieties of horseshit, which I used effectively.

"Maybe smaller prizes but spread out more across the sales force," I suggested.

"Hmmm," Dan said.

"Maybe fewer meetings but more content. Masking tape across Henrietta's mouth. Just kidding again, Dan."

"Hmmm."

"More communication." This was a real howler, of course. We already had too much communication.

"Why do you want the job, Jeanie?" Dan asked, and started cleaning his glasses.

Here I faltered. "Um, well, I want to advance. I want to be the best I can be. Is that an army slogan?" Oh God.

Then I found myself. "I want to help LotsaCoups move forward to a premier place in the industry." Now I had it. I blathered on while Dan finished cleaning his glasses.

He gave one final nod. "Okay, I'll put you on the short list, Jeanie. You're doing great in the contest, and that will be a big factor in the decision. Lou Lambaster will be here next week and you'll have to interview with him. I'd be happy to have you."

"Thanks, Dan." I wanted to hug him.

"Could you send Garrett in, please?"

I swept out the door and smiled graciously at poor Garrett, who couldn't possibly be better than I was.

Later at home I wondered who could possibly be worse. I tore the house apart. I tore the car apart. Nothing. I fixed myself a frozen entrée and ate it with a spoon, since all forks were in the dishwasher. What a loser I was. I couldn't even run my dishwasher.

It was time, past time actually, to start rounding up my regular customers, but I couldn't concentrate. Then I had a brainstorm. My car, newly obsessed with brake-fluid levels, practically found its own way to Cheng Du. My hopes were high.

"Is Rick here today?" I asked the bartender.

"Not yet. Four o'clock," he answered.

"Do you have a lost and found?"

"Oh yes. What you lose?"

"Some money, actually."

"Wallet?"

"No, not a wallet. I'm not sure what it was in. But it was a lot of money."

The bartender gave me a sympathetic look, one that I'm sure he reserved for morons.

"No, sorry," he said.

"Oh well. Thanks."

I sat in my car and rested my head on the steering wheel. My cell rang and I wondered what else could go wrong.

"This is Jeanie."

"Hi, Jeanie?"

"Yes." Sometimes I wouldn't mind being sarcastic.

"This is Carol from ColdCuts."

"Oh hi, Carol. I've been meaning to get over there and show you your ad. It looks great." I hadn't even started it.

"The thing is, well, you know my sister has a salon in Acton?"

"Oh yes." My heart sank.

"Well, like, it has the same name and the same slogo? So like my sister says it would be better for us to do the ad together? Like her salon and mine together?"

"Mmmm."

"So I'm sorry, but I guess we are going to go ahead and let this other lady do it who's been, like, really pestering my sister? I'm so grateful you're not like that, Jeanie."

"Yes. Hmmm."

"And who knows, maybe we'll, like, meet again. Okay, Jeanie?"

"Sure, Carol. Best of luck."

Now I did cry.

"From the eighteen forties and once known as the perfect ship, Gramp!"

"Clipper!" he answered from the stairs.

"Hey, Gramp. Would you let the Spotlighters borrow your stepladder? One of the kids in my show broke the one at the school."

"Awrrenbiletto."

"What?"

"All right. I guess so."

"Great. Thanks. I guess they're having all kinds of set problems."

"What kind of problems?"

"One thing is the big staircase. They're trying to get it on wheels."

My plan worked. I took Gramp with me to rehearsal. I had engaged his natural tool-loving and problem-loving curiosity, and also I think he was avoiding the new candle-giving woman. On our way out he told me to ignore the phone.

*   *   *

You thought I wouldn't go to rehearsal? Just because I faced financial ruin, loss of first place in the contest, and possible imprisonment? I figured it might get my mind off things. And it would give the money a chance to plump up, spread out, and be found. I made a solemn vow that the minute, the second, I found the money, I would drive to the convenience store and get a money order. Day or night.

"I'll get that," Gramp assured Sam within one minute of their meeting. He referred to an unpainted spot at the top of the staircase.

"Gramp," I said, but then pulled back and left him in the hallway with Sam. Inside the auditorium, the children were enjoying dark-chocolate buttercreams from a sampler someone had brought and left on the stage. Some faces were covered with chocolate; others wiped fingers up and down shirts and clothing. By the time Marianne got them tuned up, it looked more like a minstrel show with the younger ones in complete blackface.

Barton walked in. "Oh. Is the show changed to *Willie Wonka?*" he asked. "Nobody told me." The kids all laughed, except for the oldest boy, who ran back to the box of candy for another morsel.

"Get away from there!" Barton cried, and grabbed the box. The kids laughed again.

"Isabel," Barton said in a low voice. "This is my last show with kids. I'm serious." The children found this funny too, and Isabel barely looked up from her conference with Velma.

"Do-Re-Mi" sounded limp and looked a bit jerky, probably because Laura kept jumping away from the group. I figured she ought to be used to chocolate, working where she did, but she seemed appalled at each encounter with the kids. Laura and Barton giggled incessantly.

The huge snout of the staircase appeared from the wings.

"Watch out!" Barton called, and the performers dispersed. We all watched the behemoth rattle its way to center stage with only one person, my grandfather, pushing it. Everyone present applauded.

My grandfather, the ham, took a bow and had this to say: "Oh hi, Barton. Barton's dating my granddaughter, everybody, so I already know him."

There was a tiny silence and then a voice said, "Actually, that isn't true." It was my voice. I spoke from the steps to the stage and had everyone's attention within seconds. It was a little bit like a sales presentation. "Barton is not dating me because dating is hard for him. So you can't say that, Gramp." I calmly walked down the steps and grabbed my purse from the front row. I continued through the auditorium, still speaking in tongues. "But what you can say, Gramp, is that Barton owes me forty-two dollars. You can definitely say that, and if you'd like to collect it for me, I'd be grateful. If you wanted to say that Barton has odd sexual proclivities and not much talent for poetry, I wouldn't object to that either." I reached the back door of the auditorium and turned around for the close. "But just don't say that I'm dating him, okay?" I said as I walked out with a flounce and collapsed in the bathroom.

Gramp didn't know everybody at Shipley's when we got there, but he did by the time we left. Many of the older nuns had come along and it seemed clear their musical comedy experience was about to be greatly enhanced. The most surprising aspect to all this was Marianne. My mouth fell open when I saw her plop down next to Gramp and order a Johnnie Walker Black. They were discussing Mozart, I think.

Everything was different after my speech. I was the lead nun now. People showed respect. They held doors for me.

I got the best wimple. Barton came to Shipley's and made an effort to act normal. So did I, though I felt a bit shaky. Barton sat with Laura, whom I'd never seen so animated. I could only imagine the hilarity they shared during the day by the doughnut ovens. Laura's eyes sparkled and her face glowed. If she could have looked like that with Charlie onstage, we'd have had ourselves a love interest. Meg had given me a thumbs-up for my performance and gone home to Gary for once, and I was glad for that. Charlie wasn't there, so that left Susie free to be homecoming queen. I was the bitter old spinster of the group, Velma's preferred conversation partner, and a somewhat heavy drinker. After just one rehearsal, Gramp was hooked.

To: Dan Albright
Fr: Jeanie Callahan
Re: Getting Close to the Business
Things couldn't be better. A number of fence-sitters are starting to eat out of my hand. I should be able to add three more sales to my total. SEND.

Edelweiss Schmaydelweiss

Wednesday, July 15

The clock said six A.M. and I could hear Gramp coming in the slider. This was it. I was going to have serious words with him. I drifted back to sleep, and then something woke me again. I rolled over in bed and looked into Meg's face.

"I'm pregnant," she whispered.

I stared. My mouth opened. Then it shut. Then I started screaming, and then she started screaming. Then we were both jumping on the bed like we used to in grade school.

"Watch out, don't fall," I yelled.

"Gary went to tell his parents an hour ago. They'll freak!"

"How do you feel?" I yelled.

"Like shit!"

My grandfather's white face appeared in the doorway. "What's wrong? Why are you screaming?" That made us scream even more.

"Meg's pregnant, Gramp!"

"Well, what do you know. I'll make a nutritious breakfast."

"No, thanks, Mr. Callahan. Jeanie and I are going to the beach today and we have to get started."

"We are?" I said, and bounced off the bed and onto the floor.

"Yes, we have to. I've already left a message. Screw work!"

"Yes, screw work." That was what I'd been doing lately anyway.

"And screw Liechtenstein!"

"Oh yes! Screw Leichtenstein to the wall!"

"How do you think it happened?" I whispered.

"Well, let's see. Do you think it could have been that thing I do with my husband where we take our clothes off?" Our giggles made Gramp shake his head and eventually leave my house for his.

"Gee whiz," I said. "I wonder which time did the trick."

"It could have been the garter belt, you know."

"The Garter Belt Baby. I like it."

"It wasn't the painting, I know it wasn't. It's already back in the attic, thank God."

"I forgot to tell you I put a curse on it the other night."

"Gee, thanks. Let's get Isabel and Tommy," Meg said. "They'll want to go."

So we did. Isabel sacrificed a day in her new shop, Tommy Cuthbert sacrificed a day of recovering from his other show, and we all sacrificed our regular lives for a day at Hampton Beach. At Isabel's urging, we even brought Sam Yummy, who gave up a day of hauling shit. We ate pork rinds, fried dough, cotton candy, and hot pretzels. We swam in the ocean. We got sunburned. And every so often we screamed.

Flibbertigibit, a Will-o'-the-Wisp, a Clown

Friday, July 17

I made up my mind to confide in Dan about the money. He would help me. He would have to. Good thing he didn't know about my other recent crime, pilfering the expensive six-color handouts—and from his file cabinet, too. I had no intention of giving *those* back. I figured I might as well head over to Eastboro and wow the peasants with the glitzy brochures. As I stood in my closet, trying to make a good wardrobe selection, I brushed against a pair of panty hose hanging on the door and a hundred-dollar bill floated out of them.

Was it Atlas who carried the world on his shoulders? I was no longer Atlas.

I clutched the beautiful, glorious, cleverly hidden wad of money to my breast, and instantly remembered hiding it there. I'd figured most burglars in our area were fetish-free, and I couldn't picture one taking the time to sniff panty hose while completing a heist. It was satisfying to know my theory had been borne out. I enjoyed two seconds of relief, then immediately put off going to the convenience store for a money order, and began worrying about other things, such as where my next sale would come from and how I could keep fooling Dan with my memos. Sad to say, it took me five seconds to move past the wonderful news, and return to my normal, dissatisfied state of mind. Why do we do that? Meg always says people are so people-y.

Friday zest did kick in. I don't think I had ever felt so much Friday zest, as a matter of fact. I stopped at Nashoba Tire and Harassment and gave my best sympathetic listen to a psoriasis story. I collected ad copy from numerous clients and stayed sane.

"All right, Jeanie, what if I give a free yardstick to every customer?"

"You're an ice cream store, Harry."

"But I have a lot of yardsticks."

"What about a free ice-cream cone?"

"Well, a free kid's cone would be okay, I guess."

"Regular would be better."

"Okay, a free small regular with purchase of eight additional ice-cream cones."

"Eight, Harry? Are you joking?"

"Well all right, four?"

"How about one?"

"Okay. You're usually right, Jeanie. Let's see if it works."

"This is Jeanie."

"This is Stephanie Wilson from LotsaCoups."

"Yes, hi, Stephanie. What's up?"

"Where can I get a picture of a man holding firewood in his arms?"

"Did you look in the clip art book?"
"Oh no, I forgot. Okay, bye."

I spent a short time with Mort and tried to manage his coupon expectations and his Isabel expectations too. My cell rang as I walked out his door.

"This is Jeanie."

"Hi, this is Stephanie Wilson with LotsaCoups."

"Yes, I know who you are, Stephanie."

"I'd like the man holding the firewood to be smiling. Is that possible?"

"I would guess so, Stephanie. Keep looking in all the books."

"Okay, bye."

I made a few cold calls but with no results. One guy accused me of "gimmickry." I didn't disagree with him. My cell rang again.

"This is Jeanie."

"Hi, this is Stephanie Wilson from LotsaCoups."

I said nothing.

"I'm just practicing my greeting, you know."

"That's fine."

"I was wondering if someone could take my picture holding the firewood? Can I be the model in the ad?"

"Sure, why not?"

"You don't think it would be a problem with a woman holding firewood?"

"Not at all."

"Okay, bye."

I chatted with Moey the jailbird and gave him the refund for the three participants who were newly "inside." Lenny wasn't there.

"Hey, you want a kitten?" Moey asked.

"A kitten?"

"Yeah, it's been hanging around here, and we don't want no trouble with the health department."

"Oh, what a cutie," I said of the little tiger.

"If you don't take it," Moey said, "we're going to have to get rid of it our own way. You get me?"

"Oh Moey, no. I have a guinea pig, I can't have a cat, can I?"

My cell rang. I looked at it first, then answered.

"Hi, Stephanie."

"Yes, this is Stephanie Wilson with LotsaCoups."

"I'm really busy, Stephanie."

"I need to take a day off for this photo shoot. Is that going to be a problem?"

"Not for me. Do what you have to do."

"Well, we have to get it right, don't we? Shouldn't we? By the way, I need to talk to you about the border decoration on Benito's ad."

"All right, Stephanie, I'll talk to you later. Bye."

Somehow, in the confusion, I walked out of Jailbird Pizza with a kitten. Moey talked me into it.

"Cats and guinea pigs are well-known in the animal kingdom for friendship," he said.

"Oh yeah, Moey, sure. What a bullshitter. What am I going to do with it?"

Stephanie called again and asked if I would mind if she called on Honeydew Donuts. I said go ahead.

"If she doesn't get a territory soon, I'm killing myself, Moey."

"Huh?"

"Nothing. All right, I'll bring it next door and see if Dave will take it."

While I waited to speak with the pet store owner about the kitten and, I hoped, about his onerous ten-percent offer, a young man came in with a cloth bag over his arm. The bag moved by itself when he put it on the counter next to me.

"That's not a snake in there, is it?" I inquired.

"Yes. It's been abused," the young guy said.

The concept of an abused snake was foreign to me and not one I wanted to explore. I skedaddled out of there pronto and let the kitten into the backseat of my car. I would have persevered in my travels up and down the street, but Stephanie called wanting to know if Columbus Day was considered a holiday, and I lost the will to live.

The kitten seemed to like Mr. Piggy. There was a little squeaking from inside the cage, indicating the guinea pig's unease, but no catastrophes. The slots between the cage wires were fortunately too small for the kitten to get more than its paw into, so at least we were safe from a security breach of that kind. I tried not to think about the mental anguish Mr. Piggy might be feeling with a furry, clawed predator walking on top of his dwelling. The kitten found lots of other engaging activities, including scratching my mother's velvet wing chairs, scratching my kitchen table, and scratching the living room carpet. My plan was to sit at the table and make coupon-related phone calls before going back to the pet store with the kitten. My morning had been good, but I still needed ad copy from many clients for the upcoming deadline. My front doorbell rang.

"Yes?" I said to a middle-aged woman holding a plate of lemon squares, my favorite.

"Is Robert here? Robert Callahan?"

"He lives next door. That way," I said. "But he's not home now."

"Oh yes, are you his granddaughter?"

"Yes, that's right."

"Perhaps you could give him these."

"Okay, sure."

"Hello, I'm Rita Wylie, and I'm part of the group that's

suing Mr. Callahan. I just wanted him to have these. We're very grateful."

I pulled my hand back.

"Why are you suing him, may I ask?"

"Oh, I thought Gert Mayer told you about that."

"No, she hasn't."

"I think it would be better if you were to ask her. It's just a little embarrassing, that's all. Well, better go." The woman hightailed it down my driveway like a racehorse out of the gate. I kept the lemon squares for myself.

I never did make it back to the pet store. Meg thought it was so cute about the kitten that when she picked me up for rehearsal, she brought over an old litter box and some cans of cat food. I refused to accept them, and in fact brought the little feline with me to rehearsal. I figured I could palm it off on somebody.

Meg, still glowing from her recent news, wore an enormous maternity top that ballooned over her midsection.

"What is that?" I asked in the car.

"What does it look like?"

"A tablecloth."

"Christ, you sound like my mother."

"Your mother wouldn't wear a tablecloth."

"My mother isn't pregnant."

I left Meg to her own devices when we arrived at EHS. I first tried, with considerable success, to interest the von Trapp kids in the kitten. All parents present, however, nixed the idea. Some mentioned pets already at home that weren't being cared for; others just said no. I followed the kids to the cafeteria, where their newest pursuit was kicking the vending machines. Truman sometimes did it and got a free candy bar. In fact, the kids, with the exception of Jennifer, all idolized Truman and followed him up and down the hallway, he on his skateboard like a rolling Pied

Piper. Truman didn't want the kitten, but the youngest girl loved it, as I had hoped. I figured it might be a nice gift for her absent parents. I left the kitten in the lobby with the kids when I reported for chorus duty.

I found my nun colleagues sitting across several rows in the back of the auditorium while Marianne twiddled her thumbs on the stage waiting for us. I waved to her and wondered how things were at home with Mean Mom and the Muslins. A young woman was interviewing Isabel and our group for the *Worcester Tribune*.

"And how long have you been doing theater?" the woman asked.

Isabel began speaking, but Helen interrupted in a loud voice. "Only six months for me," she said, crucifix resting in her lap. "This one's up in the air so far. Ask me in another week how it's going."

"Ten years," Isabel said.

"This is my first," one of the high school girls said, and popped her gum. Her friends nodded agreement.

"What's the best part of it?"

A knitting nun answered this one. "Getting out of the house."

Everyone gave a weak laugh, though Isabel looked abashed at such an answer. "I love to sing. It's a great opportunity."

"Yes, a great opportunity," the group murmured. The reporter seemed to reach the end of her questions and looked around for another victim. Just as she caught sight of Barton, we heard a big commotion in the lobby.

"Those kids had better not be opening paint cans," Helen said.

There was no problem with paint cans. The ruckus was centered on the kitten, keeping its balance nicely on Truman's skateboard as it got pushed along between the cafeteria tables.

"Hang ten, dude!"

"Go, kitty!" The kids all cheered, and it was suggested they could try to get it on some TV show that featured animal tricks.

"I think you're being cruel to it," Jennifer said.

"Why don't you tell someone who cares," Truman answered as he gave the skateboard an extra shove.

It was indeed a night for stupid tricks, for frivolity pushed a bit too far. Even dark, suspicious Charlie seemed actually silly as he did his scenes. Susie was out in the lobby with the janitor, and her absence seemed both unnerving and empowering for Charlie. He whirled around once and caught Laura yawning.

"Do you think I'm boring?" he demanded.

"No," she said. "I'm just tired."

"You don't seem to mean it when you say you love me," he said, and grabbed Laura around her waist in a somewhat shocking embrace. "I think you have someone else." Laura gave a pale smile as she pulled away. Every now and then Charlie would walk up one or two of the steps on the staircase to deliver his lines, and Barton would caution him.

"This isn't *Hamlet*, Charlie, cool it with the oration."

But he wouldn't stop. "Stay off the staircase, Charlie," Barton repeated.

During a break, Charlie bowed to Stephanie and called her "milady," which I'm sure she enjoyed. Then he grabbed a wrench from my grandfather's toolbox, walked up the entire staircase, and extended his arms.

"To be or not to be," he proclaimed in the loudest voice we had ever heard from him. Everybody felt nervous.

"What's up *his* ass?" Helen whispered, and no one had an answer.

Near the end of rehearsal, the wrench fell off the staircase and narrowly missed Charlie's head. Barton blew up.

"Don't leave things on the staircase! Do you hear me?"

Charlie threw his script on the floor. "Yes, I hear you loud and clear, Barton. And do you hear this? *I quit!*"

Trips and Falls

Magda occasionally consulted with me on certain nuances in English that she wasn't sure of, such as whether "shithead" was a worse insult than "bastard." Today she wanted to know what a "cock tease" was, and I rolled my eyes.

"Where are you getting these, Magda?" I asked.

"Blind date I have last week."

Dan conveniently interrupted our discussion to call me into the meeting, and I hoped Magda might hunt down this definition without me. I also hoped she wouldn't use it while answering our phones.

"Okay, I have a sales exercise for us today," Dan said, and I sighed. I think most of the group sighed. Abe was not in attendance, having taken the day off to roar down to the Indian casino in Connecticut. Instead, I exchanged glances with Connie and Garrett. "Here's the premise. You are at a party approaching the buffet table. Right next to you is the CEO of a big company. What do you say?"

Silence filled the room until Florence piped up. "Do you think the roast beef is spoiled?"

Dan frowned as the rest of us laughed. "Remember, this is your one opportunity to get next to this guy. He won't take your calls in the office."

"Then ask him why he won't," Florence said.

"Hi, sir," Garrett jumped in. "Have you ever considered doing a coupon for your business?"

Henrietta leaned forward. "Sir, my name is Henrietta Lewis. I'm with LotsaCoups, and statistics show that many of your customers would respond favorably to a direct-mail promotion."

Connie took her glasses off. "If someone tried to sell me something at a party, I'd walk away."

"Well, Connie, maybe that's why you're not winning the contest," Dan said in a much more snide manner than we had seen before. The corporate guys must have read him the riot act.

"Well, Dan, maybe that's your opinion."

Dan insisted that everyone play the game. I agreed with Connie, of course, but came up with something bland when it was my turn. There's no point in falling on your sword for a piddling nit like this. By the time we finished, Henrietta was expounding by the paragraph, and if someone actually were listening to her at a buffet table, they'd have pitched forward into the mushroom gravy.

"Dan, I have a great idea," said Stephanie. "I would offer to carry the guy's plate for him and maybe give him some expert advice on some of the dishes that were being served."

"What if you didn't have any expert advice?" Florence asked.

"I would," Stephanie said.

"All right, everybody," Dan interjected, ignoring Stephanie's contribution. "Be ready to use your brains and think on your feet every Monday morning. I'd like to announce that Henrietta is now tied with Jeanie for first place in the contest." I was afraid of this, and in fact was somewhat relieved that I was still in a tie. Henrietta wore a gorgeous two-piece lavender ensemble that crushed her chest and must seriously have constricted any arm movement. Her smug smile provoked what I hoped was a smug smile of my own. I was an actress, after all. In truth, I was very worried about the contest. My vehicle was nearing the end of its days. It told me so all day long.

"So," Dan said. "I'm very pleased that the leaders are both from this team, though I'm going to have to light a fire under the North Shore and South Shore people." I, for one, did not want to see any fires lit. Henrietta was competition enough. Dan continued. "It's going to be lots of fun at the finish line, watching to see who wins." Oh yeah, it was going to be fun. I wished now I hadn't let Stephanie have Benito, but it was too late. Stephanie droned on about her first sale.

"I have an instinct for it, I guess," she said.

I could have kissed Dan when he added, "Jeanie is training Stephanie, so we know she's getting the real deal."

"Thanks, Dan," I said. Stephanie said nothing.

I was anxious to talk to Stephanie, not about coupons, but about the Spotlighters. Nobody knew what was happening with Charlie and whether he was really serious about quitting. Meg was beside herself and had spent Sunday on my minuscule patio eating saltines to keep her weight down, but with an occasional slice of banana cream pie, another gift from the lawsuit ladies. Getting to the bottom of that was on my list for the week, too. That and still trying to jettison the kitten, which was scratching everything in my house with impunity.

"What do you think will happen with Charlie?" I asked Stephanie when the meeting ended.

"I don't know. I suppose Barton will have to play the captain."

"Oh," I said, not relishing the prospect of watching Barton make goo-goo eyes at Laura onstage and off. My adrenaline rush from the speech was wearing off.

Of similar mind, Stephanie said, "He doesn't look good with her, though. She's a frigging giant." Stephanie had never commented on my outburst the other night, and this was either because she had a surprise streak of tact or more likely because she'd completely forgotten it.

Dan approached us. "Is Wednesday okay for your interview with Lou, Jeanie?"

"Sure," I said.

Then he turned to my erstwhile partner. "So I'd say you're ready for your own territory, Stephanie. What do you think?" Stephanie's eyes turned starry and I booked out of there as fast as I could.

"Hi, this is Jeanie at LotsaCoups. I'm looking for new customers. If I can't improve your business with a coupon, I'll cook dinner for you. Leave a message." BEEP.

"Hi, Jeanie. It's Mark at Nashoba Tire. Does this mean I get a free hamburger for that ad we did last year on the windshield wipers? Ha, ha. Change my logo from left to right, will you? Thanks." BEEP.

"Jeanie, it's Harry. I haven't been able to sleep with all these yardsticks. Can I give away a yardstick and a cone?" BEEP.

"Hello. I do enjoy hearing your voice. It's comforting to me, and I know you will be intrigued by my business idea. Very soon I will leave my phone number, but not yet." BEEP.

I finally bought the long-awaited money order on my way home and then spent the afternoon on the phone. I completed ten layouts, faxed them to the plant, and felt competent. I called Dog Daze, I called the karate place, I called the bagel shop, but got nothing in the new category. I was in a drought.

The kitten caught a mouse in my pantry while I

worked. I admit to a bit of screaming when I saw what was going on. I don't like little hairy rodents with tails. The mouse was almost bigger than the kitten and managed to escape, but I decided to keep the little hunter, whom I named Sheena. Mr. Piggy made a helicopter-whirring sound I hadn't heard before, and I chose to interpret it as approval of Sheena. Gramp, wearing his homeless-golfer outfit, was absorbed in some yard project next door, so I didn't disturb him.

Later at rehearsal, I noticed several "mature" women seemed to be on the stage crew now. In fact, Mrs. Mayer went sashaying by me with a stack of music books. She looked different.

"Hey, Mrs. Mayer. So you're doing the show now?"

"Why yes, I am, Jeanie. I'm assistant stage manager, helping out Meg Larson."

"Meg's my best friend."

"That's nice." She walked away and I stared at her. Mrs. Mayer had lost at least ten or twelve pounds since I'd last taken a look at her, and her hair was frosted blond. One of those library books must have had some good material.

Barton lumbered past me to jump up onto the stage. He and I went to great lengths to avoid each other, and I walked well out of my way around him.

"Okay, cast members, here's the story," Barton announced. "It seems our leading man doesn't want to do the show now. He thinks we can replace him without any trouble."

Susie Jenkins looked mortified, as nearly everyone turned to her. "He's in one of his moods. Sometimes he's like that."

"Oh, okay, that's good. It's only a mood. How many rehearsals are we going to miss while he's in his mood? The stage crew and the actors and the costume people and the house manager and the stage manager are in a mood too," Barton said.

Susie shook her head.

Marianne pointed out, "It's not Susie's fault, Barton."

"No, it isn't," Barton said. "But tech week is two weeks away."

"I'll do my best," Susie said.

As I feared, Barton stood in for Charlie and had tremendous chemistry with Laura. The Captain and Maria came to life on our stage. I wanted to puke.

To: Dan Albright
Fr: Jeanie Callahan
Re: Getting Close to the Business
Some of the business owners were absent to-night, so I couldn't sign them up. I will, though.
I will win the contest and be queen of the world. SEND.

Over Stones on Its Way

Wednesday, July 22

"How do you do, Jeanie, it's a pleasure to meet you," Lou Lambaster said as he extended his hand with a warm smile, made even a bit warmer by his enormous teeth. Not surprisingly, he was known behind his back as Bugs, and I prayed I would not call him that during the interview. I would have given him high marks for friendliness if I hadn't been introduced to him at least eight times before. He never had a clue who I was, and if he remembered me after the interview, I'd be shocked.

"Hi, Lou, very nice to see you," I said. Dan beamed in the background. I was no longer so sure that the skids were greased in my favor, but I had a feeling Dan wanted me for the job.

"Why don't we go downstairs and get a coffee or something?" Lou suggested. He whistled all the way down in the elevator to the cafeteria, where I let him buy me a sticky pecan roll. He ordered a big breakfast and told the clerk to put it on the LotsaCoups tab. I wondered if Dan knew.

"So," he said. "I understand you're a top performer here."

"Well, um, yes, I am these days." He raised his eyebrows at me. "Yes, I am a top performer."

"Oh, wait a minute," he said, and pulled out a piece of paper from his pants pocket. "That's the other gal. You're the reliable one, right?"

"Oh, well, did someone say that? Yes, I'm that one, too."

"Ha, ha, ha. Just foolin' with you. Gotta be able to take the heat, Jeanie."

"Yes, that's right."

"What's your vision for the company?" This question filled the air exactly as I bit down on the sticky bun.

"Um, I'd like to help bring LotsaCoups to a premier position in the industry." I reached to wipe off the corners of my mouth and got syrup on the back of my hand.

"Yeah, what else?"

"Well," I said, talking with my mouth full. "The company should always be looking forward."

"Jeanie? Can I be honest?" Lou asked as I took the one meager napkin and tried to clean myself off. "That sounds like a lot of bull honky."

I picked up the plate and watched the roll slide end over end onto the floor.

"You know what? It is, Lou. That's the kind of talk I always hear at meetings."

"Never mind that," he said, indicating the mess on the floor. "What do you mean?"

I told Lou Lambaster my exact opinions on contests, sales meetings, motivational speeches, and mail order. I added in commissions, paperwork, and the lag time between deadlines. He consumed bacon and eggs, hash browns, toast, and coffee while I talked, and then used a toothpick. I left my roll on the floor and I remembered not to call him Bugs.

"Yeah, you got a point there," Lou said.

My face was flushed. I almost expected him to fire me. Instead, he stood up and I followed him out the door to the elevator after indicating to the clerk how sorry I was about the mess we were leaving.

"All right, Dan, let's take a look at your expenses here," Lou said back in the office, and it was fun to watch Dan hop to. "They're a little high, it seems to me." They were undoubtedly a little higher yet after Lou's big order downstairs, but I didn't say anything.

"Okay, then, so is that it?" I asked.

"Yup, we'll letcha know," Lou said. "A pleasure to meet you, Jeanie, and thanks for your honesty." He shook my hand with a fierce grip, and I knew I didn't get the job.

I zigged and zagged across my territory, rounding up previously sold business and looking for more. I replayed the interview again and again in my head. There was a point where I'd had him, I knew it. He'd been mine. And then I went too far. I think he felt insulted. By the end of the day I was calm, knowing I'd done my best and told the truth, even if I did make a mess of the linoleum.

I picked up a *Worcester Tribune* and read the article written about us.

The nuns are a varied bunch, some older, some quite young, some in the middle. They all love to sing, and when I heard them on the stage a bit later, they were very impressive. How nice! There was a picture of the four leads, including Charlie, who looked like a space alien.

I laughed out loud several times as I read, especially where it said director Barton Columbus loved children and considered working with them a specialty of his. *The children playing the von Trapp family are just plain adorable*, the article said, and I wondered if the woman had seen the right ones.

At the end of the afternoon my cell rang, and lo and

behold, it was Dr. Leviathan. "Come back," he said, and I
did. Trying to explain Stephanie's faux pas without criti-
cizing her—a colleague hired by my company, after all—
wasn't easy. "She's a bimbo" seemed unwise. "She has the
brain of a guinea pig" did too. I was pretty good at doing
the dance of death on a pinhead, as Abe called it, but felt
unsure about this one. When I got there, Dr. Leviathan
didn't seem to remember Stephanie, so I didn't mention
her.

"What should I get, about fifty new patients from this?"
My dance had to be saved for my own skin and his expectations. By the time I left, Dr. L was enthusiastically
telling me about a new accounting system he'd invented
that could revolutionize management practice. I nodded
knowingly, watching the clock on the wall tick toward my
release.

Gramp and I had been skipping *Jeopardy!* lately so he
could leave the house early for rehearsal. He had fixed the
staircase, mended the curtain, and replaced some lights,
which he said were dangerously old. I hoped he was getting reimbursed for all of it. It was pretty lonely without
him and I ate my frozen entrée quickly. Sheena had discovered curtains and enjoyed climbing them. I watched
her claw up to the top of the kitchen window, lose her balance, and leap perilously onto the table where I sat.

"You home wrecker!" I said, but laughed. Mr. Piggy
went into one of his frenzied NASCAR circuits around
the cage. These could go on for many minutes, and I felt
perhaps he wanted more attention. Everybody wanted a
piece of me, except for Barton. I remembered to run the
dishwasher.

Cast and crew were buzzing about the newspaper article
when I walked into the auditorium. Several copies were
circulating, and quotes filled the air.

" 'Veteran actress,' " Stephanie said with a frown. "What does that mean? Is she saying I'm old?" No one replied.

The high school girls yipped and howled. "Maybe we could get a band going and be vocalists," one said as ambition began to bloom within their group.

Bill Tuxhorn walked down my row and sat next to me.

"How come you never ask people to advertise with LotsaCoups, Jeanie?"

"I do, Bill. All day long."

"But how come you don't ask any of us? I might be interested."

"Really? That's great."

"I could use some new clients. Could you get that for me? This tactic I've been using this summer isn't really working."

"What tactic is that?"

"I don't know. I guess you could call it trying to get close to the business."

I made an appointment with Bill and felt pretty good about my day. Two more new were now in and my prospects were raised.

I should have known. I should have known. When I looked up from my conference with Bill Tuxhorn, I saw Gramp playing the part of the Captain. People were paying close attention in the audience, primarily to see if he was any good. I didn't blame them.

I raced over to Isabel. "Why isn't Barton playing the role?" I asked.

"He can't be here opening night. He told us from the beginning."

"Oh yes."

"He has an audition in New York. He can't miss that."

"I see." But I didn't really see. What I saw was an eighty-six-year-old man, strong and tough though he may have been, trying to play opposite a college girl. He was tall enough for Laura, but looked more like her ancestor than a romantic possibility.

He wasn't bad, though. The more I watched him the better he seemed. That, I have learned, is the way of theater. The more you see an actor or a scene, the better you think it is. Trouble is, the real audience sees it only once. I like to think of it as self-hypnosis.

During a break, I sat down on the piano bench next to Marianne. Her sausage roll was missing. In fact, she had a new haircut altogether.

"I like your hair, Marianne," I said.

She blushed. "Thank you. It was about time, I'd say."

"Everybody needs to do something shocking now and then, eh?"

"That's exactly what I think," Marianne said. It raced back into my head that Marianne might be planning something even more shocking for opening night. I was pretty sure she wouldn't walk out to conduct naked, but what else might she do? Flash people from the piano bench? Climb every mountain, folks, and a couple of little mountains too. Is that an unmentionable body part sticking out between the French horn and the flute?

"What will you wear on opening night, Marianne?" I asked.

"The orchestra always wears black."

"Oh. That makes sense."

"Though I might be trying something new."

"I see."

"Yes, you'll get an eyeful," Marianne replied, sending a chill down my back. She turned to deal with Truman and his request for a louder cue. Truman was starting to show signs of stage fright, and every night his performance worsened. Marianne spoke comfortingly to him, and I hoped he would be all right. She surely wouldn't ruin the show for him. I caught sight of Marianne's notebook on the piano and fought the urge to steal a peek at it.

Brown Paper Packages

Friday, July 24

A number of packages were stacked by the door of Bill Tuxhorn's office.

"Sorry about that," he said. "Trying to do my own mail-order piece. It costs a goddamn fortune."

"I can help you," I said. First I pitched in on lugging the boxes into the back room. Then I listened for forty-five minutes to his story about how he got into the business. Then I consoled him about his dog that had recently died. When he started telling me about his problems with erectile dysfunction, I said I had to go. He signed my contract like a lamb. Some people are just looking for someone to talk to.

I drove to the office to pick up proofs for my ads that were just starting to come back and also to nose around and see what Henrietta might have turned in. Jailbird Pizza looked great. The artist had used a cute little guy in a striped outfit looking out from behind bars, and I thought Lenny and the boys would like it. Would pizza customers like it? I thought they might. The five-dollar offer would speak louder to them than the artwork, anyway.

"Hey, Magda," I whispered.

"Zhust a minute, Zheenie. Ya? Ya? Naw, you not dickhead. Have a vunderful day."

"Has Henrietta sold any more new?"

"Nope, no way, José."

"Thanks, girlfriend." It didn't really matter whether Henrietta had turned in new sales. She could hold on to them until the last minute and sandbag me, I knew that very well. Harry's Ice Cream looked beautiful, though there were no yardsticks showing. Proofs always look beautiful, and clients always like to see their business names in print. What they like even better than that is their picture. If you can get a client to put his picture on an ad, you will have him for life, unless, of course, you get somebody like Stephanie in there to screw it up for you.

And speaking of Satan herself, Stephanie stood in the middle of the room with a smudged-up layout form and tears in her eyes.

She wasn't technically my responsibility anymore, but I felt a pang of sympathy.

"Steph, is that still Benito's ad? You've got to send it in or you won't get a proof back in time and then you'll really have problems."

"I don't like this typeface. I just don't like it."

"Is the phone number right?"

"Of course."

"Is the address correct?"

"What do you take me for, Jeanie?"

I walked out of the office a bit earlier than I intended, and without checking in with Dan on the status of my job promotion. I realized if I did become sales manager, it would be people like Stephanie who would take most of my attention. A powerful reason to be content with my present status.

* * *

"Okay," Barton said, "listen up! Tonight is an official run-through. No matter what happens, we're running the show—front to back, top to bottom, no stops."

This sounded really professional and good. What it proved to be was chaotic and horrible. Starting with the very first scenes, most of them with us nuns, disorder and disarray reigned. Without Barton guiding our every move, we did a whole lot of standing around and looking quizzically at one another. Meg yelled to us occasionally from the wings which way to go, and Isabel stopped frequently to consult her script.

"No books!" Barton yelled from the darkened audience. A book is a script. Isabel had another bruise on her arm, and I saw her try to cover it up with a long sleeve. Since the temperature in the high school must have been in the high eighties, long sleeves were a suspicious wardrobe choice to start with, and I vowed to pursue this topic, at least with Meg.

"Lights are on in this scene!" Barton yelled again. "Do we understand the meaning of 'on'?" Meg couldn't have liked his tone. I know I didn't. "'On' is sometimes known as the opposite of 'off'!"

The real lighting, from the panel up above, hadn't been planned yet, though Sam Yummy was sitting in the booth reading a manual of some kind. For now there were two choices for lights, on or off, and I knew Meg was doing her best. Tonight she wore a huge balloon of a dress, the front of which hung down almost to her ankles, and I hoped she wouldn't trip.

By the time the nuns were off and the kids were on, everyone was sweating freely. Truman had that deer-in-the-headlights look he'd been nurturing, and stood pretty much by himself in the wings. It was hard to believe this was the same boy who could plot so much trouble else-where. Truman was so unsure of himself now, he was making Jennifer look even better, which probably added to his uncertainty. But even Jennifer seemed tentative and there were times when the only sound heard was the piano.

Barton groaned.

Stephanie carried the day. She crossed and sat and turned just as she always did, without hesitation and without insecurity. She even got a few laughs from Barton and the sparse audience. Gramp, who was allowed a book, did his best, and so did Laura, who had to keep whispering to Gramp where to go. I was worried about him in the extreme heat, and evidently so was Barton, because he asked Tommy to stand in as the Captain during the second act. Tommy read the lines okay, but was far too young and coy for the role. Though I think it hurt Gramp's feelings, he looked relieved to be back in charge of the staircase.

That was another problem. The thing had no trouble rolling now. In fact, it sailed right into the wings with Isabel still on top of it singing. This sent Barton into apoplexy and some of us into a fit of squelched laughter.

The ballroom number, otherwise known as the *Phantom of the Opera* scene, since there were so many imaginary dance partners, went about as badly as it could. What was supposed to be an elegant waltz looked more like a hootenanny or even a religious frenzy, featuring lots of solitary women with their arms up in the air. Barton stayed in the back of the auditorium, pacing and groaning being his primary activities for the evening.

Scene changes were the worst.

"We're reading library books out here!" he yelled as people scurried about. "We're finishing them and starting new ones!"

"Where's the bench?" somebody whispered.

"I just finished *War and Peace!*"

"There's supposed to be a bench in this scene, isn't there?"

"I've always wanted to read *Crime and Punishment!*"

"Get it out there!"

"And now I have time to do it!"

"It goes here," Stephanie said. I could tell the crew member wanted to kill Stephanie, who could easily have hauled the bench out onstage with her.

"Oh God in heaven," Barton moaned. "We're all getting old and dying." Finally the bench was placed onstage and Stephanie kicked it into position. It collapsed and broke.

"Okay, okay, okay," Barton said. "Take five, everybody. I need aspirin, I need Valium, I need heavy drugs."

"Somebody has to fix this bench," Stephanie said.

Not even my grandfather volunteered.

Cast members trailed into Shipley's like displaced persons from a war. Shirley Temples gave way to martinis and Manhattans, and by midnight good humor was restored to the group, even if words were a bit slurred.

Barton and Laura presided as king and queen, and I wondered idly if she would take him home and read Shakespeare to him. I also hoped she liked her zinnias a bit wilted.

There were many candidates for drunkest Shipley's participant that night, including Barton himself, who got quieter and quieter. No jokes, no sarcasm, no snappy retorts. One was Velma, whom I'd never seen drink a drop of alcohol, but tonight she was pounding down draft beers and holding forth on the failings of Velcro.

"You just don't get the same quality as real sewing."

"Tell it, Velma."

"The old ways were the best. Skirts held together and so did belts and sashes."

"You are so right."

"When we did *My Fair Lady*, everybody's pants stayed on."

I doubted that.

Surprisingly, I was not one of the drunken contenders, since I had my hands full worrying about Gramp and his own consumption of vodka and cranberry juice. Marianne once again had his attention, and Mrs. Mayer and the other stagehands had to sit across from the two of them and take crumbs. Even they were nursing drinks.

But the winner was clearly Susie Jenkins, who, by the time the group broke up, could barely stand.

"Don't leave me," she moaned to her janitor friend.

The fellow looked nervous. "Susie, I think you should have some coffee."

"I don't need coffee, darling. I need something else."

The young man no longer seemed so eager to huddle with Susie, and in fact looked plenty ready to get out the door.

"I'll take care of her," I said to the guy. "Go ahead." He vamoosed and Susie started to cry.

"I need, um, what is his name? I need him. Where did he go?"

"Susie, I'm taking you home. You can leave your car here and pick it up tomorrow."

"Oh no. Charlie won't like that."

"Well then, do you want to call Charlie to come get you?"

"No, I can't do that either."

I eventually convinced Susie to get in my car, no easy project on any occasion. She insisted on getting in the backseat with all my papers and files, not to mention bags of cat food and a scratching post.

Every time we went over a bump, she moaned, "Oh, what is his name?" Once she lifted her head and said in a clear voice, "I have perfect double vision."

"Oh. Well, that's good, I guess," I said. My potential list of replies seemed limited.

Somehow, Susie guided me to her house in Boylston, and I was shocked at its grand aspect; it lay up a huge, twisting driveway that must have been hell to negotiate in the wintertime. The house was old, antique, like something straight from an Edgar Allan Poe story. I couldn't see

any near neighbors. I pictured Susie and me getting murdered by Charlie and no one finding us until spring. I
opened the front door, which, of course, creaked like one
in a haunted house.

"Hello?" I called. "Charlie?"

The ceilings were high, really high, and I forced myself
to think of heating costs instead of chain-saw massacres. I
had to wind my way down several hallways to find Charlie,
who was seated in front of a huge television screen. I was
comforted to see that he was watching a talk show, and
not *The Shining*.

He jumped when he saw me. "What is it?"

"It's Susie, Charlie. She's under the weather. I brought
her home."

"Under the weather? You mean drunk?"

"Um, well, sort of."

He followed me back outside and we managed to drag
Susie out of the car, into the house, and up the stairs. I felt
truly embarrassed every time she moaned, "I need maintenance." It seemed so true.

"In here," Charlie said. We got her into a bedroom and
tossed her onto a child's twin bed. To my eye, it didn't look
like the master bedroom. I found an afghan at the bottom
of the bed and covered Susie with it so she could die of a
hangover and not pneumonia. Charlie took off her shoes
in a surprisingly tender way, and placed them neatly together on the floor. We walked back down the stairs and
stood by the front door. I noticed Charlie's hair was sticking up in some odd places. Captain von Trapp on crack.
That, I think, is what they call high concept.

"Thanks," he said. "That was a long drive for you."

"No problem," I answered.

"Is everyone talking about me?" he asked.

I didn't say anything.

"Yeah, that's what I thought. I'm doing all of you a favor."

"A favor?"

"It'll be a favor if the show has to be canceled."

"I don't think I agree with that, Charlie. And it's not going to be canceled."

"You want a beer?"

"Well, okay." I followed him down the hallway maze, this time coming out in the kitchen, where he retrieved two beers from the fridge. He sat at the kitchen table and so did I. The clock said 1:48 and I hoped Gramp was home.

"Don't you see how pitiful the show is?" Charlie continued.

"I wouldn't call it pitiful. Some parts of it are really good."

"Yeah, and some parts are pitiful."

I sighed. "Why did you audition for it?"

"I didn't want to. I did it for Susie. She begged me."

"Still, you didn't have to."

"She said it might save our marriage."

"Oh."

"I grew up in this house, you know."

"Wow, it's very beautiful."

"Barton thinks he knows everything, but in fact he knows very little."

"He knows about theater, though, I think."

Charlie leaned back in his chair and crossed his legs. He wore sweatpants and a faded Red Sox T-shirt.

"Barton makes doughnuts at Honeydew," Charlie said.

"Yeah? So?"

"You of all people should see his flaws," Charlie said.

I felt a blush try to make its way up my throat. "I do see his flaws. But . . ." I moved my mouth and swallowed a few times and couldn't manage anything more.

Charlie sneered. "Wait. Wait here. I'll be right back." He jumped up out of his seat and left the room. I looked around at the stainless-steel decor and compared it to Isabel's charming and colorful kitchen. I didn't see any personality in this one.

He was gone for a long time. My contacts were bothering me, and I was thinking I could sneak out when he walked back in and handed me a high school yearbook, just what I needed at two in the morning. "Look on page fifty-four," he said.

I leafed through the pages until I found it, the Brookline High School Drama Club's presentation of *The Sound of Music*. By my quick calculations, Charlie was around forty, younger than he looked.

"Is this you?" I asked, referring to the gangly kid in the back row.

"My brother. He played the Captain."

"Oh my God. Is this Susie? Was she Maria?"

Charlie nodded.

"And where are you?"

"I wouldn't have anything to do with it. It was drivel, just like this show. My brother broke both legs on opening night."

"Oh my God."

"Car accident. Drinking and driving. All those high school girls you hang around with ought to know about it."

I finished my beer and switched to raspberry seltzer. This didn't seem an appropriate story to drink to. I clenched the muscles in my legs and appreciated them. I couldn't just walk out on Charlie, who seemed to have worse problems than I did. I considered asking him a lot of questions, such as, *Why don't you have any children?* and other private things like that, but held back. He and Susie could easily visit Liechtenstein anytime they wanted. I browsed through some of the other pages in the book and found Charlie's picture in the Chess Club.

"Here you are. Charlie, you're not afraid that you're going to break your legs on opening night, are you?"

"Of course not. The show is terrible. I don't want to add my terribleness to it."

"It's worse without you, Charlie."

"Oh really? Who is playing my part?"

"My grandfather, for one. Tommy Cuthbert sometimes."

Charlie made a face. "Tommy Cuthbert? You've got to be kidding."

"Charlie, listen to me," I said. "You owe it to everybody to come back. You especially owe it to your wife, who is struggling."

"She doesn't care," Charlie said.

"I think she does."

I managed to make my exit while Charlie thought this over.

I pulled up to him in the driveway for a parting shot: "Charlie. If you were one of my clients, I'd tell you you were a fabulous Captain and inspiring and handsome and all kinds of bullshit. But I'm just going to say this. You're not the worst. Okay? You're not the worst who ever played the part. Think about it, Charlie. Please think about it."

A Name I Call Myself

Saturday, July 25

"You stooge," I said to the mirror. "You complete and utter stooge."

The word did not begin to describe the depths of my moral depravity. On the other side of the bathroom door sat Barton in his mismatched Hawaiian ensemble, holding a bouquet of grocery-store roses. If I could have gone out the window, I would have.

Barton leaped up as I walked out of the bathroom, not from courtesy but from the shock of Sheena landing claws-first on his neck from an unknown launching spot.

"Yow!" he yelled. "How many animals do you have now?"

"Just two. That's the end. No more are allowed in."

"Is there one in here?" Barton asked, looking down at Mr. Piggy's cage.

"He likes to hide in the toilet paper roll before he eats it."

Barton shifted his weight. "So do you want to go out for dinner?" he asked.

"Barton," I said. "Do you have ears? Were you listening

the other night?" I now heard the front door open and the familiar, "Yoo-hoo," from Mrs. Mayer. She had the gift of endless nerve and I the curse of endless bad timing.

"Hi, it's me! All ready to answer your questions, dear. Oh, hi, there, Barton. How are you?"

"So what's with the lawsuit, Mrs. Mayer? Why don't you tell me right now?"

"I'd rather do it in private, dear."

I sighed in exasperation. Mrs. Mayer wore spandex from head to toe and held a bicycle helmet.

"Well, when?"

Mrs. Mayer looked at Barton, who looked right back at her.

"Would you two like to come over for dinner later? Your grandfather is coming, and some of my friends."

"That sounds good," Barton said.

"It doesn't sound good to me, though," I said, my courage making a late entrance. "As far as I'm concerned, Barton, you're not invited. And if you're going, I'm not."

"But I really wanted to see you tonight, Jeanie. I've had a change of heart."

"You are unbelievable," I said. "For your information, I have another date tonight. I'll be bringing someone else to your party, Mrs. Mayer, if that's okay." Mrs. Mayer stood dumbstruck. "So I'd appreciate if you would take your flowers and go, Barton. Does that make sense, or should I try saying it in another language? I've got dictionaries here somewhere."

Mrs. Mayer came to life and began talking to Barton about props in the show as she propelled him out the door. I went to my sales notebook to look up Lenny's number.

I dressed for Mrs. Mayer's party in my air-conditioned bedroom, last year's birthday present from Gramp. The heat wave was taking its toll on my hair, which even after shampoo, styling gel, and a flatiron, was frizzing up like vegetative growth in the jungle.

Lenny rang my doorbell precisely when he said he would. In the end, I'd felt shy about blatantly asking him to be my date, so I said it was something about the coupon. Okay, so I said it was an emergency about the coupon.

"What is it?" he said with a worried look. I should have remembered his kind of emergencies could be pretty serious.

"Oh, um, the plant just wanted to know if . . . if you wanted maroon. Well, I know you do, but I didn't know if you wanted something, um, younger or edgier. So to speak."

Lenny moved in very close to me, and I got to experience the same extreme scrutiny his cons did. For me, it was not unpleasant. His eyes were the piercing blue of a Siberian husky's. "We want whatever maroon you pick for us, Jeanie."

"Oh, well, that's good," I said. "And do you want to go across the street to a party with me?" He relaxed then and smiled. He paid attention to my two pets, and they seemed to like him. I could tell because Mr. Piggy started twitching his rear end and turning in circles. Sheena attached herself to Lenny's shoelaces and had to be forcibly removed when it was time to go. I frankly hoped I wouldn't be doing the same kinds of things.

I felt exhilarated, bathed in truth and righteousness. I fluffed out my frizz as far as it would go and dabbed on a bit more lip gloss to sustain me on the walk across the street. I gave Lenny some background info and we watched Gramp walking over to Mrs. Mayer's ahead of us, decked out in an orange leisure suit from the seventies. Elvis was about to enter the building.

Lenny picked up one of the Steuben squirrels on our way out and said, "Nice squirrel." I nearly fainted.

*   *   *

Lenny didn't stay long at the party. We were barely in the door when the television news, which old people always have to watch with the volume way up, started showing an attempted bank robbery at a Shrewsbury savings and loan. Lenny said, "Oh, shit," and got up to leave. Several of the oldsters became alarmed.

"Geez, I've got money in that bank. Should we all go down there?"

"No, no," Lenny said. "Stay where you are. I just have to check out a couple of clients." I explained to the group that Lenny worked with the courts and the police.

"I think that's very exciting," one of the ladies said. "Is it like CSI?"

"No. It's nothing like CSI," Lenny said, trying to get out the door.

"I'd like to get one of those big flashlights like they have on CSI."

"No flashlights in my job," Lenny said with a smile, and thanked Mrs. Mayer for having him. Many of the ladies followed him to the door and shook his hand, and then many gentlemen did too, all thanking him for serving the community. The entire group followed him out to the front porch and all the way down the lawn to the street.

"If you need help," my grandfather called to him, "I have tire tools and a generator."

"Okay, thanks. If I need them, I'll call." Lenny waved his hand and the whole group waved back. It was like the finale in a show, Huck going off to the western territories or a young idealist leaving for the New World. I walked with Lenny across the street to my driveway, where he got into his car.

"I feel like a war hero," he said.

"You are," I said.

"I'd ask you to come with me, but it probably wouldn't be very fun," he said.

"Even though I could run the generator."

"That's true."

"Well, next time," I said.

"Yes. Definitely next time."

Lenny drove off and I floated back across to Mrs. Mayer's house and eventually remembered why I was really there.

"I don't think I get it," I said to Mrs. Mayer. She and I were whispering in the corner of her kitchen, a cute remodeled affair, not unlike her own body.

"The book said to try to find a way to do business with the man of your choice."

"Okay, yes, I get that."

"So Rita and I and the others all liked these certain lawyers."

"Coincidentally?"

"God works in mysterious ways, dear," Mrs. Mayer said, and then left me to fulfill her bartending responsibilities. Many old-fashioned dishes were on display, including Jell-O salad with cucumbers floating in it, Velveeta cheese dip, and a sausage appetizer called Jimmy Dean's Balls.

I followed my hostess onto her enclosed back porch. "Okay, so all of you went goo-goo over various lawyers at the same time. I'm with you."

"Yes, and here's one right now. Al Shorenstein, please meet Jeanie Callahan." A silver-haired gentleman shook my hand and almost started to kiss it until I grabbed it back. I was forced to make small talk for several minutes while I waited to get Mrs. Mayer alone again.

I finally did. "So you all decided to sue my grandfather?"

"Yes, we picked one person because it would be so much more efficient," she said. "We all brought little trivial lawsuits against him, which he didn't mind because he knew we would withdraw them."

"Just so you could sit across a desk from a lawyer you liked and wear extra lipstick."

"I need more than lipstick, Jeanie."

"But these lawyers let you do that? They're willing to have their time wasted on stupid lawsuits?"

"We didn't announce they were stupid. And the lawyers didn't know we were going to withdraw them."

"I just can't believe it."

"Lawyers like money, Jeanie. Don't ever forget that."

Attorney Shorenstein jumped in. "Uh-oh, are you maligning my profession, Gert?"

"Not at all, Al, I'm delighting in it," Mrs. Mayer said. My own head was spinning.

"So did it work?" I whispered.

"It sure did," she whispered back to me with a smile that made her look teenaged. "Rita's going out with Nicky Vulgarapoulos and two of the other girls have had dates as well. My own results are still pending," she said with a flush. As if I couldn't figure that one out.

"Didn't you have to pay for the lawsuit?"

"Yes, but it wasn't as much as some of the really secure and discreet dating services."

"Oh," I said, thinking of the one I had used.

I chowed down on the cheese dip, then enjoyed a thick burger off the grill, made by my grandfather. These people may have been a little cuckoo, but they knew how to eat. I finished the evening by explaining direct mail to Al Shorenstein in excruciating detail. He sat closer and closer, and I left before anyone could sue me.

Voices That Urge Me to Stay

Tuesday, July 28

"Hi, this is Jeanie Callahan. If you are the person who has been calling me about a new business, but hasn't left your number yet, today's the day to do it. The deadline is going to run out this Friday, and then it will be too late to get into our next mailing. Do it." BEEP.

"Hey there, Jeanie. This is Al Shorenstein. I met you at Gert Mayer's the other night. I know I'm a little older than you, but I thought you might have dinner with me anyway. We could talk about coupons." BEEP.

"Hi, Zheenie, big-time psychopath on phone for you. 555-8997 and de name is Zhon somebody. You and Henrietta in tie again. What obsessive she is." BEEP.

Abe and I both ordered mai tais. I felt really pressed for time, but Abe seemed luxuriantly at ease.

"Let's get some decent food here today. I'm buying," he said.

"What's indecent about the free buffet?" I asked.

"Aw, let's live large for a change. I can afford it."

"You can?"

Abe shifted in his chair. "Would you believe ten thousand big ones in blackjack yesterday? And another eight grand the day before?"

I sputtered. "Are you kidding?"

"No, my child, I am not kidding. Order what you want."

We selected a number of expensive appetizers along with a lobster dish and three other grand menu items. Rick the waiter asked us if we were expecting more people, but we just laughed and said no.

"Mmmm, thanks, pard," I said, digging in. "So what about your coupon responsibilities?"

"I'm just about to leave those behind, Jeanie Beanie."

"Argh," I choked. "Don't call me that."

Abe scrutinized me, both of us with full mouths, and I shook my head. "Don't ask."

"I figure if I can take away ten to fifteen grand every month, I won't even have to go to the casino most days. I'll just stop in when I need money."

"Abe, this doesn't seem wise."

"It is wise, Jeanie. I hate coupons. In fact, you can have the two new sales I did get. My brother is hassling me about better results for Baldwin Springs, so that gravy train might be over soon anyway."

A recording of a trumpet call to arms got played over the speakers. We looked up to see what was going on and were shocked to find it was the introduction to the General's Imperial Duck or whatever it was we had ordered. A red plastic carpet was thrown down from the kitchen through the bar to our table, to the delight and confusion of patrons on all sides of us.

Rick and two cohorts served us. "First time for Imperial Duck this year," Rick said.

"Great," we said.

Half an hour later, I put my fork down. "My body will not accept further nutrients."

"So do you want to give me some money to take?" Abe asked.

"Okay, sure, I will." I retrieved my purse and wrote out a check for two hundred dollars to Abe. If he really were on a blackjack roll, I'd win. If he went bust, it would pay him around about what the commissions were from the sales he was giving me.

"How's your show going?" Abe asked as I wrote.

"It's pretty horrible. The lead guy walked out."

"Did you ever get any sales from it?"

"Yeah, one. That's it. It's plumbed."

"How about the young sluts?"

"I told you, they're not sluts. We need men desperately, if you're interested."

"I'm too busy for that. I can't sing anyway."

"At this point, I think your little wee-wee alone will qualify you."

"Hey. Who says it's little?"

We got Rick to wrap up all the leftovers. We looked as though we'd been to Hannaford's for a weekly shopping trip as we walked out the door.

Later, as I sat in intense discomfort and watched *Jeopardy!* with Gramp, I sifted through my stack of proofs and scheduled my zigging and zagging for the next day.

"So are all the lawsuits canceled?" I asked.

"Yup. According to Gert." Gramp was just cooling down from his StairMaster regimen. "Jonathan Swift's 'A Modest Proposal'!" he yelled.

"Hmm," I said, and wondered if it would be worthwhile to call this Shorenstein guy. What could he offer, a free will and testament? I felt pretty sure he was not interested in direct mail. But the pressure from Henrietta was intense. I wondered whether she had the same feeling about me. I went into the kitchen with my cell and called the psychopath.

"Yallow!"

"Hi, this is Jeanie Callahan from LotsaCoups."

"Oh yeah, hi. *Shut up!*"

"I think you called our office."

"*I said shut up, or I'll knock your head off!*"

"Sir?"

"Yeah, that's right. My niece is almost dead and has worked a few miracles I can tell you about. She is definitely going to be canonized a saint. I'm sure there's a way to make some money on it and I figured I'd give you guys a call."

"Oh. Actually, well, hmm."

"*Don't make me come in there!* Do you want to come over here?"

"Um, no, I don't."

I hung up the phone. I called the distasteful Al Shorenstein and left a message. He would undoubtedly be thrilled.

I vowed to blitz all my towns in the next three days. If they weren't obvious scams or mail order, I would take them. And maybe I would think over the mail-order taboo.

"The bell tolls for thee!" Gramp yelled.

Happy to Greet Me

Friday, July 31

I finished my blitz at three P.M., walked into Isabel's shop, and flopped down on a chair. The store was comfy and had plenty of opportunities for flopping and relaxing. I had managed to sign one more new, another beauty shop that I prayed to God would be open by the time the coupon got mailed.

"This place looks fantastic," I said. Quick Study Photo Developing was opening the next day, and there were balloons and flowers everywhere, including the bouquet I had sent. Tommy Cuthbert was placing the different arrangements around the store, I suppose tastefully, but I was so tired I couldn't really tell.

"Thank you so much for the flowers," Isabel said. "And are you going to win the contest?"

"Your guess is as good as mine."

"You know you're going to win," Tommy said.

"But today's the last day, right?" Isabel asked.

"It's the last day for a proofed ad. I can still sell one, though, if somebody doesn't need to see a proof."

My buddies had helped me out during the blitz, and in fact the new beauty shop owner was a friend of Tommy's. With the two from Abe, it brought me up to twenty-six.

"Anything new on the show?"

"No. Barton is having a stroke every half hour. Good thing I have caller ID. There he is now."

The phone behind the counter rang a few times and then cut off. Meg walked in the door with a huge spray of roses and daisies, which got exclaimed over, and then she pulled out a bottle of champagne, which also got exclaimed over with even more enthusiasm.

"I can't have any, but you guys can," she said. Meg wore another beautiful maternity top that was mini-length in back and almost to her ankles in front.

"Uh-oh," I said. "I just realized Mort didn't call me today. Is he there?" I peered out Quick Study's window and saw Mort peering back. The champagne made me strike a sexy pose and blow him a kiss. Mort took a step backward and walked away. I wondered if he thought I was Isabel. Friday zest got the better of me.

"Can I use your fax?" I asked Isabel, and quickly dashed off a layout for the beauty shop. I was hoping to take a couple of days off soon.

The phone rang again and Isabel snatched the receiver up to her ear.

"Yes, Barton. What is it?"

She stood there nodding her head. "Yeah. Okay, yeah." Then she sighed. "Oh, all right. Yeah, I'll take care of it."

She put the phone down and told us, "Barton only wants the kids there tonight, so I get to call everybody else and tell them not to show up."

"We'll help you, Isabel," I said. Tommy, Meg, and I pulled out our cells and left messages with everyone in the cast. It took only ten minutes.

"So here we are with an unexpected night off. We should all go home and get some sleep," I suggested like the perfect Girl Scout.

"Nah," the group said.

We eventually took proofs, layouts, champagne, and other bits of our lives to Isabel's house for the evening. Isabel threw together something delicious for us, and I was glad to have it, since I'd been getting a bit weary of Imperial Duck. Despite saying we wouldn't, Meg and I borrowed Isabel's bathing suits again and relaxed poolside in the heat and humidity. I lowered myself into the deep end and held on to the pool's cement border.

"Who would we most like to kill in the cast?" I asked.

"The kids," said Meg at the same time Isabel said, "Jennifer."

"Let's not forget Charlie. He's deserving of death, I'd say."

"Or Helen," said Tommy. "Although I'd have to go with Jennifer, I think."

Large noises emanated from the back door, as though someone were throwing dishes on the floor. Isabel took a deep breath, rose, and went into the house. Shortly after we could hear Clarissa yelling.

"Why don't you shut the fuck up?" resounded very clearly into the night air. The girl had problems, we agreed.

"Can we kill her too?" I asked.

Isabel's soft voice was heard, and then Clarissa's again. "Yes! I'm telling you, I will!" Meg and I and Tommy looked at each other as the argument seemed to escalate. Isabel cried out and we looked disbelievingly at the back door, where she stumbled outside, quite obviously having been shoved.

"You are such an incredible whore!" we heard Clarissa yell as Isabel came toward us with a brand-new red mark on her arm.

I pulled myself out of the pool and stood near her.

"Isabel. It's Clarissa, isn't it? She's the one who hits you."
She said nothing.

"It is. I know it is. I thought it was your husband."

"What about him?" Meg asked. "Have you told your husband?"

"It's complicated," Isabel said. "Like I told you before. And I can't tell Ray about it. I just can't."

I put my hands on my hips. "Isabel, why on earth not? I mean, I know it's not my business, but this is ridiculous. If Clarissa is hitting you and abusing you and hates you, her father should know about it. I can't believe he hasn't noticed already."

"I can't bring Ray into it."

Tommy said in a quiet voice, "Go ahead and tell them, Isabel."

Isabel took a deep breath. "Clarissa saw me with Sam. She's understandably enraged by it. I don't blame her."

"Oh wow," I said. "That is complicated."

"She doesn't care a fig," Tommy said. "She just wants cash."

Isabel went on. "And now"—she stopped for another breath—"she's saying I have to pay her two hundred dollars a week to keep her quiet. I don't think she means it, though."

"Oh," Tommy said. "She definitely means it. Money is the one thing she really means."

We sat silently.

"She says she'll tell her dad about Sam if I don't. Listen, let's just forget it, okay?"

We all sat in a line with our feet dangling in the water.

"It's blackmail. She's blackmailing you," I said. "Pure and simple."

"What does Sam say?" Meg asked.

"Sam wants to kill Clarissa."

"So do I," Tommy said.

"I should leave Ray, and I'm planning to, if I can get the photo shop to be successful."

We took this information in.

"It will be," Tommy said. "I'm going to start taking pictures so you can develop them."

"Yeah, I'd hate to see those," I said. He poked me in the side and I poked him back.

"That at least sounds like a plan," Meg said. "Although you'd have to give all this up."

"Yes, I will have to," Isabel said, looking around at the house and acreage. "It's not worth everything, though, Meg."

I scared everybody when I jumped into the water with a big splash.

Fellows I Meet May Tell Me I'm Sweet

Saturday, August 1

"So tell me about yourself," Al Shorenstein said. I'd agreed to meet him mainly because I am always and forever a prisoner of hope. If he would buy an ad, it would be worth it. I knew this was going to be a britches account, but the big prize was leading me off my normal path.

"Nothing much to tell. I started off at—"

"I was Phi Beta Kappa my junior year at Cornell," Al said.

"I passed Chemistry at East High," I replied.

"I was a Sig Tau."

"I was a Virgo."

"What?"

"I still am a Virgo. My grandfather is too."

"Your grandfather is a great guy."

"Thanks. So, Al, if you were to advertise with us—"

"How do you like selling for a living?"

This kind of dueling interview went on all through the dinner, which I must admit was way out of my league. I met him at the Fish House in Worcester, and the check was in the vicinity of my mortgage payment.

"Sir, will this wine be satisfactory?" the waiter said.

"Mmm, no, try to find a ninety-two if you can," Al said.

I considered telling Al that my vintage requirements are on the low side, as in off the shelf or rotgut, take your choice, but he was having such a good time showing off that I kept my mouth shut.

"I was editor of the *Law Review*," Al said after we had finally deigned to accept a three-hundred-dollar bottle of wine and were sipping it. I sniffed it first just to be polite. Abe always sniffs wine or beer and says things like "impudent but amusing," so I said it.

"Impudent but amusing."

"You know, you're right. I have half a mind to send it back."

"No, Al! I was kidding again. Listen—"

"Having dinner with a beautiful woman demands good wine. I love your earrings."

"Thanks. So—"

"How is your tilapia?"

"It's divine." I wasn't sure which thing on my plate was the tilapia, but I think it was the fish, and my answer was correct in any event, because everything tasted heavenly. We went on to have chocolate panna cotta with port-and-balsamic-glazed cherries, whatever that is. The menu told us it would be a flavorful and elegant end to a summer meal, and it was, even if I wasn't sure what I was eating.

After dinner we took up residence in the bar, and though I was horribly full, I ordered a cosmopolitan, thinking it would settle my stomach. It came in a martini glass with a crooked stem, and after a while I had to concentrate very hard to pick it up in the right place.

"Al, you're making me feel guilty. I consider this a sales call, you know."

"It is, it is. Tell me about the coupons."

"But I already did the other night, remember?"

"Tell me again."

"Well," I began, and reached for the twisty stem of my drink. "The concept is very simple."

"Okay, that's enough. I'll buy one."

"You will? But you haven't heard anything."

"That's okay. I trust you." I noticed Al had one of those accrued tans you see on magazine models and disgraced CEOs. Unfortunately, he also had the middle-aged gray ponytail—if only men knew how loathsome those are— and a giant diamond pinkie ring. As Meg would say, ew.

"I won't be able to show you a proof."

"That's okay. I don't even know what a proof is."

"That seems truly remarkable, Al."

As we ended the evening in the parking lot, Al kept trying to whisper in my ear, and I kept trying to move. I found a contract in my front seat and got him to sign it. I even made him write a check, no matter what people might think as they walked by us.

"So what do you want to put on your ad?"

"I don't care. Anything you want."

"Half-hour free consultation?"

"Jesus, Jeanie, I can't give my work away for free."

Now I was on familiar ground. We worked our way all around the car as I explained to him the things I should have explained inside the restaurant. I finally agreed merely to put his name, address, and phone number on the ad along with his photograph, which sealed the deal.

"We'll have to meet again so you can get the photo."

"Okay, Al. Thank you for dinner. I've got to go now be- cause my brake-fluid level is low."

*   *   *

"Hi, this is the voice mail of Jeanie Callahan. This message is for the person with the revolutionary new idea. I want to be part of it. I can help you bring it to the world. I will be waiting for you at the Tatnuck Square McDonald's in Worcester, tomorrow, Sunday, August second. I will be holding a LotsaCoups envelope and sitting near the men's room. No, wait, I'll be near the ladies' room. Okay? I hope you can make it. If this is someone else, please leave a message and forgive the interruption. Have a good day." BEEP.

"Hey, Jeanie, it's Stephanie Wilson from LotsaCoups. What was that all about? I finally finished Benito's ad, but the plant says they can't give me a proof on it. What should I do?" BEEP.

"Abe the player here. I don't know what you're up to now, but it sounds good. I've had a little setback, but it's fine. I still have money and confidence. I have confidence in confidence alone, tra-la. Good luck with your technical week, whatever." BEEP.

And Willingly I Believe

Sunday, August 2

The first thing I saw when I walked into McDonald's was Abe, and it did not give me a good feeling.

"Well, you're certainly unshaven," I said as I took my place next to the ladies' room. He was communing with a large coffee.

"Yeah," he said.

"I could grocery shop with the bags under your eyes."

He sighed.

"I don't think you're here to pay off on my investment, are you?"

"Oh Jeanie. It's been a really bad twenty-four hours. Do you know how much money you can lose in just one day?"

"No, I don't, but I'm sure it's a number approaching infinity."

Abe's eyes filled with tears.

"That's okay, Abie. I'm sorry. Don't worry about the two hundred." Then I realized what he wanted.

"Oh, you want those two sales back, don't you?"

"I know I can use those commissions to stake myself again. If you could give me another two hundred, Jeanie, I could double it. I've figured out what I was doing wrong."

At that moment, the revolutionary guy walked into McDonald's. I know my destiny when I see it. Standing in at three hundred pounds plus, he wore thick glasses and carried a briefcase. I watched him stop at the counter to buy a sack of food as I tried to lead Abe back on the straight and somewhat narrow.

"Abe, I don't really have two hundred bucks to spare right now. But go ahead and take those two accounts back. I'm sure they'll be happy to see you. In fact, here are their proofs, which I did for you." I handed him the two proofs and tried to pretend I didn't care about losing two new sales and going down to twenty-five in the count.

"Are you Jeanie?" Revolutionary Guy asked.

"Yes, hello," I said with my brightest, shallowest smile.

He answered with his own smile, which revealed two rows of tree stumps.

"I like the way you set this meeting up. I'm into puzzles and games."

"Oh me too," I gushed.

"So what are the prices?" The guy got right to it, and I appreciated that. It isn't smart to spend a lot of time selling if you haven't qualified the prospect, but I did it anyway because I wanted the sale so badly. I hoped and prayed this wasn't a wild-goose chase.

"This is my colleague Abe McNamara. He specializes in financial activity, risky business, you might say. That's not what you have, though, is it?"

"No, indeed," Revolutionary said. "In fact, I'd rather not say it out loud, if you don't mind. There are ears everywhere."

"Fine with me," I said. I didn't really think the young family next to us with the screaming baby were corporate spies, but you never know. My potential client pushed over some kind of press release. I read only the first line.

UNDERWATER MINIATURE GOLF—CALL TODAY

I pushed the paper in front of Abe and let him read it too. He immediately excused himself for the restroom.

"Think about it," said Revolutionary, his eyes magnified to triple their size behind his spectacles.

"Mmmm, yes."

"No one has ever done this before," he said. He reached into the food sack and started to munch on some fries.

"You know something, though?" I said. "I think you'd be better off with television. You'd reach more people. You don't really need a targeted approach."

"I don't?"

"No. And you know what else? I have another appointment at Elsa's down the road, so I'm going to have to fly."

"You mean you're not going to sell me?"

"Not today, sir, though I would love to. Take care."

The wild goose was flapping its wings for takeoff when I got to my car. I couldn't look back because I'd feel too sorry for the guy. Such is my curse.

I stood dumbfounded when Abe showed up at the high school ten minutes after I did and told me what he'd done.

"You what?"

"Hey, it's a lemming sale. He's determined to do it, so I might as well benefit."

"Oh, Abe. I can't believe you would take a sale like that. What are you doing here anyway?"

"It's Sunday. Is it okay if I watch a little before I head back down to the casino?" I knew he wanted to see the girls.

"Sure. Come on in."

I introduced Abe to Meg, who had actually met him before at some shindig at my house. The weather continued to be hot, and she wore another dress of the voluminous variety, which made Abe compliment her on her condition. He then whispered to me that he was the real father of Meg's child, and I knew he was feeling better. I sat him down in the auditorium and told him we were running the show twice today, so it would be a long one.

"Don't worry about me. I'll take off if I get bored. No sales meeting tomorrow 'cause of the deadline; that's one good thing."

"Oh, right. Thank God."

An hour later, Abe was onstage and reading the part of the Captain. I felt embarrassed. The first run-through had been delayed because Barton was trying to make a final decision on the role. Abe had spirit, but was too young by far, not to mention about six inches shorter than Laura. When he jumped off the stage, Bill Tuxhorn took his place. God bless Billy, who developed an unexpected stammer as he stood there. Probably just looking at Laura set off his erectile dysfunction, though I wasn't entirely sure how that worked, since I hadn't stuck around for the details. Finally, Sam Yummy stood in and gave the whole thing a hillbilly treatment.

"Well hello there, Miss Maria."

In the midst of this muddle, another one was shaping up in the back of the auditorium.

Truman wanted to quit. First he stood alone with Meg, who tried to put her arm around his shoulders and exert her family influence. That didn't work at all. Then Sam sauntered up and spoke to him, but that didn't do any good either. Finally the boy shook Meg off, grabbed his board, and started for the door. Meg cried out, and a group of people moved to the back of the auditorium to block his way. Barton had to stop the rehearsal.

"Truman," Barton said. "You're going into high school this fall, aren't you? This is a question of maturity."

Truman didn't care.

"Do you want to be known as immature?"

Truman did.

"You'll never get another part, you know."

That was fine with Truman.

Isabel jumped in. "Truman, you're going to feel a lot better when you're wearing the costume and actually standing on the stage."

"No, I'm not," Truman said.

Marianne tried. "You don't have to sing, Truman. Just talk the song."

"That would be stupid," Truman said.

Jennifer piped up. "No, Truman, you're the one who's stupid."

"Don't call me stupid! You're a fucking bitch and everybody knows it!" Truman cried, and had to be restrained from going after Jennifer. Barton held on to both of the boy's arms from the back. Truman, in his customary heavymetal T-shirt, struggled and sniffed and started to cry.

Jennifer ran to the front row, where her mother folded her in her arms and they both dissolved in tears. Meg walked down the aisle to do the dance of death on a pinhead with the two of them, joined shortly by Tommy, who knelt next to Jennifer and said God knew what. It reminded me of dealing with clients. Say what you have to; just get them to do what you want.

"Don't quit, Truman," a voice said. "No one should quit."

It was Charlie.

He and Susie stood together near the door. People either gasped or glared, and some did both.

"I owe everybody here an apology. Barton is right. It was immature and stupid and I'm very sorry, and I hope you'll have me back."

It was quiet for a long time. Truman broke free of Barton's grasp and stood like a rodeo calf newly sprung, shifting and twitching his weight around but not leaving. He looked at Charlie and then looked down at the floor. Jennifer and her mother stopped crying. There was a lot of sniffing.

Everyone looked to Barton for the verdict. "Well, okay, we'll have you back, Charlie." This seemed to me an understatement of large proportion. Everyone relaxed slightly, and Barton continued. "We're running late, so let's get going. Places, everybody."

Charlie put his arm around Truman. "Okay, Truman?"

Truman nodded.

The two of them headed off down the aisle, where Truman and Jennifer apologized to each other in the way that kids do, with no eye contact and very little sincerity, because they were being made to. Susie joined her chorus friends, including me. She seemed to have a special smile on her face, I thought.

"Are you taking off?" I asked Abe, whose eyes were locked on one of the young nuns in a bathing suit.

"Hell, no," he said.

It was a day for surprise entrances. Just before the opening chord I ducked out into the lobby for a drink of water, and saw Lenny Sadowski with six of the jailbirds.

"Oh, my God, what are you guys doing here?" I asked, stunned.

"We came to help you out," Moey said. I had a feeling his sport shirt came from Benito's.

Lenny explained. "You said your show desperately needed men. Here they are. Desperate men for desperate times. Just kidding, guys."

"Yeah, watch it, Lenny."

"I suggested that being in a show might be a good activity for this week. Keep us busy and happy while we plan for our opening."

"Yeah, he don't want us getting in no trouble, that's really it."

"Come on, Ziggy, it's going to be fun."

"That's fantastic," I said, and ushered them into the auditorium, introducing them to Barton, whose annoyance at another delay was greatly outweighed by his glee at getting seven men.

"Just sit here and wait for the ballroom scene, okay? I'll tell you what to do when we get there." He turned to Abe, who sat like a theater critic in the middle of the house. "Sir? Do you want to be in the ballroom scene too?"

"Okay," Abe said. "Sure."

By the time we got to the scene, Vic had rolled in, literally. He had several buddies along to push his wheelchair. Suddenly there were lots of men, and we had to take a break while Barton sorted them out.

He did it well. While people got drinks and sprayed themselves with water spritzers, Barton dissuaded Vic from trying to be in the scene.

"You can be our good-luck mascot," he said. Vic nodded but looked disappointed. Tommy was summoned to do an instantaneous rechoreograph of the dance, which he did, and it worked. Well, let's put it this way: you would say it worked if you're a kind and tolerant person, which I am. Almost all of the nuns now had partners, including Helen, who got matched with Moey.

"Hey, what is that?" Moey yelled, and jumped away.

"It's been blessed by the pope," Helen told him, and held up her crucifix.

"Yeah? Well, it's sticking me in the groin. Tell the pope I don't need no castrate-ization problems, okay?"

The ballroom scene took an hour, but we finally moved forward to the rest of the show. Isabel's number was thrilling, as always, and I saw Abe and the jailbirds and everybody else watch with respect. Talent is like that. It commands attention. I wished I could have Isabel on my sales calls, ready to burst into song whenever anyone said no.

Charlie was noticeably improved. He knew all his lines and all his moves. He never rubbed his head once. Scene changes were still very long, and Barton was still very impatient. He yelled while everybody else whispered.

"Shit. Does the curtain open now?"

"I just finished *Moby Dick*!"

"Are the table and chairs in this scene?"

"It was good! I enjoyed it!"

"No, that's the next one. Hurry up!"

"Now I'm starting *Rise and Fall of the Roman Empire*!"

"What does he expect? This fucking thing is heavy."

"Mmm, I love a good book!"

By the time I sat in the audience and watched the end of the first run-through, it actually looked like a show. You could see the skeleton of it through the fat, or maybe you would call it gristle.

"Charlie looks great," I said to Susie, who sat next to me.

"Yes," she said, and smiled again. She was staying away from the entire maintenance department, from what I could tell. "He's had a revelation."

"That's wonderful."

"Jeanie, I am really grateful to you for bringing me home last week."

"Don't mention it."

"What an idiot I've been."

"Hey, Susie, I've been an idiot a few times myself."

"We're going to have the cast party at our house. We're so excited. We'll donate the food from the business."

"What business?"

"Charlie's, of course. You know that he owns Dog Daze, don't you?"

Just then Lenny sat next to me, and my handsome-man antennae went wiggling and perking upward at the same time that my jaw fell open.

"This was fun," Lenny said. "We enjoyed it."

"He owns *what*?"

* * *

Directors give what they call notes after a rehearsal. Things like, "Helen, please don't floss your teeth when you're onstage." Or, "Jennifer, don't go up and down on your toes in the middle of the song." Blah, blah. Barton had many notes to give. Then we had a dinner break, when a good number of us walked across the highway to Main Street House of Pizza, also one of my clients. The owner wasn't in or I could have actually had him sign his proof and gotten some business done. We traipsed back across Route 118, singing one of our church songs, and got some stares from local folks.

"Come to the show!" we yelled.

"There goes our staircase," someone howled as an eighteen-wheel tractor-trailer went by.

"Isabel! Don't jump!" Everyone was in high spirits.

Some of the high school girls, those wearing the shortest of shorts and under Abe's willing guidance, were painting the sign in front of the school to advertise our production. They were singing too. I had to think all the way back to junior high to remember feeling so warm and comradely. To top off the good feeling, Charlie said to me as we walked back into the school, "Jeanie, you were totally right in everything you said to me. I wish there were something I could do to show my gratitude."

Baby, You're on the Brink

Turned out there were several ways for Charlie to show appreciation. There was the big print run for Dog Daze, of course, no proof necessary, and I left a carefully worded message for Dan explaining how this had happened and why it was mine.

"You mean I don't have to deal with that odd woman, what's-her-name?"

"Henrietta. She's our top seller, Charlie. She tracked you down when I couldn't."

"She's persistent. Yeesh."

I left Henrietta a politically correct, nongloating gloating message. I felt a little underhanded and sneaky about the whole thing, but no way was I walking away from the sale, which would net me almost as much as the prize itself, if I won it. I knew Dan wouldn't care who brought the sale in. Another way for Charlie to express true love was a smaller print run for a different restaurant he owned in Boston. I gritted my teeth and suggested he give this to

Henrietta, but he wouldn't. He wanted to give me a third buy, too, but I advised him against advertising a medical-supply business that he said was the most profitable of all. Charlie thought I was a model of integrity for all this, and I basked in his misplaced admiration.

There were four days left to get all proofs approved. I still had more than thirty left to get signed, and I left the house early to track down the deadbeats. It's always traumatic when money has to change hands. No matter how well you get along with clients, no matter how eager they are to run their ad, nobody wants to pay.

"Oh no, I forgot my checkbook."

"The owner isn't in."

"I think we're going to skip this one."

I am endlessly patient with these people, and will come back a hundred times. Sometimes I hate myself for it, but that's why I hold the office record for collections.

"Will you have your checkbook tomorrow?"

"Will the owner be in later?"

"You don't want to skip this one. It's your best season."

Some people have to be sold all over again, and these are very wearying, involving hours of long-winded sagas. The Silver Star Car Wash owner made me haul out all my sales tools every time I walked in there for a check, and he'd been using the coupon for years. As I sat looking out the window of Ling's Buffet while the husband-and-wife owners screamed at each other in Chinese, I could see my car and longed to be in it.

Then again, some are easy as pie. After all his annoying phone calls, Mort always signed his proof without even looking at it and had a check ready. On proof days, I loved Mort passionately.

"Jeanie," he said in a low voice. "If I tell you what Isabel did in her window to me last week, you won't believe it."

"Yes, I would, Mort."

I stopped in at Isabel's new store, and things looked

busy. A few people were browsing around looking at frames and such, and she said there'd been a number of film-developing customers already that morning. She told me to look in the back room, which I did. Four bulging suitcases rested there, and I knew what they meant.

"Way to go, girl. You're out of the house."

"Yup. I don't know where I'm going, but I'm out."

Isabel had already paid for her ad way back in June, so all she had to do was sign. There are never any problems with those.

By the end of the day, I had ten in the bag and paid for. Fifteen more had been signed and were waiting for checks. I munched my frozen entrée and watched Gramp head out for rehearsal. Most of his tools had been moved from his garage to the high school, and I hoped he got all of them back. The musicians were scheduled that night for the first time, and I couldn't wait to see how it would go with a full orchestra. We were headed for glory.

"Glory" might not have been the right word, though, since when I arrived the kids had fulfilled their destiny by spilling an open can of paint right in front of the superintendent, who hadn't left for the day and was having a fit.

"This is going to ruin the cafeteria!" he yelled.

"We'll take care of it," my grandfather said.

"No problem," Bill Tuxhorn added, and indeed Rita Wylie and Mrs. Mayer and the senior brigade swarmed around the problem. Isabel had never produced a show with so much help.

Inside the auditorium were a number of new Category C's (dorks), most especially the violinist, who resembled Abraham Lincoln in an eerie way. He was good, though, unlike the trombone player, whose pitch seemed less than a hundred percent. It was very exciting to listen to them tune up. Marianne was in charge, and it must have been thrilling for her to receive such deference from a large group, twelve in all. Isabel had confided that the orchestra was the most expensive part of the whole production. You couldn't really put that in the program, unfortunately.

We weren't running the whole show, just the musical parts. The nun songs sounded great to my ear, but I saw Barton spouting off to himself in the back row, and when I sat down to listen to Laura sing the title song, I knew why. You couldn't hear her. Not even a little bit. Ditto for Charlie. Stephanie was okay, and I guess our chorus songs were too, since there were so many of us. Isabel was still fantastic. The orchestra actually enhanced her number.

Sometimes the orchestra plays "under" a scene, and those were the worst of all. It was like watching a silent movie. The actors' mouths were moving, but all you could hear was music.

The thrill wore off quickly. Marianne frequently lowered her outstretched palms downward to indicate legato or spiccato or whatever it is that means shut the hell up. Nothing helped.

"We have to have mikes," Barton said later at Shipley's. "There's no alternative."

"It's not in the budget," Isabel said.

"Well then, fine. No one's going to hear one word."

I sat across from the two of them and noticed Laura looking forlorn down at the end of the booth. It looked as though she'd gotten some new speech from Barton, and I felt sorry for her.

An idea popped into my head. It had nothing to do with miking and singing, but I went for it anyway.

"Hey, you guys, will you all do something for me?"

Everyone looked my way.

"When you get home, will you all send me an e-mail and tell me exactly how many minutes it took you to get there?"

"It takes me ten. I can tell you right now," somebody said.

"Yes, but would you mind documenting it for me? Then I can print it out and use it for a marketing survey I'm doing."

"Are you trying to sell Shipley's, Jeanie?"

"Could be," I said. Shipley's wasn't in my territory.

"Susie, you and Charlie will do it, won't you?"

"But of course."

"And Velma?"

"Okay."

"And Barton?"

He shrugged. "I guess so." Bingo. I jotted down my e-mail address many different times and handed it out to various participants. "Don't forget," I cautioned.

Barton looked fierce tonight, arms folded, black cloud firmly in place above his head. If he was sandman, I would soon find out.

I drove home, booted up my laptop, and waded through all the messages on my server, laughing at some of the comments.

Twelve minutes to driveway, thirteen to bathroom. It should have been only twenty minutes, but stopped for butts.

I'm not sure what time I got home, but it was during the Viagra commercial on channel thirty-eight.

Barton's message was terse. *Nineteen minutes, and why won't you go out with me?* But his screen name was Bcolumb or something like that. So he wasn't the culprit. Then I realized with a gasp that he could easily have another account and another name, and could still be the anonymous agitator of Marianne. The whole thing had proved nothing. I never said I was Nancy Drew.

It was late. I sat there hunched over the screen as Sheena tried to crawl up my bare leg. I picked her up and stroked her in my lap while she purred like one of my grandfather's motorized gadgets. "Figure this out for me, baby," I cooed to my new pet. Mr. Piggy was quiet in his cage. I didn't ask him because he's not good at complex analysis.

Then I had another idea. I went to one of those providers where you can get a free e-mail account and signed up for one. It was the same one that Marianne used. I called myself Marpet1, almost exactly like Marianne's screen name. If sandman was on the dumb side, and that seemed entirely possible, maybe he wouldn't notice.

Hi. It's me, I wrote in an e-mail to sandman. *I think I will try conducting nude. I think it will wake everyone up, just as you suggested. Leave me a candy bar on my piano tomorrow night, just as a sign, and I'll do it. Okay? Yours, M.* I pressed send and wondered what the hell I was doing.

Totally Unprepared Am I

Tuesday, August 4

"Did you have an appointment with Attorney Shorenstein?" the secretary asked me. I stood inside Al's downtown Worcester law office. I was parked illegally, and had walked six blocks. I was irritated, sweaty, and had gum on my shoe. I won't even go into my hair.

"He said he would leave a photograph for me."

"A photograph?" The woman glanced past me, like in a movie scene where she would alert security and they would haul me off for questioning.

"Yes, for his LotsaCoups ad." I held up an envelope.

"Al's doing an ad in that?" the woman asked. I gritted my teeth. Some people are just too good for coupons. Al's building had seen better days, as had the secretary in my view. Like all its Main Street neighbors, the building had many vacancies inside. The elevator had wheezed and gasped its way up to the fourth floor, and I felt lucky to be out of its confines.

"Yes, he is. Attorney Shorenstein is doing a coupon," I

said, rubbing it in as vigorously as possible. "He's already paid for it. We just need the photograph." The office itself was sumptuous in its furnishings and appointments. Dark-wood paneling, brass lamps, Oriental rugs, and, I was happy to see, lots of photographs of Al on the walls. I mo-seyed over to a couple of them and marveled at Al catch-ing a big fish somewhere, Al shaking hands with the governor, even Al gazing poignantly into the sunset on a beach. I managed not to convulse.

"You can't use those," she said. I nodded. Her phone started ringing and she started taking lots of calls and ig-noring me. I knew this technique. I was not in the mood for it. I stood around for about five minutes, long enough to cool off in the lovely air-conditioning, and then made my move. I turned my back squarely to the dragon lady with my briefcase in front of me, reached up to the fish photograph, which was closest, lifted it easily off the wall, and let it fall into the briefcase. I would have left the frame behind, but time seemed of the essence, so I turned around briefly, smiled, and split. I took the stairs down.

"Hi. This is Jeanie. If you're calling about your proof, no more changes can be made after tomorrow. If you're a new busi-ness, leave a message and there could still be time for you to get in." BEEP.

"Jeanie, it's Henrietta. I'm not going to forget what you did." BEEP.

"Hey, Jeanie, it's Abe, just finishing up at the casino. I was wrong about what I was doing wrong. But now I really DO know what it was, so I'm full of hope and still have a thousand bucks. Man, you were right about all those girls. Woo, baby." BEEP.

"It's Mort. I have a very important color change to the coupon." BEEP.

I drove to the office and turned in the proofs and checks I had, feeling more than a little worried by the message from

Henrietta. After all the sly ones she'd pulled on me and everybody else, she could eat shit and die, as far as I was concerned. On the other hand, I hoped she wouldn't bomb my house. Or throw a bucket of paint in the front door, which I'd read about someone doing. She was a formidable foe. My new were still holding at twenty-seven and seemed likely to stay there. Magda didn't know what Henrietta had turned in lately, and I was starting to get that fatalistic feeling, the one you get looking out the window of an airplane as it gains speed for takeoff. It was out of my hands. It was what it was.

I finished up the Shorenstein layout and hoped that people would respond to it. I hoped that people would figure he was good at his job if he had money for fishing trips.

Dan popped out of his office and smiled at me. "Jeanie! Hi!"

"Hey."

"Lou and I would like to talk to you. Have you got a little time?"

"Sure," I said, though I didn't. I still had proofs to be signed, and the closer you get to the cutoff, the harder they are to get. The last ones can kill you.

Dan stood up. "Let's go into the conference room."

"Okay," I said. Off to the principal's office.

Bugs—I mean Lou—was already in there, and he grabbed my hand like an old friend. He actually seemed to remember me and gave me a huge, twenty-one-tooth smile.

"Jeanie! Jeanie! Jeanie!"

"Hi, Lou," I said. I was tempted to say, "Judy, Judy, Judy," in my best Cary Grant voice, but I didn't think Lou would get it.

We sat around one end of the table, and Dan leaned back to close the door. I felt a chill go down my back. Lou offered me a breath mint, the salesman's addiction, but I shook my head no.

"Jeanie, how do you feel about Florida?" he asked with a smile.

"Good. I feel good about Florida."

Lou and Dan laughed.

"It has palm trees and Disney World."

Lou and Dan laughed even harder. They were treating me like a client.

"I suppose you mean the plant," I said.

"That's right. I want you to come to Florida and join our marketing department there," Lou said.

"Excuse me?" I said.

"You've got some great ideas, and I'd like to have you on our national team," Lou continued. Dan beamed.

"But I can't."

"Why not? You've got to be ready to go where the possibilities are, Jeanie," Lou said. He seemed much better dressed and more persuasive than he had in the cafeteria.

"You're not married, are you, Jeanie?" Dan asked. "You don't have to worry about a spouse's job, right?"

"No, but I can't leave my grandfather."

Both men nodded their heads at this, but didn't accept it. In sorority rush, this used to be called hotboxing.

They were the hunters and I the prey. They would track me down, corner me, and then I would get away. Then they would prove me wrong again and tree me. I ended up speaking from the tree.

"Can I have some time to think about it?"

The room exploded in jollity. "But of course!"

"See what you think!"

"Maybe your grandfather will want to go!" Chairs were scraped back and handshakes given.

"But what about the other job? The sales manager job?" I asked.

They didn't look at each other. They were pros. Dan answered. "Oh, you'd be wasted in that job, Jeanie."

*   *   *

The orchestra wasn't expected again until dress rehearsal on Thursday night, so we were back to just the piano, making the sound overall seem a little diminished, a bit tinny. The singing volume, however, fell back into the acceptable range, meaning at least you could hear the words, or most of them. As Marianne practiced with the children, I wandered around and thought about trivial things, like my life and my career.

How could I move to Florida? Wouldn't it be sticky-hot there all the time? But maybe the job would be great, not to mention no cold-calling. I saw myself issuing orders, coming up with brilliant concepts, wearing fabulous clothes.

I also kept a close eye on the piano to see who, if anyone, might put a candy bar on it. Barton walked by the instrument several times before the show started, and each time I jumped onto the stage and into the wings to observe him. This may have looked like erratic behavior on my part, but I have learned that erratic behavior is relative. In a theater group, if you choose to stand on your head and bray like a donkey, people will not make judgments. They will assume you have a good reason for it and will even consider braying with you if the reason makes sense. Jumping intermittently in and out of the wings and wrapping yourself in the curtain is pretty much like reading a newspaper to them, nothing special.

In the hallway behind the stage, my grandfather was overseeing the paint job on some of the scenery pieces. The flats—as they're called in the biz—have to be latched together in the back, and they are the devil to match up in front. Despite their recent successes with lawyers, Mrs. Mayer and Mrs. Wylie and all the stage crew looked to be flirting up a storm with Vic's friends. Shipley's was becoming an all-out senior-citizen meat market. Meg had abandoned the maternity clothes in the intense heat and wore spandex shorts and a sports bra. Abe hovered close by the teenagers.

"I only have two words for you," I said.

"Yeah? I have one for you," he replied.

"Jail bait."

"Roulette."

"Oh. Good. Have you got my two hundred?"

"Not yet, but I will."

"Abe, this isn't going to work. Sell some coupons."

"Psh, you're wrong, Jeanie."

"No, I'm not. You're going to lose all your money."

"Jailbait is only one word."

I didn't have time to prove Abe right or wrong, because Isabel's stepdaughter, Clarissa, had barged in out front and was causing a commotion from the back row.

"What is she doing here?" I whispered to Isabel, who had just arrived from her shop.

"She says I took her DVD player. I didn't. She's just trying to harass me."

I'd never seen Clarissa in anything but a bikini, and indeed the one she wore tonight under a loosely draped towel was an eye-opener. Our own high school girls sat up and paid close attention, to say nothing of Truman and all the grown men. I noticed that Abe sat quite near the girl and looked completely absorbed in her sarcastic spiel. If he leaped forward in support of her, I would have to kill him.

"As I already said, I want my DVD player. It's not like I called any of you losers and faggots. That would make a good theme song, though, wouldn't it? *The Sound of Losers and Faggots!* Oh, and fat people too. I wouldn't want to leave Isabel out."

"I'm going to ask you to leave," Barton said.

"You know, you're not bad-looking," Clarissa said. "But I'm not leaving till I get my DVD player."

Isabel walked out onto the stage and yelled, "I didn't take it, Clarissa. Please leave."

Just as Clarissa filled her lungs for another scathing

comment, Lenny and the jailbirds sauntered forward and surrounded her.

"Who you calling a faggot?" Moey demanded.

Clarissa took a step backward.

"And who you calling fat?" Ziggy added, hitching up his pants. We all watched Lenny have a short conversation with Clarissa, after which he took the girl by the elbow and ushered her out of the auditorium. I didn't like seeing Lenny touching Clarissa, but I'm sure I was the only person disturbed by the fact that Clarissa had a candy bar in her hand.

I ran over to Marianne and examined the piano, which made her look me up and down curiously as she resumed playing. No candy bar on the piano, and that was what I had specified to sandman. Although maybe Clarissa hadn't quite had the opportunity to put it there. Oh, it would be just like the little minx to pull something like this, but how could it be? Did she even know Marianne? Lights were going on and off in a strobe effect as Sam Yummy worked them from the booth up above.

"No! Use fourteen and twenty-three!" Barton yelled.

Different lights went on and off.

"No! I said fourteen!"

The rehearsal started almost an hour late. Because the band wasn't there, you could hear the participants for the most part, but the technical aspects were pretty sad. It was more or less three hours of hell, highlighted by the lights going on and off in strange patterns. By the time I took my first sip of chardonnay at Shipley's, it was almost midnight. Don Shipley was keeping the place open for us a bit later than usual, and he must have been making some money because I saw numerous orders of nachos and potato skins go wheeling by. Our table alone ordered six or seven appetizers, not to mention burger platters and plenty of alcohol.

"Costumes tomorrow, everybody," Velma said. "Don't forget."

"We'll be nice and toasty warm in those," I said.

"Only a few more nights," Stephanie said. "Boo-hoo. It's always so sad when the show ends." Stephanie seemed nicer than normal, possibly since she had gotten her Benito's proof after all. She still wasn't happy with it, naturally, and I didn't know what she was going to do about it.

"Hey, Marianne," I said to our newly vivacious musical director, who at that moment was giggling with my grandfather. She was showing him something in her notebook.

She looked at me with her normal inquisitive face, and I asked, "Do you know Clarissa? Isabel's stepdaughter?"

"I know who she is," she answered.

"But no more than that?"

"Years ago I gave her piano lessons. I caught her making prank phone calls once to my house."

That was it. Clarissa must be my man, as it were, and I was furious. Not to mention that I heard her calling Isabel a whore with my own ears. But I didn't exactly know what to do about it. *Hey, Marianne, in addition to eating all your food that day, we scoured through your computer too.*

I couldn't enjoy myself. I started to think about Sheena and how she was waiting up for her Meow Mix, and I thought I'd better skedaddle. The conversation had turned to early nostalgia for the show.

"Just think," Sam said. "A week from tonight we'll all be at home doing nothing."

"Not me. I'm taking up shooting, so I'll be at target practice," said Helen.

"Everyone has been so nice," Susie said. "This has even been more fun than when I did the show in high school." Cast members cooed over Susie having been Maria back then, and a few bravely avowed that she could still play the role.

"Some of those dancing pizza guys are pretty nice," Isabel said.

"Some of them, not all," cautioned Helen.

"You're right," Susie said. "Even Vic and all his friends are very nice."

Meg popped an onion ring into her mouth. "This show is the greatest. Everyone here helped get me pregnant."

"Maybe you should rephrase that, Meg," I said.

"Well," said Susie. "Let's not completely overlook the janitors. They're nice too. My old friend walked up to the piano during intermission and gave Marianne a Milky Way."

Better Beware, Be Canny and Careful

Wednesday, August 5

I still couldn't concentrate nearly twenty-four hours later. I had fewer than ten proofs left, but they required tough love. Mark at Nashoba Tire had already bobbed and weaved his way around payment three times. Every time I showed up, he had just left. His guys knew me well, and why wouldn't they?

"Hey, Jack. Is Mark in?"

"Uh, no, I don't think he is."

"His truck is here."

"It is?"

"Yup, sort of hidden out there behind the trees."

"Well, I, uh, I'll check." He picked up the phone and pressed a button. "Is Mark up there?" he asked in a tremulous voice. "Oh yeah, I guess he is here. Go on up, Jeanie."

I walked into the work area and stayed well away from the wrenches and tire tools as I minced my way up the iron steps. I had to walk on tiptoe so my heels wouldn't get stuck in the crevices.

"Mark?" I called, and knocked on the door.

"Ymklknl," came from inside. Mark was watching a Red Sox game, and I perched on a rickety folding chair to watch with him. The Yankees scored a run while we sat there, and we turned toward each other in dismay.

"Things aren't going well here, Jeanie," Mark said. He then gave a good matinee performance of his litany of troubles, including employees not showing up, customers not appreciating his service, bank problems, mortgage problems, credit card debt, and every other thing, including his wife's cake business and how he couldn't even eat from his own refrigerator at home. A good performance but not great, since it only took fifteen minutes and last time it had been more than thirty.

Finally, instead of taking the gas pipe, which truly seemed the only choice, he opened his desk drawer and pulled out several envelopes. I knew they contained postdated checks, which was against company policy and my own as well. One day something bad was going to happen with this account, but with any luck it wouldn't be mine for long.

By midafternoon I had whittled down my proof list to only three. I kept thinking about Florida and wondering whether I should take the job. I also kept thinking about Marianne and sandman. My car, in fact, kept veering in the direction of Marianne's house until it was on her street, then right in front, and then with all the bad luck I could have asked for, there was Marianne in the driveway just exiting her own car and waving at me. What could I do?

"Let's go out on the porch," Marianne said, and we walked through the garage, which, of course, meant that we didn't have to walk in the front door and encounter Mrs. Peters. We were of one mind on that. "How about some lemonade? Cold cuts?" Marianne asked, and we both laughed. She seemed much more relaxed these days.

"Lemonade sounds good," I said.

I sat on the porch and waited for Marianne to join me. I had no idea what I was going to say. I would have to try to lead up to it very subtly and carefully.

"Summer will be over soon, huh?" Marianne said as she handed me a tall glass.

"Marianne, do you ever do instant messaging on the computer?"

"What?"

"I mean, I noticed you have a computer. That is, when we were here for rehearsal, not when we rummaged through your kitchen—gee, I'm still so sorry about that—but I did . . . that is, I couldn't help but notice that you have a computer. Heh, heh."

"Yes?"

"And, well, a lot of people enjoy talking to their friends on it. I know I do. I send e-mails and memos and messages and sometimes instant messages. Do you ever do that?"

"Jeanie."

"They say little kids shouldn't go online because predators can be on there and trick them into meeting them to see a puppy or something, when really they want to attack them or hurt them."

"Jeanie."

"Usually adults don't have to worry about that, though."

We smiled at each other. I swallowed hard.

"You read those instant messages, didn't you?" Marianne asked.

"What instant messages?"

"The ones from sandman."

I considered denying it and then slumped in my chair. "I've been a little worried about them, Marianne. I'm sorry."

"Do you know who sandman is?"

"No, do you?" I asked.

"Think about it."

"Okay, I'm thinking."

"It's obviously Barton."

This raised my eyebrows. "Why do you say that?" I didn't want to say, *I happen to know Barton can't stand you.*

Marianne fluffed her missing sausage roll. "Who's the only person with a laptop open during rehearsal?"

"Well, yes, Barton. That's true," I said.

"We definitely have an attraction, he and I. I just pretend I don't like him and he does the same to me."

"Oh," I said, and thought of Barton's love for "setting things in motion." Maybe she was right.

"I know things didn't work out with you and Barton, Jeanie. He and I are meant to be together."

"Well, you're both doing a good job with the pretense," I said, and told Marianne of my clever Marpet1 scheme.

Her face lit up. "A few people gave me candy last night, and I'm sure Barton meant to. I saw him put a candy bar in his pocket. The kids got them out of the machine, which is going to get us all in trouble."

"Hmmm," I said. "I thought it might be Clarissa Cartwright. She's hateful enough."

Marianne smiled. "No. It's Barton. I know it is."

I couldn't convince Marianne to entertain other theories, so I left it at that.

"You know something, Jeanie? I don't care if Barton ever tells me. Someday"—and her face went pink—"if we're together, it will be fun to look back on."

"I'm sure it will, Marianne," I said.

"I'm not used to having fun."

Then Marianne started to laugh and I realized I'd never seen her laugh, not a hard laugh the way Meg and I do it. Eventually it infected me and I started laughing, and pretty soon we were helpless.

"Did you think I would conduct naked?"

"Not really. Well, yes, I was afraid of it."

"Wouldn't my mother love that?" Marianne hooted.

Once again my grandfather had been proven right. He

says we should mind our own business, and he's never been wrong that I know of. I should needlepoint that and hang it in my house. And I would too, if I knew how to needlepoint.

Rehearsal went pretty well. The worst part was still the lighting, which went on and off at very odd times and in unusual places. Right during one of the love scenes with Maria and the Captain, the spotlight went on, pointed directly at Charlie's crotch. Even Barton laughed at that one. Then later, when Jennifer and Truman were supposed to be singing, it pointed a thousand watts at Truman's face. This sent him into a bit of a stage-fright relapse and took some calming down on everyone's part. Though the show looked better than it ever had, Barton seemed the angriest he'd ever been. I figured he'd run out of women.

"Sam! Are you reading comic books up there?"

"No!" came Sam's muffled reply from the lighting booth. "I'm trying to do what you want!"

Barton shook his head and continued to pace.

Just as Isabel finished her song and everyone clapped on the way back to their places, a voice cried out in the darkness.

"Is Jeanie Callahan here?"

It was Roger Crandall, the poor fellow with "prostrate" problems who had abandoned Ye Olde English Scones and Tacos earlier in the summer.

Barton snapped at him. "We're in the middle of a rehearsal, sir, if you don't mind." Maria and the von Trapp children were just taking their positions on the stage, and one of them was opening his mouth to speak when Roger's voice again intruded from the darkened auditorium.

"But I need to get in the mailing! I need to do the coupon!"

"Sir," said Barton, "do you mind waiting until we break for intermission?"

"Well, okay," Roger said. "But I really need to get in."

This was all music to my ears. I walked out to my car at intermission with Roger and got him signed and paid and put back into the mailing.

"As soon as I realized I had to change the name of the shop, things started to go my way medically," he said.

"You're changing the name? I think that's a good idea, Roger."

"Ye Olde English Scones and Tacos was a bit misleading, don't you think?" Roger asked.

"Could be. What have you changed it to?"

"Medieval Scones and Tacos."

"How will they be medieval?"

"People will eat them with their hands, right? Like in medieval times, but still modern in food content. I'm really happy with it."

"So am I, Roger. You know you're not going to see a proof, don't you?" I cautioned.

"That's okay. I'm just so happy I'm feeling good." He started to regale me with medical details, but I escaped.

"Got to get back for the second act, Rog."

"Okay. Break a leg, huh? Isn't that what they say?"

"That's right. Although we're trying not to break legs."

Barton addressed the group after the show. "Okay. That's everything I have. Good job in general."

"Thank you very much," Jennifer said, as if he had addressed her personally.

"As you know, tomorrow night is dress rehearsal."

"Yeah!"

"You will have an audience. Right, Isabel?"

"Right," Isabel said. "Mostly senior citizens."

Barton continued. "These people get in free, and they're usually good laughers if they can hear what you say. Don't let it throw you. Don't wait for a laugh, okay?"

"Yeah, yeah," everybody said.

"The sound techs will be here early with the body mikes, so everybody getting one has to be here at five P.M. Okay? This is it, folks. Now everybody go home and get a good night's sleep."

Aside from Helen, who was off to a big family reunion somewhere nearby, Barton must have taken his own advice, since he was the only person who didn't go to Shipley's.

I Go to the Hills

I stood in the pet shop, proof signed and in hand.

"We're done, aren't we?" the owner asked. "I signed the thing."

"Dave."

"Oh, don't start. Please, Jeanie."

"It's not going to work."

"Well, then let's call it off."

I tried to think of a new and innovative way to convince this guy not to fall into the ten-percent trap. But I couldn't.

"Can I just ask you a question? One question. And will you answer it honestly?"

"Okay," he said.

"Would you rush into a restaurant to get ten percent off?"

He thought carefully. "Yes. I would."

I spent another fifteen minutes watching Dave clean fish tanks. The only thing he said was, "I'd be willing to do fifteen percent off any gerbil." If I'd had any gumption, I'd have walked away and told him to forget it. But I still wanted to win the contest, and he was a new customer, so, being that I was slightly hungover from the night before anyway, and being a sniveling jellyfish at my core, I gave in. I wondered if Stephanie, who had wowed everybody with her "Cabaret" rendition at one A.M. from the top of the bar, was even working at all.

I finally walked out, tail between my legs, and went next door. Jailbird Pizza was starting to look very spiffy, with an awning outside and a most cool neon sign in the window. Another most cool element was the blue dress shirt and tie on Lenny, who sat at a table looking worried.

"Hey," I said. "You guys ready for tonight?"

"Yeah!" exclaimed Moey. "I got a little somethin' for Helen."

Lenny frowned. "Moey, no little somethin's for anybody, okay?"

Moey smirked.

"Jeanie. I'm glad you're here," Lenny said.

"Why don't I like the look on your face?" I asked.

I sat down, took a good gander into his eyes and liked it even less.

"I should have made all the guys come be in your show," Lenny said. "They're enjoying it and they're not getting in trouble."

"Yeah? But?"

"Someone named Henrietta Lewis has filed complaints in three of our towns. Something about ex-cons shouldn't be able to run a business in our midst. They're a menace and a danger, yadda, yadda."

"Henrietta Lewis?"

"Yeah. Probably some old biddy. I'd like to know how she got the information."

I was on the verge of spilling everything to Lenny, but held back. He probably wouldn't be too happy to hear that someone from LotsaCoups was trying to sabotage him. He didn't know the sabotage target was me.

"But what will happen?" I wailed.

"Nothing will probably come of it, but I don't think we can go forward with the ad in those towns this time around."

"Oh, brother. Oh, gosh." After leaping forward to twenty-eight last night with the scones and tacos, I was back to twenty-five today before even eating lunch.

"I'm just worried that she's going to do it in all of our towns," Lenny said. He started to chew on his pencil.

The door opened, and Dave from the pet store stood on the sidewalk peering in.

"All right, Jeanie. Let's do it your way," he said, and closed the door.

Lenny cocked his head to the side. "Boy, you've got 'em falling at your feet, don't you?"

"I wish," I said.

I drove to the office in a rage. How dare Henrietta pull a stunt like that? I fully intended to get her in as much trouble as I could with Dan, until I started to think things over. Maybe Dan wouldn't like the sound of Jailbird Pizza, the particulars of which he did not know. Maybe Dan would nix the whole deal. I left Abe a message on his voice mail, though I was quite sure he was either passed out at home or playing roulette at the casino. By the time I stomped up to Magda's desk, I was thoroughly undecided.

"Hi, Zheenie. Henrietta just turn in big stack of contracts. Now I get to put all in computer at last minute."

"Yeah," I said. "The old sandbag routine. Henrietta would have been a good wartime spy."

"Not in my war," Magda said. "We frag that bitch first thing."

I walked into Dan's office and closed the door without

asking permission. He looked bewildered, and I couldn't blame him.

"Dan, you'd better not be giving Henrietta the sales manager's job."

He said nothing.

"And I don't want to go to Florida."

He took off his glasses.

"I can work for Garrett or Connie or anyone else."

He leaned back in his chair.

"But if I have to have her as my boss, I'm quitting."

"Good morning, Jeanie. How are things with you?"

I sighed.

"Isn't tonight your show?"

"Dress rehearsal."

"I'll be there tomorrow night. Where is it, East High in Worcester?"

"Oh Dan, that's very nice of you. You don't have to come. Abe's in it too, you know."

"I'm glad he's accomplishing something for the summer," Dan said, and I worried about the tone in his voice.

"Did you get all your proofs in?"

"Yes, I did."

"Money?"

"Yup."

"Good offers?"

"Yes."

"Okay then," Dan said.

"No, it's not okay."

I talked nonstop for ten minutes. I told Dan of my frustrations with clients and how nobody had any brains and everybody was out to get me. I shared my concerns over my car, my grandfather, and my cat. I told him all about the show but nothing about Jailbird Pizza. Most of all, I complained about Henrietta. He was quiet through it all.

"Is that everything?" Dan asked.

"Yes. Unless I think of something else."

"You're good at what you do, Jeanie."

"I am?"

"I'm very glad you don't want the job in Florida."

"You are?"

"Hang in there, kid," he said. "You're making me look good."

Dan turned out to be a good manager, one of the best I ever had, even if he did like memos a bit more than most. But even though he calmed me down slightly, I was still pissed off.

I drove to the high school that night with the radio on. I normally don't like loud, angry music, but I was in the mood for it. I turned it way up. My own favorite fantasy of violence is smashing an ATM machine with my fist. That to me would feel satisfying. Meg thinks throwing a gourd through a plate-glass window would be better, but I don't agree. It's not immediate enough. When the window cracks, you're not actually present, you're not actually doing it, the gourd is. Plus, think of all the seeds.

As I pulled into a parking place, something in one of the songs clicked in my head. I sat there for a moment and a few things came into focus. The scales fell from my eyes, so to speak, although so did my troublesome contact lens, and I had to stop to find it and clean it.

The young kids were running or skating up and down the hallways, some in makeup, some without. It felt funny as a nun to be putting on makeup, but the high school girls were experts.

"Jeanie, cover your whole face and then put on the headpiece."

"Oh yeah, duh. What was I thinking?"

My costume felt very itchy, and the headpiece kept drifting down onto my nose. Several others had the same problem.

"We look like creatures on *Star Trek*," Helen said, and

she was right. Velma came to each of us and pinned our costumes together. The leads were fully made up and trying to get used to the big, boxy microphones they had to wear strapped inside their costumes.

Stephanie put it best. "I can't walk around with this sticking out of my ass." I think a lot of people enjoyed seeing Stephanie's distress; the clunky protrusion was a bit disconcerting to view, even for the Abraham Lincoln violinist, who seemed thoroughly charmed by Stephanie and walked around doing her bidding until he had to go join the orchestra and tune up. Mrs. Mayer, my grandfather, and Meg wore headphones and I guess were talking to one another. I'm sure it was wicked fun.

Barton summoned us for one last talking-to. It was a good one. He thanked us for our help and urged us to make the show all it could be.

"I'm officially handing over the show now to the stage manager. She's in charge now. Meg, good luck," Barton said, and handed Meg a rose, a bit past its prime.

"Awwwwww," everybody said, but I knew Meg wasn't all that charmed. Barton apologized that he would not be there the next night, but reminded us that the show was the important thing.

"If something happens out there, you don't break character," he said. "If you have to die, get offstage and die. You don't stop the show for anything. Got that?"

We did.

Dress rehearsal went okay. The entrances up the aisle from the back of the auditorium surprised and delighted the old people in the audience. The lights were bright in my eyes, and it felt as though the whole universe were watching me, though I could see that only the first two rows had people in them. The nuns got a few laughs and so did Stephanie. The applause was new for us and sounded deafening.

At intermission I ducked out of the girls' dressing room

to get a drink of water and experienced a rare stroke of good luck. I watched as a lone figure ambled down the dark hallway away from the rehearsal and toward the regular classrooms of the high school. I could hear people calling for me back in the dressing room, but decided to slink along the wall of lockers behind the person until I saw a light come on up ahead. It was the computer lab, as I knew it would be. After a suitable interval, long enough for anyone to boot up, I moved silently to stand in the doorway. My luck held, and I was able to inch forward and sneak my way up behind the screen until I saw what I wanted to see.

"Hey, sandman. What's up?" I said, and Truman nearly jumped out of his skin. He clicked out of what he was doing, but it was too late, and he knew it.

"Hey who?" he said.

"Sandman. That's you, isn't it?"

Truman was silent.

"Not a very nice trick you're playing on Marianne. But you know, if you hadn't called Isabel a whore, I probably wouldn't have cared."

He still said nothing.

"Why'd you do that?"

He looked the other way.

"You know how I figured it out? Metallica, dude. 'Ride the lightning.' You shouldn't wear those shirts."

Truman swallowed hard. "Yeah, so?"

"Yeah, well, Marianne is a very nice person, you know. What about her feelings?"

"I was trying to end it."

"Oh, were you?"

"Yes."

"Huh. It didn't seem that way from your latest messages. Conduct naked? What are you trying to do?"

The boy's eyes glazed over. We were both going to be late getting back. "Are you going to bust me?" he finally asked.

"Why did you call Isabel a whore?"

"I hated everybody in the show then. I didn't want to be in it, my father made me."

"So?"

"I don't hate anybody now. Well, except Jennifer."

"Well, that's just great. You don't hate us now."

"What do you want me to do?"

"I don't know, Truman. I'm going to have to think about this."

"I can apologize. I have some money. I can—"

"I don't want your money."

We sat silently for a moment. "Let's get out of here," I said. I flipped the lights off and ran back down the hall.

All in all, our costumes looked good that night. We had to rip our nun habits off and change to ball gowns and then back again, though our headpieces the second time out looked a little worse for wear. One of the nuns forgot and left hers hairpinned to the back of her head during the dance sequence. I suppose she could have been a disgruntled nun who left the convent in a huff, became a socialite, and got invited to a ball all on the same day. It was funny to see the men leave the dance, rush offstage to put on Nazi armbands, and rush back on.

"You traitor," I said to Lenny. "You lousy Nazi traitor." It became our joke.

Again Barton urged us to go home and get a good night's sleep, and again we ignored his advice. I saw Truman carrying all Marianne's music to her car.

Ford Every Stream

Friday, August 7

If there were a meter to measure Friday zest, it would have been off the chart that day, right up there with the temperature readings, which were hot and steamy. I do admit now that it probably wasn't a good idea to spend the day of our opening night at the casino, and I can't even remember whose idea it was. But Abe no longer cared about working, Meg certainly didn't care about working, and people like Tommy and some others didn't have jobs anyway. Stephanie came along, and she and I carefully didn't mention coupons to each other. Abe picked us up in a huge van, yet another gift from his dead uncle. I wondered how much of the unfortunate gentleman's estate had been redeposited into the casino coffers. In truth, it was probably all headed there.

Not everyone was asked to this event, most especially my grandfather and his female posse. Isabel was staunch in saying that she couldn't leave her store until two of the high school girls said they would watch over things, and then she escaped. She had to pay them minimum wage and also promise that she would bet their numbers on keno. Sam Yummy was easily talked out of his workday, and we were ready to launch when I boldly demanded that Abe stop in front of Jailbird Pizza, where I ran in and absconded with Lenny. He was deliciously willing.

"Youse guys is up to no good," Moey said with a smirk.

"We're Austrian patriots, Moey. We're good by definition," Lenny said. He wore another beautiful shirt, and we held hands in the van. I felt very bold.

All the way to Connecticut we sang songs from the show, including our new favorite.

"High on a hill stood a lonely goatherd," Abe trilled.

"Lady-oh-de-lady-oh-de-lady-hoo," we all yelled.

"What will you give for a win at blackjack?" Abe continued.

"Lady-oh-de-lady-oh-de-lady-hoo."

"Can't you people be serious?" Stephanie whined.

"Lady-oh-de-lady-oh-de-lady-hoo."

"The lonely goatherd wins a huge jackpot!" Abe yelled.

"The lonely goatherd narrowly avoids a car in the breakdown lane!" Sam yelled back. "Be careful!"

"Hey Abe, the lonely goatherd wants to stop at Dunkin' Donuts, okay?"

No matter what was said, we repeated our yodeling mantra. Stephanie complained repeatedly about the sound system and the stage and thirty-seven other things. The rest of us upped the volume so as not to hear her, and I felt I was a better alto for it.

The Lonely Goatherd Memorial Trip arrived at the casino around ten A.M. Abe promptly trailed off after one of the Indian-maiden waitresses. I hoped he still had his shirt when I saw him again. Lenny and I stood in front of the same slot machine for three hours, behaving in a somewhat sappy manner. Poor Lenny had to take cell call after cell call from various criminals and probationers, including our very own Ziggy, who seemed to be in some kind of new hot water.

"You don't want to know," Lenny said to me, and he was right. Surprisingly, the casino will allow you to make out openly on the gambling floor.

"Shit! I've already lost twenty dollars!" said Tommy at one P.M.

"Twenty dollars is nothing," Abe replied as our group reconnoitered at the bar. We had agreed to no drinking because of our theatrical obligations that evening, but some of us were wavering.

"I will if you will," Tommy said to me.

"I'm only in the chorus," I said.

"Fuck, I'm only in one scene," said Abe. "Give me a Dewar's with a twist, please."

By three in the afternoon I was plotzed. Lenny was smiling nonstop at me, which I loved, Stephanie reeked of cigarette smoke, and even Tommy seemed a bit tipsy. Abe had run up and down through several thousand dollars but somehow ended up ahead on the day.

"I'm feeling it!" he yelled. "I'm in the zone!"

"We've got to go," Stephanie said. "I have a five-o'clock call."

"Well, lah-dee-freakin'-dah," said Meg, the only sober person. "I have to be there by five too."

"Come on, Abe, we have to go," Stephanie whined, giving Meg a dirty look.

I was down a hundred bucks by then, which didn't seem too bad. Meg had won a hundred on a slot-machine jackpot, but Isabel was the big winner with a huge bucket full of silver dollars.

"Yaay," Sam said. "The hills are alive!"

* * *

To my surprise, stage makeup was easy to put on in my condition; it slid easily into place and I soon saw the face of Sister Jean, my stage persona, staring cockeyed back at me in the mirror. Stephanie's butt protrusion didn't seem to bother her either, and in fact her entire personality seemed improved.

"Jeanie, thank you for helping me with Benito."

"You're welcome, Stephanie." I thought I was dreaming.

With Barton not there, things seemed a bit more casual altogether. Truman helped the musicians set up their music stands and I clapped him on the back.

"Keep it up, dude," I said, and he nodded.

Sam was smiling for the first time that week, without the director yelling at him. He and Isabel kissed openly in the hallway while Meg led the preshow talk.

"Everybody knows what to do. Let's just do it."

"Can we do the circle of power?" Jennifer asked, referring to one of the motivational warm-up techniques that Susie had introduced to us, and which about half the cast thought had mystical effects and the other half thought was bogus. Personally, I don't mind bogus activities, since I'm so used to them in my work.

"Sure," agreed Meg. Pretty soon the whole cast stood in a dark gymnasium, minutes before the curtain went up, holding hands. When your hand gets squeezed, that means "power" is being sent to you, and you in turn will squeeze the person on your other side to "send" it to him or her. This little pocket of power goes around the circle a couple of times until people are totally entranced or totally bored. I always wondered how I could use it in my sales presentation. *Sir, would you mind giving me your hand so I can send you some power?* Mort would probably love it. See, now that's why these things don't work for me, because my mind wanders too much.

Meg ended the exercise. "Break a leg, you guys," she said. "Well," she amended her statement with a nod to

Charlie, "not an actual leg. Be careful. Are you all okay?"

"Definitely," Abe said, about to fall over. Somewhere on the premises I knew was a sequestered bottle of Dewar's.

"All right, then, places, please."

Moey gave Helen a prayer book that he said had inspired him in his childhood. Everyone was very touched, most not knowing that his inspiration had landed him six to ten at Walpole. My grandfather wore his Indiana Jones outfit, but after a while took the hat off.

Marianne was a vision. Her hair had blond streaks and bangs. She wore a one-shouldered black dress and looked glamorous if severe, possibly the first time for her, and she knew it. Abraham Lincoln looked handsome himself, and even the off-key trombonist looked dapper in his shiny tuxedo. The overture, which we could hear from the cafeteria, where we waited for our surprise entrance, sounded positively philharmonic.

The house was nearly full. I hadn't realized it until I first walked into the auditorium, but there they were, the big, dark, silent mass of watchers, turning in their seats to see us walk up the aisle. Where had they all come from? I opened my eyes wide and then very wide. Susie and I looked at each other as if to say, *Here we go, and what have we gotten ourselves into?* The audience loved our entrance, as we expected them to, and we walked carefully, knowing how good we were. In a way, we were like the starting pitcher, handing it off after a good run to the actors. Close it, babe. It's all yours.

As we ascended the stage steps, I had a sense that something wasn't right.

"Where are the lights?" one of the nuns whispered. I saw Meg out of the corner of my eye, speaking vigorously into her headset and waving her arms around.

"Are we in the dark?"

"What's happening?"

"Just keep going," someone said, and we did. The lights eventually came on in the middle of the stage, though not at the edges. The scene with the nuns and Maria was fine and had lights on it, though those of us placed on the periphery of the stage were pretty much standing in the dark. Then they went off completely for a few seconds and came on again. Soon it was like a disco. I could hear Meg hissing into the headphones, and as we made our subway exit, a distinct burning smell filled the air.

In the midst of all this, the secondary leads, especially Stephanie, were great. The laughs they got somewhat made up for the checkerboard lighting, which I knew must have had Stephanie in a rage. Plus, her body mike actually fell off and clunked on the floor. She picked it up with great hauteur and made a face at it, which the audience loved. In addition to that, Stephanie had the great good presence of mind to march over to wherever the lights happened to be to give her lines. The audience caught on and clapped for her. Jennifer's song went fine, and although the crowd was a bit silent at the end of it, they applauded graciously. Even Charlie was okay, though he didn't get many laughs. Isabel brought the house down, as expected.

At intermission, Sam and Meg conferred frantically while he told her that a couple of the lights had burned out and he was trying to compensate for it by trying other combinations. Meg told him not to experiment any further. Meg, in fact, looked so red in the face—and so did my grandfather—that I decided to break the fourth wall, as Barton would have said, and race into the lobby to get them some ginger ale. My strategy was to run so fast that no one would notice I was in costume. The cafeteria was packed with ginger ale consumers and cookie eaters too, so packed that I knocked one poor guy's beverage onto his shirt. He wasn't dressed very well, and he may have been part of the state hospital group that had been brought in. He had that kind of a pleasant but mindless look to him. I wore Stephanie's red velvet cape, so at least maybe no one in the lobby noticed my prom dress. In the end, Velma had told us prom dresses were okay for the ballroom scene, and I was proud that mine still fit with only one safety pin.

Meg slurped down the ginger ale and barked out orders: move this, change that, we're going ahead. She marched out onstage and announced to the audience that a light had burned out and no one should worry about it; it was under control. Her new maternity dress hung down almost to the floor.

The wedding scene of the Captain and Maria smelled like a forest fire. The audience stayed put, probably because of Meg's cautionary address, but everyone in the building, including us, was worried. It must be said that had the mishaps stopped there, everything would have been all right.

As Laura recited one of her lines, a stream of water pegged her in the eye. *Ping.* She flinched, of course, though it was over quickly and didn't look any worse than if she had tried to avoid a mosquito. Later, as Stephanie stood in the same spot, it happened to her too. *Ping.* A few titters could be heard from the audience, but since Stephanie had them eating out of her hand anyway, they laughed at everything she did. Then Laura took another one and another. *Ping. Zap.* Then Stephanie. *Zap. Ping.* Minutes later, a powerful chest-high surge of water nearly knocked Charlie backward and caused him to rub his head. Old habits return in the face of adversity, I guess, since Charlie rubbed his head almost to the end of the show. Another smaller salvo of bulletlike precision hit him at shin level, but Charlie stood back and continued with his speech, which got him high marks from me for perseverance, but a few outright laughs from the crowd, especially when the spotlight crotch shot showed up again on Charlie and several of the patriots.

"Squirt guns?" whispered a nun.

"Sprinklers," said Helen as we stood in the wings wearing our ball gowns. She still carried the crucifix. "Sprinklers are on."

"Fuck!" cried Meg, but we were unstoppable, a show-business juggernaut going forward no matter what.

I doubt there was ever a ball held like the one we portrayed, unless it was in Atlantis, underwater, or in Revolutionary Guy's dreams—good thing no one had to play miniature golf. I had new respect for Gene Kelly in "Singin' in the Rain." The waltzing couples were drenched. Moey's thin hair was plastered onto his skull, and I was surprised to see dye dripping down Ziggy's neck. Everybody's makeup was smeared, and some looked more ghoulish than others, including Helen, whose nose looked much larger on her face. No one broke character, though, and when Abe swung by me during the number, he merely looked sweaty instead of drunk and soaking wet. I saw Mrs. Mayer's face in the wings once, her mouth in a perfect O shape. The orchestra kept playing, and I saw a couple of them steal curious looks at us. It was very cooling for the actors and sobering as well for some of us, but I was glad Barton wasn't there to see it.

Things did not get better. The postwedding return of Maria and the Captain was a sauna bath for all, and a couple of times Charlie got drilled square in the face. Another time it was Laura. The audience was into it by now, and every line took on a double meaning.

"We must escape," Laura said, and the audience roared.

"My life is different now with you," Charlie said, or something like that, and the auditorium rocked with laughter. The kids sang their good-bye song bobbing and ducking up and down as streams of water pelted them, and Jennifer's reprise could have been renamed "I Am Sixteen and in the Shower." The floor was tremendously slippery, and Austrian patriots slid this way and that, a couple of them taking dives onto the floor. Two uniformed Nazi guards entered stage right and tripped in tandem, legs flying out from under them in exact synchronized motion. Ziggy made one exit crawling on his hands and knees.

That wasn't all for Ziggy. As I pretended to make small talk in one of the conversation groups dotted across the stage—"Gosh, it must be raining! And how are you?"—I noticed a new person enter, a man who squinted in the bright lights, adjusted his cap, and made a beeline for Zig. Beelines were hard to make just then, so I suppose I should say he trod gingerly toward Ziggy. This person fit in well with our group in some ways, since he wore a police outfit, not of the homemade Velcro Nazi denomination, but of the Massachusetts State Police. I recognized the uniform and, in fact, knew it well from my unfortunate habit of speeding on Route 2 and other places in my quest for coupon sales. This gentleman was immediately joined by another of his ilk, and the two troopers made a handsome pair as they circled around the dance floor, trying to approach Ziggy.

Don't ever think that your state policemen are brutes. They may well have better manners than you do, and indeed these two courteously tried to cut in on Susie twice as she twirled around with Ziggy on the glistening wet dance floor. Susie may have thought they wanted to dance with her, and maybe in her mind it was some puzzling new blocking from Barton, but it soon became obvious that she was not their target. I missed the actual takedown. I had to turn away to waltz—one-two-three, one-two-three—and when I looked back, Ziggy was on the ground. The handsome troopers had their guns out and pointed toward him, which had a downer effect on some of the dancers, including Abe, who swan-dived across several waltzing couples onto the floor trying to make it to the wings. All concerned went out stage left, and the whole thing was over in less than a minute, but our male ranks were considerably diminished, not only by the absence of Ziggy and some others, but Lenny too, who went running out after them. This left me without a partner. I didn't know what to do, but remembered Barton's instructions about staying in character, so I walked over toward the orchestra, curtsied, and pretended to be the conductor. It was easy. I just followed Marianne's motions, more or less, and pretended to guide the other dancers offstage. The audience applauded for me, and I felt like a star.

The staircase made a final unannounced voyage across the stage with all the von Trapp kids on top of it and a couple of stagehands, rolling out of control and crashing into the circuit-breaker box in the wings, which dimmed the lights one more time. The kids jumped off and were fine, though somehow Mrs. Mayer was pinned to the wall by the incident and required some later attention from a chiropractor in the audience.

Finally, the big Austrian flag tacked to the back of one of the flats became waterlogged and collapsed on top of several chorus members, male or female, I didn't know. They floundered and fumbled underneath, but got themselves offstage with a little help, resembling a giant patriotic centipede being led off to an unknown fate.

There's no point in telling all of it. It was a disaster. It was more than a disaster. Half the cast was crying and the other half triumphant as we took our soaking-wet curtain calls and listened to the prolonged standing ovation. I heard later that Charlie Jenkins walked all the way home.

Till You Find Your Dream

Monday, August 10

"One hundred and thirty-nine pounds."

"Ha!" I said. "How do you like *that*, you killjoy!" I couldn't help myself. That weight even included Sheena, who stood on my feet on top of the scale, so I felt positively svelte for the first time in weeks. I marched straight to the refrigerator and selected yogurt, a courageous sign of control and virtue, but then noticed the expiration date had come and gone, so I was forced to throw it out and have more scalloped-potato leftovers from the cast party, and it only seemed prudent to suck down the last of the seven-layer dessert, also from the cast party. I took the opportunity to pitch all Imperial Duck remains into the trash.

I stood in front of the kitchen slider to savor my high-energy breakfast and saw Gramp outside in his Juan Valdez outfit, albeit with a slightly larger hat than Juan wears in the coffee commercials. Gramp was doing something to the lawn mower and looked restored, recovered, and normal.

After the weekend we had been through, I was very grateful.

I turned the treadmill on, another sign of courage and virtue, but then turned it off when I saw the clock. The treadmill itself groaned and sounded weary, and I didn't want to push my luck with machines.

My car wasn't making the emphysema sound anymore. It had now progressed to a death rattle. I promised it, the vehicle, that it would have my complete attention after the sales meeting, and it accepted this bargain, showing good faith by getting me there.

"Your carburetor is failing."

"I know; just hang in there."

"Your carburetor is failing."

"Just a little while longer."

I parked in a pretty good spot and noticed the new Dunkin' Donuts was open, though I didn't have time for a Coolatta, and was entirely too stuffed. I saw Abe's car and, in fact, Abe, or at least the back of him, leaning into the passenger seat. He finally stood up, holding a tremendous stack of papers and files, and headed for me.

"Hey, sweetie," I said. "How are you feeling?"

"I'm feeling great. Have we got our reviews yet? Have they been in the paper?"

"I don't think so," I replied. "The reviewers were there Friday night. What else are they going to say except that it was hilarious in an amateur, juvenile, slapstick way?"

"Yes, but Saturday night the show *was* great."

"I doubt they came back on Saturday night."

"Will you take these inside for me?" Abe asked.

I looked at him.

"I'm quitting. I left Dan a message."

"Not to be a gambler at the casino, Abe. Please tell me you have some money left."

"No, not to gamble. That's ridiculous. I don't know what I was thinking."

"Well, good."

"I still have the rest of my uncle's estate left, and I've made a decision."

"Yeah?"

"I'm going to New York to be an actor."

What followed was mostly me with my mouth hanging open being told by Abe how it wouldn't be that hard and how badly all segments of show business needed good men. I knew that I no longer wanted to go to Hollywood, and I told him how I had considered it myself, but I wasn't able to budge him. It was, as Abe would have called it, a lemming sale. I eventually took all his papers and files, balanced them in my arms, promised to meet him in New York for drinks, and kissed Abe goodbye.

"Oh yeah!" he said. "That file on the top is Baldwin Springs. My brother is expecting your call." He winked and took off.

Magda was wearing a beret when I got to the office, a sure sign of trouble. I asked her how her weekend had been, and she made a fist with one hand and a middle-finger salute to the sky with the other. I smiled and looked in my mailbox. Several checks had come in as promised, and I blessed all the business owners silently in my heart. Speaking of my heart, it was pounding like one of those cars that drive by with the bass turned up so loud the whole vehicle is vibrating. I glanced into the conference room and saw just about everyone except Henrietta.

Henrietta wasn't there because she too had resigned, not to go to New York, but to go to our competitor Coupon Busters for a big job. The real scuttlebutt, though, was that she hadn't won the sales contest and was appalled, ashamed, and *wicked pissed*.

I didn't win the sales contest either. The winner was Bob Bordeaux, who turned in more than fifty new customers at the last minute. It seemed a little shady. Probably because of that, the new owners decided to give a hundred dollars for *each* new customer, and I got a very consoling twenty-seven hundred clams. Added to my Dog Daze commission, it was a most excellent haul.

And I got the sales manager job. Dan made a big to-do about announcing it in the meeting, and everyone congratulated me, and it was all very nice. Stephanie groveled on the floor about how much I deserved it and how wonderful I was and well dressed and nice and even not too horrible a singer. I was Nobel laureate for coupons in those few minutes, and I enjoyed every second. I accepted all the accolades and praise in the conference room and then went into Dan's office and turned the job down. They say your life passes in front of you when you face death, but my life passed in front of me in those few seconds of Dan's announcement. Everything crystallized. I didn't want to work nine to five. I didn't want to worry about how much other people were selling or whether they were parked on a bar stool at Cheng Du. I didn't want to be burdened with other people's concerns. Mort's Hardware was enough for me.

I saw a play once—was it *Our Town?*— where a girl comes back to her earlier life after she has died. She walks around the kitchen looking at everything and wishing so much that she could be there again, living it again and this time appreciating it. It's not possible to feel stupendous elation every minute, not unless you're on heroin or something. So in that sense, that not-being-on-heroin sense, I'd always thought I wasn't terribly happy. But I know now there's no point in appreciating it later; there's no point in looking back and saying wow, I was happy then and I didn't know it.

I got in my car and drove to the car repair shop. I was as happy as I could be.

From the August 9 *Heywood News*:

WORCESTER SPOTLIGHTERS NOT ALL WET
BY PATTY CARSON

WORCESTER—There were some technical problems in the Worcester Spotlighters' Friday-night performance of *The Sound of Music*, but for the most part no one noticed them. The performers were so talented and so wonderful that a little lighting difficulty didn't matter.

Laura Wheeler of Marlboro played Maria and was lovely in her shy and soft-spoken portrayal. There probably could have been more attention paid to the sound system, since Ms. Wheeler's songs weren't always heard in the back row, but that was outweighed by her convincing performance as the ebullient novice nun who falls in love with Captain von Trapp.

Portraying the Captain was Charles Jenkins of Boylston. He gave the role a dignity not even seen in Christopher Plummer's film rendition. Mr. Jenkins has never been onstage before, but undoubtedly looks to a bright future therein.

In the secondary roles of Max and the Baroness were veterans Dennis Macklinski and Stephanie Wilson. They were quite simply hilarious, and when Ms. Wilson's concealed microphone fell onto the floor, she picked it up with great aplomb.

The children were wonderful, and you just wanted to take them home with you. Special kudos to newcomer Jennifer Albright-Phelps, who wowed them with "Sixteen Going on Seventeen." She and Truman Larson did a superb job playing older teenagers. I especially like the scene where the children moved up the staircase saying good-bye to the revelers at the ball. And speaking of the staircase, it was a construction marvel as it rolled back and forth at different intervals.

Music direction was by Marianne Peters, whom we all remember as Mrs. Snow in last year's *Carousel*. Stage direction was by the brilliantly talented Barton Columbus. All in all, a most enjoyable evening.

From the August 10 *Worcester Tribune*:

DROWNED OUT IN WORCESTER
BY GENE KRUMPEL

Unfortunately for the actors who must have given time and effort to this clunker, the final product had a few more laughs than intended. For starters, the orchestra was flat and frequently just plain off-key, though that was more of a groaner than a laugher. I listened carefully and decided it was mainly in the deeper notes—trombone? bass? Who knows?

The lead role of Captain von Trapp, head of the family and Austrian hero in the pre-Ah-nold days, was played by the very tall Charles Jenkins, who gave new meaning to the word "wooden." His leading lady, the also altitudinous Laura Wheeler, was not much better. I got used to their height while they were onstage together, but I never got used to their dullness. I sometimes thought I was watching Celtics training camp or *Gulliver's Travels with a Girlfriend*. I'm only twenty-five years old, and found myself wishing I had a hearing aid for the first act, but then I was glad I didn't have one as time and this stinker went on.

The supporting cast was a relief, particularly veteran actress Stephanie Wilson, who ably played the Baroness, though she might want to consider a less brassy hair color.

Children onstage are almost always a disaster, and this production fell right in line with what I expected. I still have one question—was there no one else to play the part of the teenage girl? She is sixteen going on seventeen in about ten years, though since I almost felt my own age had been doubled when I left the place, maybe it was true.

Don't even ask me about the accident in the second act that caused great hilarity and a real mockery of actual theater.

Who directed this mess? Barton Columbus couldn't possibly have designed the lighting board. I've seen Columbus's work, and it is usually competent. Rumor has it he wasn't present. The show should have been stopped, and everyone thought it would be when a woman in a fairy costume walked out at intermission and told everyone not to worry; it was only one light that had failed. I'm sorry to say it was the Spotlighters who burned out.

From the August 12 *New York Times*:

HELEN GRACE UNDER PRESSURE
BY DAVID WILTONBRUNNENFREUNDER

WORCESTER, Mass.—Family reunions can be heartrending and tearful as one hears about the ups and downs, and mostly downs, of one's long-lost relatives. Poor relations, rich relations, again mostly poor it seems, at least in the case of my wife's family tree and its various limbs. Here was the bargain: She would accompany me to a particularly onerous professional meeting in Las Vegas and I would trail behind her to an equally distasteful (in my view, not hers) family reunion in Massachusetts. My obligation came first, and I met it, if not with a glad heart, at least with an open mind.

And so I met the various cousins and aunts and nephews, regular folks all and likable to a man—or a woman, I should say, though these people are not sticklers for feminism or political correctness or even refined table manners. My wife tells me all the time that I don't get enough "regularness" in my rarefied life at the *Times* and that it is to my intellectual peril. I tell her that table manners at work are no different than around the Lathams' picnic table, and that's regular enough for me.

I met one young man at the reunion who works three jobs and goes to school at night. How can this be done? I asked. With great inventiveness and perseverance and luck, it seems. Another senior gentleman talked about the son and daughter who live with him and help in his daily quest to live with dignity. I was too ashamed to say I review plays on Broadway. What's dignified about that?

I skip to my wife's great-aunt because it was her story and her influence that made the trip first bearable, then pleasant, then irreplaceable. She was born Helen Grace Latham somewhere in the Berkshires, entered the convent in the 1950s, and stayed there for fifty years, more or less having to leave because the place was shutting down. During the weekend, I received lectures from Helen on morals of young people, why aluminum siding is no good, what should be done to the Red Sox pitching staff in the off season, and how to get to heaven.

If you think Helen stays home and enjoys her golden years, you don't have much imagination. Her favorite activity these days is community theater, and, in fact, she talked my wife and me into attending opening night of her current undertaking, *The Sound of Music*, in which one might argue she is eminently qualified to participate.

A busman's holiday for me, as I complained to my wife, but the gears of this bus were oiled and engaged, and it drove its route precisely according to schedule. What I saw was no less than a brilliant, sometimes sarcastic send-up of the tired old chestnut. Most of it was done silent-movie style, lights flickering on and off while the actors pretended to talk and the orchestra played. It took a while to get used to, and in the beginning people thought it was unintentional. But in the end the technique proved ingenious.

The young child playing Liesl sings that she is sixteen years old, and points out to us the fleeting nature of youth and how we are forcing adulthood entirely too early onto our society's children. Helen herself, my own great-aunt by marriage, carries an almost life-size crucifix in a bludgeoning, menacing manner that announces the clear dangers of the brutal fundamentalism we see all around us these days in an Ingmar Bergman-esque manner.

A woman in a gunnysack told the audience at intermission not to worry about the burning smell of the lights—another clever way to contrast humorously to the sugary-sweet nonsexual heroine of the piece, and to somehow suggest the "expectancy" we all have, certainly of a meaningful second act.

Then they got the sprinklers to work. How they choreographed the precise squirts and leaks and drenching waterfalls I do not know. I have seen so many "modernized" adaptations of *Richard III* and *Romeo and Juliet* (one cringes at the memory of poor Leonardo) that this production took a while to win my heart, but by the time the chorus members were waltzing about in their slapstick rendition of a ballroom scene, I was laughing so hard, my wife was embarrassed.

They were amateurs, of course, and I saw some confusion onstage. But along with the bewilderment I saw dedication, perseverance, and willingness to deal with reality, all the things I so liked about Helen and the reunion attenders. Helen in a formal gown waltzing with a Danny DeVito type was worth the price of admission. The Mother Superior character had a decent voice and, given the right circumstances, could almost certainly be welcomed on a New York stage, that is, if she would be willing to give up the great, beautiful confines of New England. And why would she? New York is nasty, dirty, unpredictable, and fast, everything you won't find there.

I always pick my favorite chorus member, and so does my wife. Hers was Helen, and you may say that she was biased. Mine was the young woman who walked to the front of the stage and brought the audience together as she curtsied. It was just after some kind of strange, impressionistic wrestling scene with police and partisans. This girl soothed us, and we loved her for it. I must admit that she spilled ginger ale on me in the lobby and then hunted me down with a dry-cleaning coupon. If she wants to call me, I will hire her to be my assistant.

Mostly on that stage I saw love of theater, the real kind, the kind all actors start out with and have respect for and then lose somehow along the way. I compared it to the cynical spoiled-brattiness of the actors I normally see every night, and though I would in the end choose to see a Broadway show over a Worcester Spotlighter production, it was an instructive night out. And Helen saved us some scalloped-potato leftovers to take home. Would Patty Lupone ever have done that?

Afterword

Okay, okay, okay. Slow it down. Nix the happy banjo music or whatever is playing in your head. If you pictured me sipping chardonnay in Manhattan after a glamorous day of work at *The New York Times*, put that dream away. Of course I didn't go flocking off to New York City to grovel at the feet of the Broadway guy. What do you think? I did it on the phone. And guess what? He didn't really want me. He sounded like a show-off and a grouch, if you want to know, and I can get that in Worcester. He did agree to go see Isabel next time she performed somewhere.

Isabel lives with Sam Yummy now and seems happy. I think they're having a lot of sex. His kids adore Isabel and are trying to talk her into a tattoo. The photo shop is doing okay and Isabel is a regular coupon customer. Mort has officially given up on her.

Meg quit her job at the high school to prepare for the new baby. By the time she was six weeks pregnant the nursery was complete, a year's supply of diapers was laid in, and a wagon and two-wheeler bicycle were purchased and stored in her garage. In addition, she sent away for application forms to summer camp, put a down payment on a piano, and started subscribing to scholarly journals in order to help with college admissions. I am not afraid to say that the *Brontë Society News* is a snoozer. By the time this child arrives, Meg will have its wedding clothes selected and nursing home picked out. She's gained only twenty pounds, no thanks to me, and Great-grandma's portrait is missing.

Mr. Piggy turned out to be a girl. I discovered this not from anatomical or veterinary knowledge, but from the four wormlike offspring that appeared in the cage one morning. Not being exactly sure what to do, I knew I had to get rid of them before they reached puberty and had any kind of urge for incest. So one fine fall day, I put them in a shoebox and forced Dave at the pet store to take them, incest being okay at his store.

Jailbird Pizza is thriving.

Barton went to New York, where he attends poetry openmike nights and makes doughnuts.

Abe went to New York and then to L.A., where he has a featured role on a well-known sitcom.

Gramp spends most evenings with Mrs. Mayer. Sometimes they wear the Bozo getups and go entertain children at the hospital, and sometimes they get into complicated yard and garden projects. In colder weather, they upholster furniture. Sometimes they just sit around and watch *Jeopardy!* with Lenny and me. That's going okay too.

As for me, the Spotlighters' winter production is *The Pajama Game*, and the auditions are next week.

NAOMI NEALE

CALENDAR GIRL

Name: Nan Cloutier

Address: Follow the gang graffiti until you reach the decrepit bakery. See the rooms above that even a squatter wouldn't claim? That's my little Manhattan paradise.

Education: (Totally useless) Liberal Arts degree from an Ivy League university.

Employment History: Cheer Facilitator for Seasonal Staffers Inc. Responsible for spreading merriment and not throttling fellow employees or shoppers, as appropriate.

Career Goal: Is there a career track that will maybe, just maybe, help me attract the attention of the department store heir of my dreams?

No way. That's a full-time job in itself!

- -

STEPHANIE ROWE
UNBECOMING BEHAVIOR

Shannon McCormick is about to be fired from her job at a snobby Boston law firm. So what if she accidentally flashed the newest hotshot attorney? The egomaniac spent his first day slamming doors in her face and usurping her secretary. And it's *her* behavior on trial!

Just to confirm there's no justice in the world, her younger sister is about to become Mrs. Rich Plastic Surgeon; her mom invites her ex-boyfriend to all the wedding festivities; and her crush for the last twenty years suddenly notices her as a woman.

Shannon will have to take a stand and make a case for living life on her terms. She's going to prove how far a little unbecoming behavior can take her.

THE MILE-HIGH HAIR CLUB

NAOMI NEALE

When worlds collide: My life in a nutshell

By Bailey Rhodes, talent producer, Expedition Network

NYC and Dixie have little in common. In New York, I have a fabulous career in cable television, incredible friends, and exciting culture. In Dixie, there's relatives who are, shall I say, two bubbles shy of plumb crazy. New York has the boyfriend who can't commit; Dixie has the agronomist with the heart of gold and biceps by the pound. Shrill, talentless anchorwomen try to claw their way into my programming in New York, while loud, talentless contestants try to claw their way into the sixty-fourth annual Miss Tidewater Butter Bean Pageant in Dixie.

But there's one thing New York and Dixie have in common: Big mouths, big heads, and even bigger hair in...

THE MILE-HIGH HAIR CLUB
